Harry Jones

Holiday Papers

Harry Jones

Holiday Papers

ISBN/EAN: 9783337293673

Printed in Europe, USA, Canada, Australia, Japan

Cover: Foto ©Andreas Hilbeck / pixelio.de

More available books at **www.hansebooks.com**

HOLIDAY PAPERS.

BY

HARRY JONES, M.A.,

Incumbent of St. Luke's, Berwick Street, Soho.

LONDON:

ROBERT HARDWICKE, 192, PICCADILLY.

1864.

COX AND WYMAN,
ORIENTAL, CLASSICAL, AND GENERAL PRINTERS,
GREAT QUEEN STREET, LONDON, W.C.

PREFACE.

The following Papers were written during, or at the edge of, occasional holidays in the midst of heavy Pastoral Work.

As they recall to me with healthy freshness the scenes where most of them were jotted down, and have stirred, not unpleasantly, the sense of quiet recreation in many of my friends, I have ventured to string them on the thread of holiday thought after the fashion now in your hands.

I push my little boat out into the great paper fleet which daily risks the wind of public opinion, in hope that it may carry to you some of the spirit of glad rest which I found in shaping the pieces which I have here put together.

I beg to thank the Proprietors of *Chambers's Journal, Once a Week,* and the *Leisure Hour,* for their permission to reprint such of these Papers as have appeared in their respective Periodicals.

HARRY JONES.

May, 1864.

CONTENTS.

	Page.
Holidays	1
Work	11
Looking Back from Half-way	27
How we Stocked the Mere	45
Dabchicks	59
Rooks	67
Nuthatches	77
Larks	82
Pond-fishing	91
Bird-murder	103
Our Feathered Visitants	110
Starlings	127
Insect Warfare	137
Insect Appetite	146
Dogs I have Known	153
Out of Town	170
The Language of Flowers	182

viii   *Contents.*

		Page.
Garden-games		188
Dreams		198
Association		206
Sight-seeing		221
Nursing		240
Temper		262
Poking the Fire		272
A Dinner at Greenwich		279
Waiters		292
London School Treats		299
Hedge-popping		310
The Stamp Office		323
Short Cuts		332
Mobs		344
Sea-side Life		353
Sea-bathing in France		368
Bretons and Britons		379
Mont St. Michel		391
Going Abroad		408
Back Again		419

HOLIDAY PAPERS.

HOLIDAYS.

HIS word is one of mockery to the idler, but of magic power to him who works, whether he be schoolboy or man, whether he be ploughman or premier. I question whether age makes much difference in the enjoyment of a holiday, so long as we have tolerable health. The boy is of course more demonstrative: he expresses himself about the tyrant pedagogue, who keeps him to his task, more freely than paterfamilias does about inexorable business. He shuts his book with a buoyancy, if not sauciness, which the elder holiday-maker does not feel; but for all that, the latter accepts the change with a depth of enjoyment of which Master Tommy is incapable. A man's holiday finds much of its

B

charm in the sense of escape from responsibility.   He sheds the daily capricious demands
of a profession.   When he leaves his house,
his office, his chambers, or his shop, he drops
the burden of command, which is even heavier
than that of obedience.   For days, we will
suppose, he has drawn the threads of his work
together, and wound up the machine to go
during his absence.   When the luggage is
labelled, the room in the litter of departure,
the cab called, the last summary made of wraps
and umbrellas, the man feels a steady sense of
imminent relief, of which the boy knows nothing.

A friend of mine had once just reached this
crisis of a holiday.   His carpet-bag was ready;
in a few minutes he would have been off to
Spain, when a messenger arrived, red in the
face, with news which obliged him to stay at
home for a month.   He took his knapsack out
of his bag, he re-entered the littered rooms,
went up again into his tumbled bed-chamber,
put his new travelling suit of dittoes into the
stale old wardrobe, locked up his passport with
its last gritty ·visa, and worked hard for a
month.   I look on my friend as a man who has
been through the agony of disappointment, as
one whose banns have been forbidden at the altar.

The essence of a holiday is change.   This is

more important than mere rest. I do not
know, however, whether change would not be
more refreshing if it were preceded by some
rest. We are apt to leap too suddenly from
work to play, and many a man gets knocked
up by racketing off from the bustle of business
to that of pleasure without an interval of rest.
He would enjoy his tour more if he would take
two or three good long sleeps, and have his fill
of yawning. Then he would wake up and
enjoy himself. The great want of many professional men is sleep. Nature demands that
first. However sincere your purpose of as-
cending the Matterhorn as soon as you reach
Switzerland, however capable you may be of
that feat, don't despise a few disgracefully late
breakfasts before you gird yourself for the
exertions of your holiday. If you don't thus
" knit up the ravelled sleeve of Care," you will
very likely find the unusual exertions of an
active tour rub your health out at elbows.

Change, however, is the great restorative.
The sedentary man laces on his highlows, and
pants up the hill ; the weary mountain-shepherd
lounges in the valley. The townsman flies to
the country ; the countryman takes the train for
town. The landsman rejoices in a cruise ; the
sailor gets leave for the shore.

I live in London myself, and therefore enjoy
the country with a relish unintelligible to rustics.
To me, the country is the land of ease : I see
the ploughman halting in the furrow, the milkmaid with her pail, the hedger with his bill-hook,
the reaper with his sickle, but they convey no
sensation of toil.   They enliven the stage of
the country ; they are pastoral performers.   I
am not quite sure, though, about the reaper
with his sickle.   In fact, I believe that a sickle
is as rare, say, as a boomerang.   The corn, I
am aware, is now cut either with a scythe or
reaping-machine, a chattering subversive affair,
before whose insidious knives the stalks sink
and the ripe ears topple.   But, in spite of this
mechanical fuss, the country is the land of ease
to me, for it is synonymous with holidays.   Of
course, it is a different thing to the countryman,
who breaks the monotony of his year by a visit
to town.   He would tell me, no doubt, that the
harvestman is hot and weary ; that many a
peasant does hard work on weak food ; that the
milkmaid expresses herself in a vulgar way
about early hours, and has been heard to swear
at the butter when it won't come.   I dare
say.   But for all that, the countryman cannot
understand the appetite with which I 'devour
the lanes, the beach, the rippling fields of corn,

the crawling waggon yellow with wheat, the
shadows of the clouds sailing over the sea and
the down; to say nothing of that wonderful
insight into the universe which you get by
lying flat on your back and looking up, or
rather down, into the sky. You turn away
from the world, and gaze upon the infinite,
with swallows wheeling about some hundreds,
it may be thousands, of feet beneath you, and,
if naturalists may be believed, filling their bellies
with little red enterprising spiders, which cruise
about in space. There are men who ascend
great heights to have distant scenes beneath
them. I lie on the grass, and get a deeper
view with one half-turn of the body. Conceive
the change, when I look up, in London, and
see smoke streaked with telegraph wires. By
the way, these last have been multiplied wonderfully within the last few years; it will be
impossible, soon, to get a good photographic
view of any of our chief places. Mr. Reuter
is like a spider with a great web converging
over his offices at the top of Waterloo Place.
There is little to choose, however, especially in
the neighbourhood of our public buildings ; the
metal web is being spun over the town, until at
last we shall see ourself shut in like tame birds,
and London will be a gigantic cage.

Next to change, exercise is essential to an effective holiday. I don't pretend to write about it medically; I don't know what it does for your diaphragm or mucous membrane; I don't know the specific gravities of the leg of a postman and the arm of a blacksmith; I can't tell you how much your chest will expand with a six weeks' course of gymnastics, or how rapidly healthy muscle is replaced by unwholesome fatty matter if you lie late abed, or loll about all day on a sofa, when your girth grows, indeed, but below the chest. I don't know how many miles a man in good health ought to make a point of walking in the course of each twenty-four hours. There are books enough to teach us plenty of scientific facts about the neglect and use of exercise. Indeed, to say the truth, I cannot help feeling a suspicion of this self-conscious management of the body and limbs. It is a questionable thing to obey Nature only by art. The charm, and therefore, to a certain degree, the benefit of all such things as diet and exercise, is endangered if we are always consulting printed wisdom to know when we ought to eat, walk, ride, yawn, sneeze, sleep, bathe, and have our hair cut. We may, on the other hand, attach too little importance to the when and the why of these things. There is a contempt of cause and effect which shortens many persons' lives, who yet need not have prim cut-and-dried regulations about the common machinery of health. Perhaps exercise is just one of those things which ought to have more regard paid to it than it has. If excessive, especially before the frame has become well developed and knit, however exciting at the time, it wrings the joint and strains the heart. It is a fine thing, no doubt, for a boy to find himself in the winning boat, though at the cost of white lips and a thumping pulse. He soon comes to—youth is elastic —and eats a famous supper; but maybe years afterwards the little evil seed then sown will show itself, possibly with fatal haste.

Let me then advise you, my friend, if not already well seasoned, to resist the charm of emulation on your holidays, at least at first. Don't be run off your legs directly you start on a walking tour. If you allow yourself to be carried away at once, you will perhaps spoil the whole thing. Protest, and secure the gratitude of others who have small moral courage, as well as your own digestion and sleep; protest, and win eventually respect and health.

Indeed, to enjoy a holiday thoroughly, there is need of more decision than appears at first. Remember that it is a holiday, and drive away

the working thoughts and cares which will
sometimes follow in your track. If possible,
do without letters; it has been found that they
will answer one another if allowed to accumulate
at home. Shuffle this coil off; the world will
move round still, though you take your hand
altogether off the crank. Determine to relax,
to rest, and the recreation will be effectual.
Let what boyishness you have come uppermost,
and follow the innocent whim of the day.
Holidays, to be profitable, must be entertaining,
absorbing; if anything which is legitimate
attracts and influences you, don't be ashamed
of its appearing to be too childish. Tumble
on the hay, throw stones on the beach, gape
about in the market. There is much harmless
amusement to be got out of your fellow-
travellers, and the coffee-room acquaintances
you make. Avoid the idolatry of guide-books,
which tell you not only where to go, but what
to feel and think while you are making the
prescribed excursion. Explore, to some degree
at least, for yourself; test your wits and native
resources. The practice of taking a return-
ticket for your holiday is also questionable.
You will be haunted by the remembrance that
you must take such and such a route, and,
moreover, by the suspicion that the thing will

be lost before you get its whole value. You
will peep at it in your pocket-book in unsuitable
places. It will bring back the vision of the
London terminus when you pay some boatman
on the lakes, or buy a draught of milk at an
upland Swiss chalet. You will see a Hansom
cab and your office while you are looking for
some foreign coin. The charm of a mountain
pass will yield to a whiff of Oxford Street. No,
let the holiday be cut off as cleanly as possible
from the rest of the year; they will both be the
better for the severance.

While we are on holidays, I must protest
against the sneers aimed at the excursionist.
Do not despise his baby and his bundle. If he
should chance to be vulgar, he will be doubly
so on his excursion. His black satin waistcoat,
his bottle, and food in greasy paper, his ungainly
frolicsomeness, his snobbish gallantry, are then
inevitable. But I rejoice to see them all. He
enjoys himself heartily. It is all very well for
fine ladies and gentlemen to smile in superior
dislike or condescension, which are pretty nearly
the same thing. Probably you owe more than
you fancy to that buoyant holiday-maker with
his cheap Sunday clothes, and gin and water.
Likely enough, he knows how to make the
engine which drags you both. Perhaps he

printed the refined book off which you glance
with a half-reprehensive eye at the liberties
which are being taken with the respectable
society of the second class. Don't be shocked
at the thorough way in which he wipes his face,
and returns the red cotton handkerchief into his
hat with a dab. His holiday is but a short one.
Let him take it as he will, with an ease and
openness which lose much of their vulgarity
when we reflect that they are natural. Don't
refuse the shrimps he offers you, haughtily.
Whatever you take with you on your holiday,
take a stock of good humour, and it is astonish-
ing how much enjoyment you will continue to
receive which stuck-up people altogether miss.
If you must always have your accustomed little
proprieties about you, you don't deserve a
holiday at all.

WORK.

ORK is divine. No doubt; but not more than Rest is. Do not let us be called off from a quiet wholesome estimate of work by any big epithet which, as likely as not, suggests an idea of it at variance with dry daily experience. There is nothing more true than the first three words of this little essay, and yet there is in some who accept them a mental shrug, and raising of the eye-brows, when they pass back from the loftiness of the adjective to the fatigue of the noun. Work is divine. Perhaps; but the outward sensible signs of it are sweat, blisters, head-ache, ink, chips, dirt, noise.

Don't let us, however, affect to slight the reverse of the fabric; don't let us exclaim, when the exhibiter displays it: "You have made a mistake—that is the wrong side!" To some unaffected eyes, this is probably as interesting a phase as any. I don't care what the work is, whether it be a pin or a frigate. It is most

attractive to some when inside out. The fine
ladies and gentlemen, indeed, who so often
constitute themselves the sole judges of work,
don't think so ; to them, the last finished result,
when the sawdust has been swept away, the
paint-pot removed, the brush, hammer, oil-can,
and adze carried off, is the only test of the
deed. They promenade on the deck of the
newly-launched ship, and compliment — one
another. But the true lover of work potters
about in the dock-yard, fingering, measuring,
calculating, and getting his coat torn and tarred.
He is not shocked at the picks, the barrows,
and rough fag-ends of the builder's trade, which
litter the cradle of the palace. I should not
wonder if he looked with greater interest on the
toiling organization of the printing-house, in its
daily throes of complicated parturition, than on
the smooth-ironed sheet upon the breakfast-
table : not that he fails to appreciate the result ;
not that he underrates that which alone the
other admires, not he ; but, as work, he enjoys
the inspection of the cause as much as of the
effect. He dwells with discriminate attention
on the converging lines and branches of the
process. And even when he admires the velvet
and the ribbon, he is as likely as not to think
rather of the bare-armed sinewy mechanic

tending the loom, than of the persuasive dandy who "dresses" the plate-glass window of the Regent Street shop, and serves the customer with feigned though courteous sympathy.

But the common preference for the result which marks the majority of observers, has an effect which is mischievous ; for every one has some work to do himself. You can't blame a man for skipping over all thought of the trouble which other people have been at, in the way of business, to produce what he enjoys. You are not expected to feel an interest in the construction of locomotives when you take a first-class ticket, or to sympathize with the perplexities of the engineer, while you lounge on a corner cushion of the express which flies over Chatmoss ; but when you have got anything to do yourself, nothing is more unwise than to ignore the details of the act.

Never allow yourself to turn away in disgust from the dry minutiæ and vulgar drudgery which is required for the perfection of the noblest work. The conception is brilliant. The mind warms with enthusiastic haste, as it contemplates the object you desire to see fulfilled. You feel the loftiness of the aim ; you pat your aspirations on the back, and say to yourself, Well done ! Not so fast. You must tramp many a tedious mile, and make many a tiresome blunder, and pull to pieces many a day's fabric; you must ink your fingers, lick postage-stamps, conciliate snobs, bite your nails, eat dirt, write after supper, get up with a headache, and keep your temper; you must bear to be interrupted, delayed, misunderstood, opposed, snubbed, cheated. You must make up your mind to all this, and then crawl patiently through it, before you can say, Well done! The conception is very fine. Your ideas are enlarged, and very creditable to you. Your friends applaud your intention, and walk off apologetic. Then comes the tug of vulgar work ere the thing can be done. He will surely fail who does not know that none are really helped except those who succeed of themselves. Unto him that hath shall be given.

The astronomer who maps the heavens, and reveals the planet, must add and watch; he must use his multiplication table, lose his rest, polish his lenses, peer till his eyes ache, confer with his printer, and correct his proofs, before he can verify his hypothesis in public, and claim the attention of the world.

The engineer, who revolutionizes the locomotion of mankind, who seams the face of his land with iron ruts, and carries kings, coals, and armies with the speed of a swallow and the safety of a waggon, has tedious ground to travel before he can realize the grand conception of the locomotive and the railway. He has to make experiments with files, and oil, and coke; he has to model, subtract, and divide. He has to convince incredulous philosophers, and educate the prejudiced hand. With patient brain, and cunning finger, he has to peel off the outer husks of ignorance and opposition which hide his bright idea from the eyes of the world. And then the victory is won.

The general whose name thrills a nation with grateful pride, does not become a hero by the force of lofty conception, but by the patient acquisition of military details, and constant business-like care for the food, dress, and health of his men. Ten thousand tedious trifles attended to, and disappointments borne, go to the making of a triumph. "See the conquering hero comes," is an excellent tune. But before this, he has had to march in the mud, pore over crumpled maps, and work vulgar sums after midnight, by a flickering lantern, in a gusty tent. While you were snoring in a feather-bed, he has slept on the ground in wet clothes and with the toothache. He has had to taste

rations, economize rum, order floggings, disarm
jealousy, hire mules, eat mouldy biscuit, digest
opposition. He has studied with buoyant interest during the dull routine of peace, he has
met the common-place emergencies of warfare
with strong common sense; he has been blessed
with a good liver, and has kept his wits at his
finger-ends year after year; and now, but not
till now, has the steady fire of his life burned
up into a national triumph, and the mob claps
its dirty hands at his approach.

We must be careful not to confuse work and
toil. In toil, there is a haste and strain to keep
pace with the exigencies of the demand—there
is incessant pursuit and no capture. Work, on
the contrary, however severe, involves a certain
mastery and progress on the part of the worker.
It is the slave who toils; he bends his weary
back over that which does not profit him, in
which he takes no interest, which brings no
gain, but leaves him where he was. I do not
refer to Sambo alone. Sambo enjoys himself
ever so much more than Smith the overdriven
artisan, who hammers or stitches hour after
hour, year after year, at the same stale window
in the dingy street, till his hair grows thin and
gray, but who never gets an inch ahead of his
task; whose life is a scrambling dream with the

phantom Beggary at his heels. Now Sambo has no such tribulation. In many instances he does not care. I will grant you that Massa bullies and swears at him sometimes; possibly, if cross-grained, he may have him whipped a little, but he gives him food, clothing, shelter. This is what many a free slave in the slums behind Regent Street can hardly get; I don't mean the skilled mechanic, but the man with an improvident wife, and perhaps not over-cunning hand, who is not first-rate at his trade, but has an excellent appetite, a large family equally sharp set, and a scanty cupboard. He is not fed so well as the slave; his skin is not so plump, his muscle not so hard, his pulse not so good, his spirits not so high as Sambo's. It is all very well to talk about the elevation of the poor fellow by the education and development of his finer feelings; but don't you think that, after all, perhaps, for the present, this mill-horse in the second-floor back had better remain rather thick-skinned, if possible, than otherwise? Do not let us wonder if such as he do not fill reading-rooms, or in any sense study a book. Suppose that when they do read they want plenty of mustard with their meat—lively stories, strong positions, sensationalism, in fact, to whip the jaded draggle-

tailed mind. What then? Elevate the masses.
All right. But suppose, Mr. Philanthropist,
that you had been elevating bricks all day, or
carrying hods of mortar up a ladder in sullen
succession—what would you be fit for in the
evening? The delicate play of wit, or the
skilful combat of intellect? Cannot you conceive a bricklayers' club finding some relief in
a change from dogged toil to fierce contradic-
tion? Bless you, they can't talk without it.
Bill gives Jack the lie within six inches of his
nose, and in a voice trained on house-tops; but
Jack doesn't care. They are mates throughout.

An acquaintance of mine was one evening
walking down a crowded back-street with a
native; as they passed a public-house, a gust of
savage shouts (so my friend thought them)
made him stop in alarm. He thought murder
was being done. " Bless my heart," cried he
excitedly, " do you hear that? What is it?"
" That?" replied his companion, "oh, that is
an argument."

And, I suppose, as with most of us, each
thought that he had the best of it. Nay, on
reflection, there is something definite, a prospect of some unanswerable ultimatum in the
hodman's logic. Somebody will get hoarse first,
some windpipe will hold out longest, and win.

Now, tell me honestly, would you have these sturdy fellows refined, as the term is generally understood? Mind you, I would have them sober and honest—they are brave and enduring —but would you have them refined and thin-skinned? Would you wish them to wear gloves, read the *Saturday Review*, and invariably use a pocket-handkerchief? There are exceptions in this class as there are elsewhere, perhaps more than we think, but the main bulk of labourers are happy in having thick skins and coarse feelings. Those who, from natural dulness, never can get above the lowest rung in the social ladder, whose work is little more than hand-labour, who merely wait upon the artisan, would suffer in proportion as their sensitiveness was increased. The man with an eye for the principles of his work, who catches the spirit of the thing—and there are more intellectual differences among the men in fustian and flannel who build a house than you think—will respond to the touch of refinement, and catch it himself.

There is one feature of modern work, however, which cramps the best workman—I mean the minute subdivision of labour. Nowadays, a man is tied down to one item in a complicated process. If I could summon the people who have a hand in making the pen which now

scratches over this paper, they would probably
fill the room.   The restriction to one part of a
process, moreover, not only narrows the man's
mind, but sometimes whets the desire for a
change into fierceness.   Nature avenges herself
when she has been tied up too tight.   How
frequently the skilled mechanic "breaks out,"
as it is called, and drinks for a season, as if he
were impelled to create some diversity of sensations.   Human nature cannot bear such pro-
tracted attention to one monotonous act as the
present minute subdivision of labour demands;
and hence the mechanic denied healthy change
of work, is hurried into the violent stimulating
contrasts of debauchery.

But although work may degenerate into toil,
and so become exhaustive, imperatively de-
manding pseudo-recreation, there are occupa-
tions which depress men by their very emptiness and vanity.   The dullest labourer sees his
share in the result.   The palace stands partly
by his aid.   Without him, the railway would
have remained in the portfolio of the projector.
He may point to his deeds.   The man who
blows the organ must be honoured as well as
retained.   Those, however, who see no immediate result, who have nothing to show for it
after a day's labour, are sorely tried by the very

emptiness of their occupation. A shopman, for
instance, works incessantly, but sees no end to
his labours. A man wants something more
than wages to keep up his spirits and interest
in his vocation. Take the professions, too.
Can you conceive any post more trying than
that of a cemetery chaplain ? It is said that he
not unfrequently becomes insane. And no
doubt the monotonous character of much work,
though not so dismal as the forced decorum of
incessant interment, tends to multiply nervous
and mental disorders. There are undeveloped
capabilities of lunacy in all; any man in time
and with care might be driven mad. Drink,
worry, and vice can produce disease in the
strongest brain. In work, there is nothing
more trying than apparent want of result.
Who can pump heartily at an empty well ?
The mere turning of the barren crank in
prisons, where it was nothing but a "hard-
labour machine," degraded prisoners as much
as it fatigued them. But they generally saw
an end to their labours. There are some, however, who, though legally free, grind on year
after year, at full strain, and meet with no
response whatever; they work up to high-
pressure, but no one appears to regard them.
Nothing seems to follow from their anxious toil.

These need the rare faith which can look beyond what men call success, which can steadily bear witness to truth and righteousness in spite of indifference, which does not depend for its energy upon the artificial stimulus of praise or opposition, but draws its life from a divine and invisible spring; bearing up buoyantly in the still deep waters of cold isolation, holding fast to noble principles in the midst of petty stratagems and ephemeral expediency, still blowing at the little spark of right in the great black heap of wrong, aiming high, though all around are mean, suspicious, or unconcerned. This faith is of the divine prophetic sort, but more or less must warm all leaders of the people to their work. There must be some of it in the statesman who looks beyond the commercial prejudices of the day, and dares to act on principles at which the mob are sure to hiss for years and years to come. There must be some of it in the divine who dares the heresy of progress, and rests his title of reformer, not on the victories of men who conquered centuries ago, but on his own solitary struggles against prevailing favourite errors, and respectable corruption.

There is much work, or rather toil, which seems inevitable. Who shall dig the coal?

Who shall stoke the furnace of the steamship? It is all very well saying that these are employments beneath the dignity of man. But what is to be done with the undignified man? If we are to perform no brute labour, how shall we employ the asses? Had not men better sweep the chimneys and the streets than see the only work they can do performed by a machine, and themselves shut out by their incurable defects from the great market of labour. Some of them might probably be trained to higher manual work, but in the end most will be found to have done what they could do. There is something very fallacious and productive of disappointment in the incentive to *rise*, set before men in the example of such men as George Stephenson. All can't rise. Excellence must be comparative; and though the copy-books say that comparisons are odious, we must not forget that they are necessary. In fact, Stephenson did not so much rise, as find his level; he followed his true calling, and nothing would have kept him down. But depend upon it, fewer people are kept down—except it be by their own leaden brains — than they think. Mute inglorious Miltons languish because, in spite of their many admitted good parts, they lack something which the famous possess. Some little defect mars their other excellencies. The cannon is complete, all but the touch-hole. The balloon would rise; there is gas, ballast, and a car, but there is a hole in the dome. The engine is elaborate, and would work, if it were not for the twist in the piston. These ambitious fabrics become at last merely oiled silk and old iron, and find a price in the marine store instead of applause in the world. So is it with many men : their labour is valued at as much as it is worth. They bewail their misfortunes, but so, no doubt, would addled eggs if they could speak, which are so like the rest, but so dishonourably inferior. There is some mysterious deficiency inside the most gifted failures.

While, however, we must not be accused of injustice in suspecting a vital fault in most of those who fail, however hard they labour, there are some drawbacks upon the effect of work which can be removed. There are some industrious fellows, for instance, who do nothing because they don't finish up their work as they go along; they unravel as much as they weave; they sweep the leaves towards the wind. Others exert themselves, but make some great omission : they forget the knot at the end of the thread; they complain that they are condemned to fill a sieve, but, in fact, they have forgotten to stop the bunghole. Again, many are barren, because they take too long in making up their minds ; they think too much. A loaf baked is better than a harvest contemplated. You were within an ace of inventing a steam-plough, but your neighbour dug his field.

Moreover, many people attempt too much. One man sickens over a feast, while another thrives on mutton. It may be well to have several irons in the fire, but you must leave yourself time to hammer one. This eagerness to multiply operations is a fertile source of failure. Much work is abortive, because it is manifold. There is all the difference in the world between the ability to turn your hand to anything, and the attempt to do everything at once ; the man who tries the last, generally disappears in a debris of odds and ends. Had he contented himself with one chief work, say cutting hair, he would have become a flourish-ing hairdresser, had a vote for the borough, and dined, at least on Sundays, in plenty and peace.

It is true that change of work is a great relief ; but there must be one governing object in our efforts. Above all, we want more holidays ; men live too fast, and labour too

hard.   They want something more than change
of occupation — they want more sleep, more
unmitigated play, more unruffled repose.   He
is a wise man who knows how to idle well.
He will do most who knows how to do
"nothing."   Depend upon it, work is forwarded
by occasional seasons of judicious vacancy,
when we neither read nor think—when we
clear out the workshop, and give the entire
gang, hand and brains, a whole holiday—when
we sweep the floor, and are content to leave the
skull silent and empty.   The tenants will come
back rosy and fresh from their play in the fields.
Doubtlessly, this clearance of the intellect is
by no means an easy feat, but we may be sure
that those will, in the end, prove the best
workers who know when and how to rest.

LOOKING BACK FROM HALF-WAY.

HERE is one great advantage frequently enjoyed in middle age, denied to the old and the young —I mean the pleasure of revisiting childhood's scenes, with youth enough to find most of the old faces still there, and age enough to feel as no schoolboy can the re-creating properties of a holiday. Happy the man of mid-life who has a father or mother living where he was born, where he is still called a "boy" by his parent, and "Master John" by the old gardener. When he went back from college, he used to give himself airs, and stick up for his manhood—contradicting his father, speaking contemptuously of the family small-beer, and showing that he felt his late escape from the uncertainties of hob-bledehoyism. But now, he loves the house for the very reminiscences of childhood which are forced upon him; he is now silently thankful for what, fifteen years ago, he kicked at, or accepted with protest.

There is a charm in his old home, which his own proper address in the Post Office Directory will never possess—although that has charms of its own by no means to be despised.

In the latter place, when he lands after a day's swimming, however successfully, against the stream, he cannot quite shuffle off his coil of citizenship along with his Inverness wrapper. He cannot lay aside all his cares with his umbrella.

There is no use making wry faces about it. I daresay you have been hard at work all day; well, you are not singular. Some would be thankful beyond the bounds of even melodramatic gratitude, at having such a home to hide in, out of the din of the great crowd which still throbs under the glare of gas. There are better men than you grinding away yet; so don't grumble about the cares of a household. Suppose you had no house at all!

Still, there are special charms in the old home, far away, past lighted stations, through noisy tunnels, deep in the pleasant East. There is a charm in the old home which you cannot find in Tyburnia; a capacity for yawning, a general uncoiling of one's self, which is possible nowhere else. There you can defy the pressure of a profession; there you can

escape all sense of responsibility and master-
ship. It is a place to rest in, to loosen each
button of one's being, and breathe peace at
every pore.

The effect is improved if at the same time
you are happy in finding those there who spoil
you. An impartial friend or relation is a pest
of society. As if you didn't know your own
weak places and dark corners, but must have a
friend to help you to keep your eye upon them.
With such, absence makes the heart grow
fonder. No, no ; give me a partial friend who
likes me. Give me one who loves without
ever wishing to know the reason why. Who
does not like to be spoiled ?

To me, one of the greatest enjoyments of
such a visit as I have mentioned is to moon
about, and let the stream of old associations
and memories, started by long familiar objects,
flow on without interruption.

Three days ago I was a drop of blood in the
great "pulse of the world's right hand ;" I was
a grinding-wheel—I helped to raise the hum of
Babylon.

Now, I am a fungus, pushed back through
all the steps of species, a placid, happy fungus.

A guinea ticket did it all in three hours.
When the fly I rummaged up at the inn of the

station, where the hens were already at roost,
took me up the carriage-drive of my home, all
the house was stirred—for I had not announced
myself—asking itself what the noise of wheels
could be ; and the inquiry struck me as a fair
indication of the gulf I had crossed from
Babylon to the dear old home.

How full of memories an old house and
garden is ! To those who knew it young, every
seat, shrub, nook, and view about it has a charm
and value of its own. My saunter the next
morning gave me pleasure enough, and as most
old gardens and homes are alike, or have at
least a suggestive kindly relationship to each
other, will you share my idle reverie ? There
is something in you, I hope, which responds to
the memories of boyhood. Look, sir ! there is
nothing to you in that beech-tree ; but once, I
may say, I lived in it for years. That is the
bough on which we nailed a board for a seat,
with nails drawn out of the garden-wall—blunt,
gritty, cast-iron things. But the board held on,
and the branch flattened itself out beneath it,
like a boa-constrictor which had swallowed a
gun-case. I spent many odd hours and half-
holidays in that tree. Who has not had some
similar pet retreat, the favourite cliff, the familiar
bridge, the bend in the stream, the wood, the

beach, the cave? Mine was a tree. I invited
my friends to see me there; we hauled up cap-
fuls of fruit thereto, and were sociable aloft. I
remember, though, a little boy I knew, having
a grand lesson on greediness in connection with
that same tree; no one set it him. He was not
talked to, but punished silently by the inexorable law of cause and effect, and I am sure took
a new interest in the value of experience. It
came about thus. He had been reading the
story of *Peter Wilkins.* When the ship, loaded
with iron, had become quite fixed to the load-
stone rock, and he had recovered from the first
gush of terror, he was hungry. The story says
that he hunted about till he found some cheeses
cased in lead; having opened one of these with
his axe, he "dined off it," and felt considerably
refreshed.

" I should think so," was this boy's comment
(he was nine years old)—" I should think so; no
bread, nothing but cheese." He felt that the
disaster of the wreck was almost compensated
by such a delicious and uninterrupted meal.
The scene haunted him. One day, having
found lying about in the house an irregular
block of cheese, about a pound or so in weight,
he climbed to the seat on the beech-tree, and
fell to. After a quarter of an hour, a large

fragment was still unconsumed; I believe he buried it. I know that he did not touch cheese for months, and had his first useful hint given about a check on appetite. Depend upon it, these children's follies often teach more than the most elaborately illustrated lesson in print.

How sharply some things stand out in the past! On what does your eye rest in the dim background as you peer into the twilight of infancy? While I paced about the familiar, though long unvisited garden, the water-worn pebbles in the gravel-path recalled my earliest memory. It was that of .the shingle beach. I can see it now close to my eyes. I am told I was not more than three years old when taken there for the first time, but that I spent my time in filling baskets with the store of precious stones.   Before that, I suppose, I had possessed a marble or so, and prized them with the exaggeration of youth ; but here were round pebbles without stint.   To this day, looking back, the last distinct object in the series is that beach, those priceless innumerable pebbles.   I do not remember having noticed the sea.   How truly, as Bacon somewhere says, first thoughts and third thoughts agree.   Middle-aged, mediocre, pushing men affect to search the sea.   Newton and the child know better; they pick up their shells by the ocean-edge, without the hopeless distraction of deeper soundings. In God's kingdom, though the things be only rounded pebbles on the sand, they are hid from the wise and prudent, and revealed unto babes.

When do children begin to think? When does the fancy open? When do we first step without ourselves into the magic world which lies around, and feel the fresh current of new thought? Children are more deeply impressible than we imagine. I remember feeling quite awed by what seems a simple thing. You see that grey church tower standing up among the trees. Within those hard old walls lives the sweetest, softest voice that ever spread its fairy rings in the still air. I was wandering about by myself early one summer morning in some low meadows, where a spring bubbled up out of a heap of silver sand. It was August. I was looking at it, wondering how it flowed up so full and cool through all the long hot summer, when the ponds shrunk down, and even the deep dark wells returned a stony clang to the bucket which came up dusty and bruised. I was standing over the spring, and watching how it waved away the little bits of stick and even stone I tossed within its mouth, when all at once the bell began to toll its morning signal to the gleaners (such was our custom there) to start for the new-carried fields of wheat. It touched and loosened a new world of thought to me. I knew not what it said, but the voice I had heard so often had now a mystic power it never had before.

Who first chose great bells to summon men to prayer? There was a throb of inspiration in that thought.

I try to recall my first sense of the purpose of a church, and feel it very indistinct. Perhaps the growth of my ideas was stunted by our pew. I shouldn't wonder. It was a very Saul among the others—a head and shoulders higher than the rest. It was lined, moreover, with green baize, which had retained its colour only in the shade; elsewhere, the hot summer sun and cold winter light had changed it to a dingy yellow. Just beneath the top edge ran a row of brass-headed nails. I never could count them; they were so much alike, that when you got to seventy or eighty, you lost your place. I tried, I suppose, a hundred times.

The queer old church! There were pews for all, gentle and simple. The old men's pews were close to the door, and I remember it grew to be quite an office for one of them to push it to with his crutch. The pulpit and desk

were opposite in an arch which divided the
congregation, like the two players who join
hands in the preliminary part of "French and
English." But that old church was well filled,
especially a space behind the organ, where the
hobbledehoys cut their names, and muffled the
sound of cracking nuts. There was a man,
however, who crept about with a stick; it was
a long peeled hazel wand, and I used to watch
the tip of it go by bobbing up and down above
the edge of the pew.

Now the church is restored. The pulpit
and desk have loosened hands, and stepped
back at the architect's bidding; the old men
are brought into a warmer corner, and most of
the nuts are eaten in the porch. But the part
of the church which, I confess, pleased me most
was the belfry, where I was sometimes allowed
to help chime. Raising the bells was a feat
of after-years. Oh! how grand, though it
was merely to see it done, when the ropes all
poured down through the slippery auger-holes
in the beams above, twisting and coiling up
upon the floor like the tangled heaps of macaroni
which you see in the grocers' shops. Each
ringer has a pyramid at his feet; there is a
moment's pause, and then it lashes up like a
fountain through the roof. Woe! if you set

your foot on that sudden heap! No mortal
hand can check the return-swing of the bell.
Up you must go, to be smacked against the
beam, and the next instant deposited on the
floor with a comminuted fracture of the knee
and skull.

More than one man has thus tried his hand
—say at a marriage-festival—and caused the
sounding only of a passing bell. I remember,
however, once seeing my little brother whipped
up thus by a bell-rope, and his head stop within
two inches of the beam. Perhaps he didn't let
go when he found himself upon his legs again!
But we used to creep about among the bells by
the hour together, when the starlings were laying. What a charming place it was, the very
bell-chamber itself, with its huge rough beams,
and the upper surface of the bells spotted with
white birds'-dung, while an unconsecrated dove-
cot sort of air filled the sense. Not but that
the belfry was ventilated too; those wooden
cross-barred windows which showed the map
of the country beneath, in little squares, were
always played on by the wind, which soughed
and swept around the metal rims, making them,
I thought, hum in harmony, like bells asleep
dreaming of a peal.

But how on earth did we get to talk about

the belfry? Oh, recalling early memories as we
walked about the garden, and caught at a turn
a sight of the old grey tower. But in a visit
to the scenes of childhood we find some of the
keenest recollections by no means grave.
There is a gable-end in a garden I sometimes
visit now (far away), but which I can never see
without thinking of cats—a gable-end with a
doorway in it leading into a loft, ivy on both
sides, and a sloping roof. The doorway had a
south aspect and a broad threshold, and was
reached by a ladder, the top of which only
appeared above an ivy screen. There, on the
elevated threshold, whenever the sun shone—
and it used to shine in summer then—the cat
would sit like a picture of herself in a frame,
with the inner darkness of the loft as a background. On a terrace-walk immediately opposite was a fruit-shedding apple-tree. I fear I
threw a great many pippins at Pussy. Pincher
—that was my terrier—always expected it, and
used to wait below. I have the scene before
me: Pussy asleep, or looking at her finger-nails
in a half-dose; thud comes a pippin; cat
vanishes, a moment occupied in the descent of
the ladder, then the invisible but not inaudible
alighting on Pincher. Out they both come, cat
with a tail as big as a muff, ventriloquating past

with spangs a yard and a half long, Pincher
trundling after her, all teeth and hair, till they
reach a tree, whence she curses him till he
tires of capering round the trunk, and barking
upwards.   I had a good reason for disliking
cats.   When I was a boy, they used to steal
my young rabbits.   We had a hole like a saw-
pit, boarded and covered over with wooden
bars, in which we kept, or rather tried to keep,
our rabbits.   One day, however, the gardener
caught two cats working together at the theft,
the thinnest getting down, and handing up the
young rabbits to the accomplice.   This was his
account of the matter, and I can well believe
it; for Argus—a red-eyed, evil-favoured New-
foundland we had—was once detected lamb-
killing, then washing himself in a pond, and
finally getting back to his kennel, and putting
his head in the collar before he thought any of
the household were up.   There he was before
our breakfast, with no evidence of guilt about
him beyond the pleasant secret sense of early
digestion begun in his own inside.

It is a curious thing that dogs, which can not
only learn of man, but show such natural cunning, should yet never seem to teach one
another.   Probably they accept an accomplishment as an instinct.   They don't know that

they learn, do not notice their progress. Did you ever consider what an isolated life a dog leads? He is occupied mainly with the passing moment; he rarely meditates or looks forward; he seldom listens except when spoken to. No wonder, poor fellow, that he delights to bark and bite; his life would be otherwise dull enough.

Dogs are very fond of children; they understand each other thoroughly—the dog appreciating the indulgent supervision of a mischievous boy, and the boy glad of a companion chiefly characterized by unscrupulous high spirits.

But a truce to dogs. No one can look back upon his childhood without seeing serious mistakes of management in those who were full of anxiety for the young ones under their charge.

Children are often, they think, unfairly treated by those who desire to exercise all kindness. Sometimes, however, it must be almost impossible for the senior to view the question in dispute, as he ought, from the boy's side as well as his own. I recollect an instance. There was a very large pond near my home. I was constantly worrying the authorities to get a boat for me, that I might row and sail

about. At last they said :—" If you will build
one yourself which will carry you, you may
navigate at discretion." Well, I set to work.
I got boards, nails, pitch, and did it. Certainly
the result ominously resembled a coffin, with a
triangular box, like a large spittoon, forming
the bows, nailed in front. But I pitched it,
got it down to the pond, stepped in, made a
small cruise, came back, tied the ark up to a
post, and met public opinion with confidence.
Sir, the next day the bottom of that craft was
broken all to smash by the gardener with the
back of an axe. I saw him doing it, and set
my teeth. The joints, over which I had bent
my brain and pitched my clothes, were violated;
the breach was hopeless, the whole fabric being
rendered so shaky that it clearly could never
float again. I don't think the boat ought to
have been thus rudely wrecked, though I somehow felt it was doomed. Of course, had I
been humoured, I should have been drowned.
Probably there was some material compensation
arranged at the time. I know I had but one—
the short, but, as I believed, the thoroughly
satisfactory trial of my boat.

Would it not be an excellent thing if there
were a national head-gardener always prepared
to smash rickety craft before any harm was

done? Going about with the back of his big
axe, now dropping it on the green-board of an
aspiring joint-stock company, before the widows
and the orphans had begun to pour upon it the
precious savings of their toil or wreck: now
cracking the shell of an addled bill, ere yet the
heat of the great parliamentary hen were
wasted in trying to hatch it into life: now
cutting through a growing tie before it grew
too strong for any but some successor of Sir
Cresswell Cresswell's fingers to unloose; now
knocking a hole in the bottom of a *casus belli;*
now letting daylight through a hollow irritating law; making dangerous projects and silly
schemes impracticable.

No, we must go to sea in our own craft,
otherwise we should blame the hinderer, and
never allow that we were at the edge of loss.
We must burn our own fingers and scald our
own throats, or be content to leave a gap in our
education far worse than the loss of all the
Greek whipped into the system. Your tenderly protected boys can hardly learn to be
men.

But if I was disappointed about the boat, I
remember having some very enthusiastic but
erroneous notions corrected by indulgence.

Of course every boy has wished to be

Robinson Crusoe, and probably tried to realize his independence in one way or another, building huts, and, most especially, cooking some raw provision of his own. Regular meals, bedtime, and lessons certainly mar the effort to produce the solitary's life, especially if you make the attempt in company with three or four boys. Even a half-holiday hardly allows time enough for the full flavour of the scheme to ripen. Still, the thing must be tried. We had our fit of resistance to the conventionalities of life, chafed at civilization, and set up the savagest establishment practicable under the circumstances, and within sound of the dinner-bell. We built a hut, with a fireplace, cut cabbages of our own planting, and shot small birds for meat. With an old iron pot, and a string for a bottle-jack, we despised the cumbrous apparatus of the household hard by.

But I may now confess that the cabbage was not only gritty, but tough, and the birds, when done, were sometimes as hard on one side as they were soft on the other. They were not improved, either, by the occasional burning through of the string, and tumbling down into the cinders, just when the development of gravy made their surfaces adhesive. Though they were uncommonly nice, we didn't indulge to excess; and by degrees we gave Robinson Crusoe up, though we pronounced the experiment perfection.

Oh, how much of what is blamed in children as too childish is tied down till mistakes are like to mar a life! The young beer must be set to work, and sputter if need be. What is the use, Mr. Squaretoes, of your having tried so much of life (as you phrase it), if you can't distinguish between vice and utter gladsomeness of heart, between mischief and high spirits?

O man, or madam, with tall high-backed children's chairs, and wretched unseasonable narrow tests of good-behaviour, how should you like Methuselah to fiddle about after you, and see that *you* didn't get your feet wet, or eat pastry, or lounge in company, or go to sleep in church?

Doctors and sanitary inspectors say there are no more delicate tests of the healthiness of air than little children. What is depression to a man, is death to a babe. So, depend on it, demonstrative little boys and girls, instead of being set down troublesome, and *ipso facto* excommunicate, are themselves often the truest gauge of what is wholesome in Mentor's

society.   They cling to those who are simple,
frank, unselfish.   The best compliment is the
confidence of a child.   I never was more
pleased with myself than once when sitting,
not in the best of humours, by the Lake of
Geneva smoking a pipe.   At the other end of
the seat was a poor woman, with a child some
four years old.   The small foreign thing toddled
about while its mother knitted.   Presently, I
was roused from my sulks by a chubby little
hand coming timidly on my knee with a limp
dirty piece of paper, on which the child had
drawn a scrawl.   "Voilà!" said the little trot,
putting its stump of pencil in my hand.   So I
drew magnificent faces, for which the mother
sent her back to courtesy.   I tapped the ashes
out of my pipe, and walked back more cheerily
than when I had set out for my stroll from the
Hôtel des Bergues.

HOW WE STOCKED THE MERE.

Y grandfather lived in a house called B——n Mere. It was a low rambling building, with rooms all opening into one another in a sociable sort of way ; while a number of offices stood respectfully at a little distance off, like servants waiting at dinner. The very inconvenience of its arrangements was its greatest charm in the eyes of a boy twelve years old. You could hardly go anywhere about it under shelter. The barn, coach-house, and stables were more than one hundred yards off. The back-kitchen, laundry, beer-cellar, knife-house, and apple-store were set round a court called the stone-yard. Beyond this, through an archway, was the pump-yard, fringed with humbler offices, of which one was a covered tank for hogs' wash. This I was instructed to consider unfathomable. Many a time have I watched the yardman baling out swill for the pigs, with a ladle ten feet long, and thought the worst possible form of death would be to slip over its edge, and be left inside with the great wooden door shut down upon me. It was only two feet deep, but I did not know that then. Beyond the pump-yard was the cinder-house and wood-shed. This last was a precious preserve to me and my brother. The Duke of Athol never set more store by Glen Tilt than we did by the wood-shed, for it swarmed with sparrows. They built their nests by scores in the ragged moss-grown roof. Every beam and rafter in that shed was as familiar to me as a mountain-pass to the deer-stalker. Year after year, we climbed, tore our clothes, and the skin off our knuckles, in probing the holes in the roof for eggs; and when, in after-days, the shed was condemned, and pulled down, I felt as if one of the strongest links which bound me to my childhood had been broken.

There were many other attractions to the place. The banks around were drilled with rabbit-holes; and I believe we could have challenged any warrener as to the making and setting of rabbit-nets. We had two ferrets, Pug and Polyhymnia by name, and with these two we kept the household, and many of our neighbours, supplied with rabbit-pies throughout the winter.

But the charm of the place was the mere. This was a piece of water of about ten acres, with sloping grass banks, and a plantation along one side. Here and there, at the further edge, grew patches of strong rush, which a blind man was allowed to cut for the purpose of making into mats. Poor old fellow! I see him now. He used to come in the summer with a sickle, and a child to lead him. Once set on the bank, opposite to a bed of rushes, with his face in the right direction, he waded in with outstretched arms, and his sickle in his right hand, like old Time. When he reached the rushes, he cut an armful, sawing away down below the surface till the long green shafts sprang up into his embrace. Then carrying the bundle back to his child, who spread them out in the sunshine to dry, he groped darkly backwards and forwards all the day. He was a great favourite of my grandfather's, and the servants used to take him out beer, with a dash of gin in it. When the mats were made, he sold some of them to his benefactor at considerably above cost price, and hawked the rest about the neighbourhood.

The only drawback to the mere was its want of fish. When we were quite young, little tots in the nursery, it had been dried up by a succession of very hot summers. Most tantalizing were the tales we were told about the fish which had been taken out as the waters grew low—one pike was said to have weighed twenty-seven pounds. It was so large, grandfather said, that it was cut up and sent piecemeal in presents to the neighbours round.

When we were about twelve years old, my brother and I had serious consultations about re-stocking the mere. It was a work of faith —we could not hope to see much result for several summers : but still the work itself had immediate as well as prospective attractions. We began. There was a small deep pond about a mile off, choke-full of little perch, which bit as fast as we could drop the bait among them. They never reached any size there ; the biggest was not more than four or five inches long—indeed, they had no room to grow. The great difficulty was to catch them without killing them in the process. They were so greedy that they generally swallowed the hook at once. However, by striking the moment the float bobbed, we used to twitch them out before they had time to gorge themselves. Provided with a pailful of water, into which we put them, we worked on the whole summer, carrying the vessel back, one

on each side, with several rests, and carefully
emptying it into the mere. Thus we trans-
planted many score of little perch, who had
long been sick of one another's society, and
turned off on their tails, each one for himself,
directly they had an opportunity of being
independent.

We felt that perch alone would not be
enough, so we set to work snaring pike.
There was a fen in the parish traversed by a
slow stream. From this a number of straight
dikes, about five feet wide, stretched right and
left. In the spring, the pike, which abounded
in the river, used to penetrate up these to
spawn. This was our opportunity. Armed
with a pole tipped with a wire noose, we crept
along by the side of the ditches, till we saw a
pike basking in the shallow, over the warm
black mud. Hist! be quiet. Here is one.
Lowering the pole gently about a yard before
him, the wire having been previously tried to
see whether it slipped easily, we passed the
loop slowly over his nose. If we could do
this without touching him, and coax it on past
his gills, he was ours. A sharp jerk tightened
the noose—a tug, a splash, and out floundered
Mr. Pike sideways, very much astonished and
woke up, but none the worse, except, perhaps,

for the displacement of a few scales where the wire closed and nipped him round. Thus we sometimes caught half-a-dozen on a holiday. We took them all scrupulously to the mere, where they darted off after a moment's consideration, each one believing he had cleverly given us the slip after all, so difficult is it to judge of another's motive.

We got on well with the pike and perch. The next thing was to get the former supplied with food. For this, we dragged the moat of a farm about two miles off. This belonged to my grandfather, and swarmed with carp. It had never been fished, and on a clear day, you might see numbers swimming about, probably in the belief that theirs was the only world in the universe. One of our neighbours had a drag-net; this we borrowed; and under the direction of a good-natured gamekeeper, prepared for the great event. First, as the wood-stack adjoined the moat, many logs and sticks had found their way into it, and had to be removed—otherwise, they would not only have torn the meshes, but lifted the net up, and let out the fish.

So my brother and I spent a half-holiday in wading about with rakes, and stirring up, along with the sticks we hauled out, much accu-

mulated nastiness; besides this, we dug a
trench at the end of the moat, and lowered
the water about a foot by letting it off into a
ditch. While we were clearing the moat, the
farmer, a red-faced old gentleman, named
Moses, who wore a thick black neckerchief,
which, I believe, he put on over his head of
a morning like a horsecollar, excited us with
promise of the sport we should have; he had
counted the carp by hundreds—thousands, he
might say—and the yardman, last Tuesday,
when he went to fetch a pail of water to wash
his cart, after coming back from market, saw
one as big as a sow.

At last the day came. We carried the net
in a cart, and fitted up a tumbril with a large
tub, to bring home the fish. The drag was
about six feet deep and ten yards wide, with
a rope at each corner, and a long pocket in
the middle. It was not quite wide enough
for the moat, so a man walked at each end
with a big stick, thrashing the water and
kicking about, to keep the fish in the middle.
We paused occasionally to let the corks float
up, and to remove several sticks which the
leads at the lower edge of the net scraped
up. Presently the prey began to show—some
flopped over the net, and others escaped

at the edges, knocking against one's legs in their excusable hurry to be off. Still, many remained; and when the net came opposite the sloping place where the horses used to drink, we ran it on shore, filled with a mass of animated mud. Flop, flap, splutter—some 200 carp, many of large size, were flurrying about, slipping out of our fingers, and splashing the filth into our faces, till we were as muddy as they. Of course, we boys dashed into the thick of it at once. Some few got off, but we tossed most of the fish into the tub before they knew where they were. After this we groped about at the edges of the moat, specially among the roots of some trees, and found several great cunning fellows, who had shoved their noses into holes, and were waiting quietly till the fuss was over. These we tickled, slipping the hand coaxingly along their backs; then a quick dig of the thumb into the gills, and a firm gripe, secured even the strongest; but no one who has not tried it knows how strong and slippery a large carp, say of four or five pounds weight, is under the water. Even when fairly raised above the surface, he will surely fling himself out of your grasp, unless you get your thumb well into his gills.

We dragged the moat several times again

that day, and carried quite a colony back to the mere—once there, they served only to furnish food for the pike, for we could not catch them. The seniors were too big to be swallowed, and so the supply was kept up.

Sometimes, however, even the larger ones were attempted by their voracious neighbours. Several years afterwards, I was fishing there from my punt, and saw an odd movement at the surface of the water about ten yards off. Paddling up, I found a biggish carp swimming about with a pike of less than his own size hanging upon his nose. The pike had been dead some time, for he had begun to decay, and leeches were clinging to his side. He had tried to swallow the carp, but could get only about half its head into his mouth. Having gaped to the full stretch of his jaws, he could not open his mouth wider to draw his teeth out, so he remained attached to his intended dinner, and died a victim to gluttony. The poor carp, not being able to get rid of his enemy, even when dead, had to go about his business with a corpse as big as himself on his head. Growing weak, he rose to the surface, where I found him, swimming feebly round and round, with this hideous incumbrance. I took him into the boat, slit the pike's jaws open with my knife, and released the carp, who paddled off with a light heart and a very sore nose.

But I must not anticipate. We transferred a large tubful of fish from the moat to the mere, where they multiplied, and served the pike. To these and the perch we added store of tench, mostly taken with the hook in neighbouring ponds.

For three or four years we made no attempt to catch any fish in the mere. The first trial was for pike, trolling. After a few throws, my brother had a run, and presently landed a fine fellow of about five pounds weight. From this time he went on; but no success seemed to keep their numbers down, so prodigiously had the pike multiplied themselves. The place swarmed with them. The perch, too, gave excellent sport. On a cloudy summer day, with a soft wind, I have taken two or three dozen very respectable fish. They were no longer the sickly pale little fellows we used to catch in the ponds, but strong, dark, and fat, weighing, on an average, three-quarters of a pound. We seldom caught a small one. They were so well fed, that cook said when she fried them she never had occasion to use any butter.

The tench also grew fast. We sometimes caught them with a hook and line, but by far the greater number were taken in bow-nets. These are nets made in the shape of a large drum, the ends, instead of being flat, opening inwards, leaving at last only a narrow aperture; so that it is easy for a fish to swim into the interior of the drum, but next to impossible for him to find his way out.

The inducement for the tench to enter is a nosegay of bright flowers. This excites their curiosity. Not content with looking at it from the outside, they are never satisfied till they can touch it with their noses. The nosegay is suspended in the middle of the drum, which is sunk in water about its own depth. The tench congregate outside, at first only asking one another what it can be. Presently, some adventurous spirit is overcome by curiosity, and finds his way in; the rest soon follow, and I have taken up a net of this kind, which had been laid down only for one night, with as many as a dozen of these fish within it—all large. Few fish but tench are thus inquisitive. Occasionally, a strong pike will charge the net, and go slap through, thus letting out others as well as himself; but the gentle, timid tench, if left to themselves, hardly ever escape. But though the pike sometimes broke through our bow-nets, they, in their turn, were deceived by the trimmers. A common black quart-bottle, with ten yards of line twisted round its neck, and then stuck in a notch in the cork, leaving an end of about a foot, is attached to a dead fish, with the shank of a double hook passed through him, the point sticking out on each side of his mouth. The motion of the water makes the bottle bob about, and the bait move as if it were alive. Mr. Pike swallows it, and swims off, little thinking of the fatal evidence to his whereabout that accompanies him in the shape of the bottle. You have only to take up the bottle, haul in the line, and the pike necessarily follows at the end of it. We caught numbers thus, when the water grew too weedy for us to troll.

The carp we never saw again, except on two or three occasions in the summer, when they got into a shallow bay with a narrow neck, which ran out of the mere. Once we were sitting in the library, when the coachman came up to the window in great excitement to say that a whole shoal of large carp were playing about there. We happened to have the old drag-net in the coach-house; so we ran it down in a wheelbarrow; laid it across the neck of the bay, to prevent the return of the fish into the mere; and running into the water, chased the carp about till we caught them with our bare hands. There were about a dozen, all large; one weighed more than nine pounds. I remember throwing myself down upon him, and getting him between my knees; then I seized him, with my thumb in his gills, and bore him out above my head with great splashing and triumph. They very seldom, however, gave us a chance like this, and it was impossible to take them with a hook—they were too shy. We tried over and over again with the most delicate worms and prepared paste, but it was of no use. There was a deep hole in the middle of the mere, and we had reason to believe that the large carp generally lay there, for, except on the occasion when they made the fatal trip to the shallow bay, we never caught even a sight of them in the water. But they served the purpose for which we introduced them into the mere, inasmuch as they kept up a continual supply of little ones for the pike.

I have gone into these details, as perhaps a young reader may be tempted to stock some barren pond in his neighbourhood. Our patience was rewarded; we learned not to despise the day of small things.   In a few years after we had put in the first fish, B——n Mere got the credit of being one of the best angling-places for miles around.

DABCHICKS.

PROPERLY, I ought not to call them dabchicks—not at least in capitals, and at the head of my paper—for the true distinctive English name of the bird is "The Little Grebe." But "dabchick" is so happily expressive of the habits and appearance of the animal, that it recalls in a moment its nervous jerky motion on the water, and its sudden disappearance with a "flip," as if, instead of diving, it had unexpectedly jumped down its own throat. Oh! those long spring summer days, when I lay in my punt among the rushes of the mere, and watched the manifold incessant business of its watery world. The mere, so called, of my youth, and which my brother and I stocked when we were little boys, was a pond of about ten acres, swarming with life above and below its surface. It lay about 200 yards from our house, and, with gently sloping green banks, was skirted on the further side by an irregular belt of trees, among some of whose trunks the water rose when the mere was full. My brother and I had built (with considerable assistance, it must be confessed, from the village carpenter) a punt, after the recipe given in Colonel Hawker's book on shooting. We built it in the coach-house, and when it had been carried down to the brink, in, or rather on, a tumbril, we watched its launch, and gloried in its capabilities with an interest worthy of the "Warrior." A great portion of my subsequent holiday life I spent in that punt, and baled out of it, in turn, I was going to say, half the water in the pond. Like most things which are in the main a success, it had its weak points, and one was an occasional trick of leaking. Moreover, it was a bad sailer; being quite flat-bottomed, however close-hauled and with the helm jammed hard down, it invariably moved before the wind, like a leaf. We boys concealed this unredeemed lateral motion from ourselves for a while, by saying that she "paid off" rather. But it would not do; after trying scores of times to sail across the mere with a half-wind, and always drifting sideways to the lee shore, we laid up the mast in ordinary, and stuck to orthodox punt propulsion. The place simmered with life. It was famous, among other products, for leeches. People used to

stand in the shallows, with bare legs and
expectant faces, like human floats waiting for a
bite, being themselves their own rod, line, and
bait. Every now and then the watcher would
slip his hand down his calf and transfer a leech
to his bottle. When he had enough, he sold
them to the apothecaries in a neighbouring
town, at so much a dozen. Beside the leeches
there were many pungent but less valuable
animals in the weeds, which at some seasons
of the year would drive an incautious bather
wild for a week. There were also many shell-
fish, beside an abundant stock of pike, perch,
carp, and tench. When the summer sun grew
hot, and quickened the rank growth of weeds,
animal life was multiplied in proportion. The
swallows slapped the surface with their wings,
as they snapped up their constant day-long
meal ; the dragon-fly sat in motionless brilliancy
on the rush, while the cows and horses greedily
cropped the succulent water herbage, leg-deep,
whisking their tails round and round, like ships
with their screws out of water. There were
many birds in this busy aquarium, especially
coots and waterhens ; but my especial friends
were the dabchicks.

Wriggling about everywhere, all over the
pond, in a state of chronic fuss, as if they had

only five minutes left to get through the work
of a day, now popping up *à propos* to nothing
at all, and then turning head over heels, as if
to catch their tails between their legs, these
birds fidgeted through life in a ceaseless bustle.
Was it sheer idleness which made me love to
watch them by the hour together, lying in my
punt, while the rushes grated pleasantly against
its sides as I moved?   There is a reception of
nature's truth in these seasons of seeming lazi-
ness, which, though one is not conscious of
the strain of observation, stores the mind with
healthy useful memories.

The family of grebes, to which the dabchick
belongs, represent the freshwater divers. They
remain during nearly the whole of the year in
the same mere, spending a large proportion of
their time under water, whence they drag the
material which their nests are composed of.
The grebe seldom takes to the wing, and
makes a very bad hand of walking, its legs
being placed so far astern as to render it
difficult for the body to be supported when on
dry land.   It has not the sense to hold its
chin up and jump along like a kangaroo.

The dabchick swims at a great pace under
water, and when disturbed will remain for some
time with its head alone above the surface—

sometimes sticking up only bill enough to breathe with. The bird, which is reddish black, with ash-colour below the water-line, weighs about six ounces, *i. e.*, to provide a more intelligible idea, say about as much as a rook. The young ones dive from the cradle; indeed, unlike the mother of many little folks, its anxious parent takes care to keep its feet wet during the whole course of its youth. Master Dabchick is never obliged to put on dry stockings when he comes home, for the nest is always dripping wet through. The eggs, about five in number, are laid in a squashy heap of weeds; the mother, defying the danger of a damp bed, incubates in a puddle, and when she leaves the eggs even for a short time, drags a few soaking weeds over them, so that they are not dried even by the mid-day sun. The effect of this upon the eggs is remarkable; when laid they are quite white, but before they are hatched become of a dull blotchy reddish brown— exactly as if they had been smeared all over by bloody fingers and then put back. This is caused by the juices of the decaying materials of the nest. The eggs of coots and waterhens, on the contrary, are hatched dry, never change their colour, and are always left exposed when the parent quits its nest. But the dabchick's egg might set would-be zoologists together by the ears, as much as the chameleon did the opinionated travellers. 'Tis white! 'tis mottled! no, 'tis red. The dabchick flies but seldom, but when he does, he pegs away at it furiously, working his stumpy stiff-looking wings with all his might. The rapidity with which he dives enabled him to duck at the flash of the old flint guns; before the priming had fired the charge he was off, and the sportsman saw a bubble instead of a bird on the water. It is wanton work, however, to kill these cheerful little creatures. No skill can be developed in the practice, *i. e.*, when the percussion gun is used; and when obtained they are worthless, the flavour of the dabchick being, I should think, easily realized by putting some rank fishy weeds into a wholesome dish of some other small fowl. No, leave the merry fellows alone; but if you care to watch the capricious frolics of a waterbird, you cannot choose a better than the common, but most interesting dabchick.

I cannot help making an apology to the great crested grebe for thus dwelling on the manners and customs of his small relation, the dabchick.

The great crested grebe, or loon, is a giant compared to our little friend the dabchick, and altogether makes a more respectable appearance, both in picture and pond. The habits and figure of the two birds, though, are much the same.

There are numbers of loons in the "broads" of Norfolk. Indeed, it is in East Anglia that I have most especially watched the dabchick. These loons, like the lesser grebes, incubate and leave their eggs in the wet, and meet with the same ridiculous failure when they attempt to walk. Like them, they are capital divers, and begin from the egg. A most accurate and patient observer and friend of birds, beasts, and little boys (the Rev. J. C. Atkinson), with whom I have had many a day's nesting and rabbiting, states that "the first lessons of the young loon in diving are taken beneath the literal shelter of their mother's wing." In this case, supposing the instinctive expectancy of the newly hatched led them to wait for the signal from the parent hatcher, and defer their infant plunge till the old bird dived with them, these young loons would prove an exacting family to a domestic hen. Possibly she might fancy them less disappointing than ducks;

while in truth, like many an anxious and gratified mother, she would be attributing their abstinence to nature rather than to artificial deference, or absence of contagious example.

ROOKS.

I WAS brought up in the society of rooks, and taught from earliest childhood to look upon them as sacred birds. My grandfather never would allow them to be shot. They used to walk up quite close to the windows of the old library, where he sat among his books, as much at home as he. And when he went out, as he often did, to look at the cows, and scratch the pigs with his spud, or give a carrot to his favourite old piebald, now past work, and made free of the paddock for the rest of his days, the rooks knew him well. They filled two clusters of high trees close to the house; the carriage road passed through one, and my grandfather always said he could tell when a stranger came, by the observations of the rooks; their note was then uneasy: if the stranger stopped and made gestures at them with a stick, such as putting it to his shoulder like a gun, the rooks were unequivocally offended. They took short

flights from tree to tree, and tremendous break-
neck hops among the upper boughs, as much
as to say, " Can't the fellow see he is troublesome !"

The language of rooks is very effective. I
do not know a more plaintive lamentation than
that of the parent birds, while their young
ones are being shot. Afraid as they are of a
gun, ready as they generally are to be gone
directly they catch a glimpse of one, they will
not leave the rookery then, but beat the air
around the trees from morning till evening,
while their full-grown children drop in helpless
succession. The young rooks, or perchers, as
they are called, leave the nest—which indeed
would not hold more than one of them by this
time, they having grown as big as the mother
bird—about the latter end of May, and sit on
neighbouring twigs.

Some morning, while all is going on as usual,
after the parents have been out in the fresh
early sunshine gathering food for their families,
while they see their young ones on the very
edge of flight, in a few days ready to plunge
with them from off the top branches of the
elm, and swim for the first time in air—just
when the critical moment of joy at the perfect
success of a hatch has come, and father and

grandfather, the young couple now proud of their firstlings, and the many-wintered crow who long has "led the clanging rookery home," are cawing gravely but pleasantly about the joys and trials of the passing season—some brisk snobs arrive beneath the trees. They have come for the day, evidently; they have brought a hamper with lunch.

"Picnic?" says a two-year old rook, to an elderly bird sitting close by him, who shakes his head.

It is a day's rook shooting. Presently the snobs get out their neat little pea-rifles, and load; and then, there is wailing in the air; the perchers hop and sidle as bullet after bullet whistles by. Phit! crack! puff! phit! thud! down they tumble, and spread their tails, and clench their claws as they lie where they have fallen to the ground.

They will be picked up and counted in the evening—perhaps while the gentlemen are at lunch.

Meanwhile, the helpless ranks are thinned, and the screaming parent birds fly wildly round and round, now and then plunging down to alight for a moment by their doomed offspring. Ay! yes, down on the very twigs from which several have dropped already, till the agony of fear gets for a few minutes the better of the love of children, and they watch the slaughter from the wing.

The whole scene reminds me more of what the sacking of a town must be than anything else I know. You can hear it going on from a great way off—all over the place.

It is remarkable, however, that rooks bring up their young only to part with them for ever. I imagine that a pair of sparrows could very soon colonise the thatch of an old barn; a couple of rabbits quickly people a warren; but each successive generation of rooks depart, unless—this is the curious part of it—unless they are shot. When the whole hatch throughout the rookery is allowed to grow up, they outnumber the old birds, the original inhabitants, altogether, and emigrate as a matter of course. But, when most are shot, the remnant, the cherished survivors, settle down in the old place; they are not numerous enough to make a colony or a dangerous minority, and so they stay.

Thus the rookeries which are "shot," increase more than those which are let alone. Ours diminished, sometimes for several years together; then the old folks apparently reconciled themselves to a few immigrants, and the census returns looked up again. This year (I paid the old place a visit lately) they are more numerous than usual.

Rooks are gentlemanly birds, and conservative in politics. They respect tradition, and eschew excitement. There is a steadiness and solidity about their way of living and general conversation, which is brought out strikingly by the flippant impertinence of some of their acquaintance and companions. Look at the contrast between the rook and the jackdaw. You always find them together, but the latter are pert and busy chatterers, while the others converse. To an unpractised eye they look alike at a distance when the grey head is undistinguishable. I think, however, I could pick every jackdaw out of a flight of rooks. They are not only smaller, but the pulsations of the wing are much more rapid. Their note when flying is much more frequent than that of the rooks; indeed, like most chatterboxes, they appear to the inexperienced more numerous and influential than they really are.

Rooks are sociable and domestic—often living near men; they keep their own distance, however, and do not suffer liberties to be taken with them; still, they will take a hint. We had an avenue of elms, partly overhanging the house, which it was absolutely necessary to prevent the rooks from building in. Sometimes, however, in spite of the traditional prohibition, a couple, young in the world, I suppose, would begin their nest in this avenue. By shooting at it while in progress the birds would not only leave off building there, but pull to pieces all that they had done. It is asserted, I believe with truth, that old rooks are occasionally obliged to punish the thieving propensities of some lazy associate in the same way. I don't mean by shooting, but by destroying the nest constructed with stolen materials. I have several times noticed a great palaver in the rookery during building time, which has resulted in the demolition of a half-built house. It must be a temptation for an unprincipled rook to see many suitable sticks brought up to the tops of the trees, and laid about in preliminary confusion.

Rooks mount guard. You may often notice one sitting up in a tree, while the whole community are grubbing away in a field below. It is marvellous how soon they notice whether you have a gun in your hand or not; so quick is their sight when they know their movements are suspicious, or position equivocal, that the people in my part of the world aver that they can smell even unburnt gunpowder from afar.

But when they know they are doing no harm, they approach close to man, following the plough at the very heels of the peasant, wheeling round his head, and pouncing down on the worms and grubs which are discovered in the fresh-turned furrow. Then their caw is fat and cheery, like pleasant dinner talk.

They are often accused, like others, of doing harm when they are actually conferring good. Indeed, they are one of the farmer's best protectors against the ravages of the wire-worm, from which they often help most materially to free the crop.

It is true that a rook cannot always resist the temptation of fresh-set potatoes and dibbled corn; it looks so tempting in the neat circular hole, that he sometimes picks it out, though probably to look for grubs. A cruel trap has been thus sometimes laid for him; viz., a funnel of paper, fitting the conical hole made in the ground by the dibble, but smeared inside with birdlime. When the intrusive rook takes out his head he brings out this on it, like a cap drawn over the eyes. Thus blinded, he flies up, round and round, till he is worn out, and drops, like what sportsmen call a "towered bird."

But the means mostly taken to keep rooks from doing mischief are less severe. It is quite a calling for boys to "Holloa the rooks" during seed and spring time. Sometimes the urchin has a gun, but the sly thieves soon find it won't go off, or that, if it does, the result is more alarming than dangerous. Sometimes the boy carries a dead rook, which he throws up into the air as high as he can. A few nervous birds think this the rising of their own appointed sentry, and make off.

It is very pleasant to watch the rooks at play; no animals enjoy the first fine days of early spring or late winter with greater glee. They then romp about in the bare trees like kittens. But I think that on the whole they find most pleasure in autumn. I remember one late September day, watching them for a long time. The air was perfectly still—you could hear the light tap of a falling leaf as it rustled to the ground. There was not a cloud in the sky but, as it seemed, unusual floods of warm silent sunshine. The rooks made a great to do for a time; they were at some council and could not agree. Presently, however, they rose in a body and began flying upwards in wide circles till they looked like a parcel of little birds high up in the air—still sweeping round and round. Then, all at once, the whole community slid off in the same direction with level wing, till they passed away out of sight. They had flown so high to get this glorious launch. Their notes, when they dashed off down the air slope, were a chorus of corvine laughter. Two or three fell out, and came grumbling back; they had forgotten something, I suppose, or were bilious and unsociable—all the rest were absent for the day.

Rooks do not always sleep at home. Sometimes the trees in which they may be said to live are deserted at night; generally when they are absent it is in company. You may frequently see many hundreds about sunset flying steadily in one direction : they are going to bed. Their only thought when turning in is to go to sleep with their noses to the wind.

Rooks' nests are built to last, being merely repaired from year to year. Indeed, I have known them put in "a stitch in time," even before the usual building season commenced.

They choose the sites for their dwellings

with much apparent caprice—sometimes fixing on low accessible firs, sometimes even solitary trees in the heart of London itself, though generally they prefer the "windy elms" near a country house. They lay four or five eggs, of a dull blotchy green, and place their nests close together on the tops of whatever trees they select for the purpose. Thus they are obliged to look very sharp after their proper sticks, and punish theft—sometimes even trespass—with strict severity; for they are occasionally as jealous of new comers, who try to settle honestly among them, as they are indignant at the discovery of fraud among the recognised members of their own community; in some cases uniting to drive them quite away, in others only pulling their half-built nest to pieces, when they try to build them too near to those of the original proprietors. But, on the whole, they agree pretty well among themselves.

WHEN I was a boy I lived in a house which had an old mulberry tree a few yards from the dining-room window. Its ragged bark, and, in several places, cracked decaying boughs, afforded shelter for a number of creeping insects. These, of course, were eagerly sought by various birds. There were always some tomtits prying and peeping about for such imperfectly concealed animals as their short soft bills could manage to pull out. But, besides these, we frequently noticed a pair of nuthatches, which not only chipped away lustily to lay bare covered dainties, but used the cracks in which to fix, as in a vice, the favourite food from which they have received their name. Whatever they ate, they liked nuts best.

Being generally considered shy birds, we were surprised at their venturing so near the house, and determined to return their confidence. At first we stuck nuts in crevices of

the tree, and amused ourselves by watching
these birds split them with their chisel-like bills.
Presently, however, finding that they grew more
constant in their visits, we cracked the shells
for them, and pinned the kernels to a flat place
where a bough, right in view of the window,
had been sawn off. They soon found this
out, and instead of hunting about all over the
tree, would fly at once to the ready-spread
table, and pitch into the nuts might and main.

Seeing their increasing confidence, we next
nailed a piece of board, a foot square, to the
top of a stake, which we then drove into the
ground about half a yard from the window,
and furnished it with nuts. Next day the
birds came, and, finding their old table empty,
began to look about, wondering what it meant.
Presently they espied the fresh arrangement,
and after a little hesitation would light on the
board for a moment, chip a morsel off, and then
wait to see whether any harm followed. Finding none, in a few days they came as readily to
the board as they did in the first instance to
the tree, and pegged away at the nuts, though
two or three persons stood close by watching
them through the window.

It was very amusing to watch the jealousy
with which they always drove the tomtits away

from their feast. These poor little fellows soon
found out that nuts without shells were nice
eating, and were always ready, in case the
tyrants were unpunctual at breakfast. If they
were a minute behind time three or four tomtits
would peck away the instant the nuts were
fastened down, eating as fast as they could
during the precious interval; when, whack!
down the nuthatch came among them, sending
them them off in a jiffy to watch him take his
breakfast, while they made a pretence of
examining the tree for small deer of their own.
Not sharing the nuthatch's objections to the
society of the tomtits, we contrived a plan by
which they might eat without interruption. By
stringing nuts on a strong piece of thread, and
stretching it from the tree to the window-
frame, we made the tits quite happy and independent. The nuthatch cannot feed without a
strong grip for his claws; he then uses the
weight of his whole body to give force to his
blows, catching the chips as he strikes them off.
The tomtit, however, hangs on, and nibbles away
gently, swallowing each morsel as he bites it into
his mouth. The strung nuts were indeed nuts
to him; he ate them thankfully, and topsy
turvy, while the enraged nuthatch had no purchase for his foot, and consequently could not

possess himself of a morsel; unlike the tomtit, he was unable to breakfast comfortably on a tight rope. However, they had neither of them reason to complain, for they were both fed as they liked.

We found this sociability on the part of the nuthatch not peculiar to those which frequented the mulberry tree; for some friends who lived a mile and a half off, on noticing a pair of them about the garden, soon found them appreciate the arrangement with the board. In their case it was laid upon the window-sill, and the nuts sewn to it through gimlet holes. The board was no sooner set out than the two birds were down upon it, and hard at work. Nuthatches are always found in pairs—matrimony appearing to be a permanent institution in their society. Any one living in a wooded part of the country, where these birds are found, might easily thus tame a couple. Ours became so sociable, that they would often set up their short note when they saw one of us come out of the door of the house. However frequently fed they always asked for more, carrying off and sticking in the trees about, for future contingencies, any pieces they did not feel inclined to eat on the spot.

They soon got so tame as to superintend

the process of setting out their breakfast, from the nearest boughs, hopping about within a few yards, in great anxiety, till the nuts were pinned down. They would leave any neighbouring tree directly they saw their friend come out of the house and approach the table with their morning meal. We always fed them at our own breakfast time. At last we tried whether they would take food from the hand, and threw them some. By this time they had grown so bold that after a few days' trial they would catch the nuts thrown towards them— not, as I have seen it mentioned in some book of natural history, with the claw, but with the beak. They always darted down and caught the nut from beneath. They were now so tame as generally to remain in the neighbourhood of the mulberry tree, and fly towards us when we tapped on one of the branches— looking out sharp for a catch, which they very seldom missed.

G

LARKS.

ARKS are perhaps the most familiar of all small birds to us English. The robin commits himself more fearlessly to the society of mankind, but then he is essentially a country bird. The swallow skims the parks of our great towns, as well as the meadows by the far-off stream where no wheel is heard, but she comes to us only in the summer. The sparrow, indeed, remains all the year, and may be found everywhere—as fearless as the robin—a bird of catholic impudence; but even he does not pretend to sing, only to twitter. The lark, on the other hand, may be heard in the field and in the street, in the sky and in the cage. We find him on Salisbury Plain, and in Hungerford Market; up at "heaven's gate," and down in the bird-shops about the Seven Dials. Moreover, he possesses the (to him) questionable recommendation of being eatable; he is a delicacy to the tongue as well as to the ear; he is pleasant to

see, to hear, and to taste. Sparrows are
seldom cooked, except, perhaps, at the urgent
request of spoiled little boys who have caught
them; and roast swallows or robin-pie are
delicacies yet to be proved. But the lark
combines in himself almost all that a little
bird can offer. He is very beautiful, though
not brilliant; sings the sweet songs of liberty
even when a captive; and after all, stripped of
his bright brown feathers, and with his melo-
dious throat twisted, gratifies his owner to the
last mouthful, when eaten with gravy and fried
bread-crumbs.

Call not this horrible, dear reader, but recollect that I have here put down the truth, the
whole truth, and nothing but the truth, about
the advantages and excellence of larks. It is
indeed this fulness of my record, this anxiety
to say all that I can bring in rightly about
them, which causes the painful transition from
song to simmering, from the vault of heaven
to the spit. Such contrasts may be horrible
to some; there is perhaps more of the horrible
than you think in most quiet histories, if you
did but—as in the case of the larks—know
all.

Don't suppose, from the readiness with which
I passed on to the gastronomical properties of

the bird, that I myself am fond of eating larks ;
I am not. I like to hear them sing ; to see
them mount. As for eating, most men hold
that birds are tedious and provoking when
small. They like bigger cuts, though they
don't inherit that appetite of our ancestors, the
record of which survives in the saying : " A
goose is a foolish bird—too much for one, but
not enough for two."

Larks are not only, as I have said, good to
see, hear, and taste, but they provide more
similes and illustrations to humanity than any
other birds. I have not forgotten the eagle,
of course ; how some people are " eyed " like
him ; how he sets forth the conquering far-
seeing soul, when he is seen " sailing in
supreme dominion through the azure fields
of air." I have not forgotten that a man may
be as hoarse as a rook, as greedy as a vulture,
as pert as a sparrow. I have heard a little
pretentious fellow compared to a tom-tit on a
drum. No doubt there are some as wise as
owls, and as silly as geese. There are others
who swim like ducks, more who chatter like
magpies. The local magnifico, when carried
away by his pride, is compared to a turkey-
cock ; lovers bill and coo like turtle-doves.
The persistent sot boasts of being able to sit

like a hen; the high feeder lives like a fighting-cock. Birds and their belongings furnish abundant imagery. Nothing can be lighter than a feather, nothing can be softer than down. The locks of the hero are as black as a raven; the neck of his lady-love is as graceful as the swan's. I believe that these illustrations might be carried out to much greater length by any one who would take the pains. The thoughtless little school-boy repeats his lesson like a parrot. The confident assertor of his vulgar rights claims his privilege of speech, crying, "Every cock on his own dunghill," with which savoury simile we will pass back to larks.

The lark excels in supply of illustration. I cannot find out whether there are any ornithological elements in the mudlark; but the exhilarated disturber of our first sleep, the ravisher of knockers, is said, by what connection I know not, to be "sky-larking;" the "sky," however, is now generally dropped, and the misguided "gent." sums up his exploits simply as a "lark." How the little bird we are considering came to have his title so dishonoured, may of course be accounted for in various ingenious but unsatisfactory ways. Probably, there is some reference to the over·

flow of spirits which seems to distinguish the songster.

But to leave these questionable illustrations, we come to a group both obvious and happy. The early man rises with the lark. Do we want to express a pleasant combination of brightness and activity, we say such a one is as fresh as a lark. And when we have listened to the joyous flexible song of an unaffected girl, we feel we are paying no ill compliment when we say she sings like a lark. Now, there is no other bird which provides so many illustrations. The lark has touched our hearts oftener than any other songster of its size, and made the most varied and distinct impression on the memory.

Larks are found all over Europe, but being hardy and prolific, survive in large numbers the war which is continually made against them. Being, as we have seen, good to eat, they are persecuted even in England, where so few small birds find their way either into the market or on to the table. Abroad, as we know, all manner of small game are sought after and cooked. I remember once, while going down the Rhone in a steamer, being offered a bunch of raw water-wagtails to eat at one of the villages where the boat touched.

On some parts of the Continent the lark's curiosity is employed to destroy him. He is an inquisitive bird, and will hover over an object for the purpose of inspection. Knowing this, the sportsman fixes into the ground a little whirligig, covered with bits of looking glass, which he spins by means of a string.

The larks, seeing the glittering machine from a great distance, hasten to investigate, and hover over it within shot. With us, they are killed for the table in winter, especially in the snow, when they congregate in large flocks, and sometimes enable the pothunter to bag several at one discharge. They are also netted in large numbers. Lark-shooting, however, is carried on in some parts quite in a sportsman-like way; I mean the birds are put up by walking the stubble, and are killed singly on the wing. This is considered good practice for young shots, and may be had best during the months of November and December, if the weather be open. In frost and snow, the birds flock, and when once disturbed, will often rise to a great height, out of range, and fly away to a considerable distance. But they are so fond of some spots, that, however persecuted, they are sure soon to return.　They love mostly warm upland soils.　I remember some fields, about a mile from my home, when I was a boy, where larks were certain to be found, whatever the weather. There they sang earliest in the spring; there they flocked when the snow fell, and the frost hardened the ground.　These fields sloped towards the south.

Probably most of my readers know that the lark alone of all our birds sings while on the wing, and never alights but on the ground. I say never, but I have once or twice seen a sky-lark make a bungling attempt to perch for a minute on a hedge.　Its claws are not formed to grasp a twig, the hinder ones being very long.　This bird, however, will some-times remove its eggs and helpless young by taking them up in its feet, when circumstances render the position of its nest dangerous. This removal of the household is strictly a "flitting."　Its nest is always on the ground, and often carelessly built; the eggs, four or five in number, vary in colour, being suited, doubtlessly, to the prevailing tint of the soil.　I noticed some last year in a slate district in Cumberland, tinted exactly like the broken pieces of that material; while in earthy-looking soils I have observed a useful tinge of brown.

We cannot but admire the Providence which enables this bird so readily to drop upon the very spot where its nest is concealed, after soaring long up in the sky,—a nest which seems to have nothing to mark its position, and which a man may sometimes search for in vain, even though he may have marked the spot within a few yards. I was much struck with this last summer. I was climbing a mountain covered with short grass, a huge stack of turf, joining the Helvellyn range ; a lark brushed up at my feet, and flew far away. Stooping down, I discovered a nest with five eggs.

How could she, thought I, find this warm little home again; this tiny hidden spot on the great mountain's breast, where for miles there was nothing but a monotonous green carpet, unbroken by bush or rock, not a path, landmark, or signpost to guide her back to her home? Nothing but the unerring instinct, unassisted by any sense, which God had given her for a guide ! Sure, thought I, here is a little parable, without words, telling those who will learn, that though to all appearance the helpless be deserted—and it would not be in man's power to show how they could be cared for again—yet the right comforter and protector will come, guided by a spirit whose ways we cannot explain, but only receive and bless.

OUR grand salmon-killers turn up their noses at us, but we don't care. Look at those little boys coming home in full chatter after a half-holiday's catching sticklebacks. Most of their game, it is true, has died, from having been handed about too long for inspection ; still, they have got one alive in a physic-bottle, poor beast !—probably as much perplexed as a mermaid would be in a water-butt; but its captors are happy as Scrope when he shot his biggest stag. Don't those boys recall your days of triumph when *you* caught sticklebacks ?—when you took a worm, tied him round the waist with a thread, and let him down into the middle of a shoal ? Didn't they bite, one at each end ! It was not so much of a bite, though, as a shameless gobble. Often the worm, excusably enough, threw them off when they had got half an inch of him stowed away inside; but your stickle-back is a bold feeder, and soon gets over a

check. One at each end, the rest fussing
about, and trying to help, the two lucky fellows
persevere, and swallow on till their noses meet
in the midst; then you gently lift them out,
and draw them off their dinners, the worm
doing the same service over and over again,
till he grows limp and white.

From these early essays, to the finished
diplomacy employed with shy, heavy carp,
Pond-fishing has held its own as the favourite
pursuit of thousands. Look at the floats in
the tackle-shops, where a varnished pike swims
in mid-air, like Mohammed's coffin between
heaven and earth.   Look at the floats, I say—
fat, tapering, transparent. Do not they recall
pleasant visions of the days you spent by the
weedy moat, where the water-hen crept under
the hollow bank, and the dragon-fly sat upon
the bulrush? of the dark hole beneath the
willow, where the conscious cork made circles
in the still water, and then sailed sideways off,
or sank with unequivocal decision? Talk of
the small skill needed in any humble sport.   I
should like to see a deer-stalker catch moles.
No, no! We grant you all the respect you
ask, ye fly-fishers ; but do not suppose every
tench caught with a float is a fool, or that it is
easy to fix a hook in his leather jaws, because

you hide it with a worm instead of a hackle.
In the first place, worms are not all alike; and
if you will listen for a minute, I will tell you
how best to provide this first essential in pond-
fishing. Take a spade, you suppose. No
such thing. Wait for a clear dewy night, and
then, provided with a candle and a pot of moss,
step quietly on to the lawn; there, as you hold
the flame low down, you will see the subter-
raneous population of the soil taking the air.
With the tip of his tail left inside his door,
Mr. Worm stretches himself out at full length
in the cool wet grass. Some, you see, are
large, coarse, and dark; let them lie; they
might be of use, if you wanted to catch
eels, but to other fish they offer small
temptation. Look again: there is a superior
animal, made altogether of finer clay, and
quickened with purer blood. Notice his form
—head elongated, tail flat, colour pinky, with a
dark line running down his back. Pick him
up; he is the right sort. Yes, I thought so.
You laid hold of his head, and he slipped
through your fingers quick as thought, back
into his hole. No—press his tail first just
where it dips into the ground; then gently
taking him by the body, he will lose his
presence of mind and gripe of his threshold at

the same time, and come up easily enough. There; put him in the moss, and go on. Thus hundreds may be taken. But mind you don't stump about like Rumpelstilskin, or you will jar the ground, and frighten the worms back into their holes before they can be touched.

To-morrow we will try for some tench.

Which way is the wind? East. Then you might as well fish with a bare boot-hook, for not a fin will you touch. No; not east—south-west. Ah, well! then we will try; but I fear the sky is too bright, even though the wind is in the right quarter. What I like to see is a soft gray underflight of clouds slipping slowly along; or a warm rain; or a mass piling up ammunition for a thunder-storm, while the horses stand head to tail beneath the chestnuts, with mutual civility, whisking off the flies, and pounding the dusty grass. No; the day will be too bright—the sun reigns; the hot shimmer rises from the heated soil, making the hedges tremble, as though quivering with wind; the mown hayfield is slippery beneath the soles of your shoes, and the grasshoppers raise their strident chorus as you brush them up with your feet. No fishing to-day—we will look over the tackle, and try in the evening.

What line have you got? Ah! it is as well
we didn't start at present. Just add three or
four more lengths of gut; and, please observe,
don't try to tie them together when they are
dry, or they will crack. Put them into your
mouth, if you have no water handy. See how
I manage it. Now that the gut is soft and
limp, I tie the end of one piece simply on to
the other, in a common knot; then I tie the
end of the second piece on to the first in the
same manner; then I pull the two free ends
till the knots slip along and catch against each
other. Fastened in this way, gut will neither
fray nor part.

Now for the rod! Yes, that will do—long,
light, stiff in the hand, supple at the point, with
rings not hanging loose, but fixed, and large
enough to let, if need be, a kink in the line
pass through. In the evening, we will try our
luck.

What shall we do meanwhile, do you say?
Ground-bait? Oh no; not for tench; nor often,
indeed, for any fish. I remember a friend of
mine who was promised a day's sport in a
piece of ornamental water. He threw in store
of bread and clay, mingled in orthodox proportion; and coming the next morning to the
spot with rod, gaff, and creel, found a dozen

ducks with their ends up, full of glee and his ground-bait. If you like, you may take my casting-net down to the mill, and try for a few of those dace : we want some bait for Jack.

Now it is past six o'clock, and we must be off. See, the horses have left the shade, and the cows are licking up the cool grass in the middle of the meadow. It is feeding-time, and the tench will be sharp set.

Here is the pond, an old clay-pit, with crumbling sides, and clear spots among the weeds, showing where the water is the deepest —just the place for tench. Now, then; put your rod together, and leave a good length of gut beneath the float. Bait with one of those clear-complexioned worms you found upon the grass-plot. Yes, put a big one on—if you want a big fish—and with shortened line, lower him gently by that patch of weeds. There let the float rest, and do not be in a hurry to strike when you see it move.

Bustling men, who cannot work and wait, may sneer if they will at the silent patience of the angler; what know they of the still charm which creeps over the senses, helping them to take in with half-unconscious appetite the blessed influence of evening, when the coolness of the earth meets the sinking fire of the sunbeam, and sends an equal pulse of life through every blade and leaf. Then the watcher who stands beside the pool receives into his being that calm which marks the brethren of his craft. He is angling, it is true; he speculates on the indecision of the fish, which—maybe even now deep in the cool water—are circling with suspicious hunger round his bait, loath to swallow, still more loath to leave, the luscious worm. Yet, meanwhile, he gathers in, through open senses, store of Nature's truth; he sees and marks, with tenacious observation, countless traits of life—the persevering industry of the insect, the sociable intelligence of the bird, the short history of the summer plant, the steady progress of the growing tree, the shifting architecture of the clouds, the ceaseless machinery of all around that dies to live and lives to die in perpetual succession.

But, look! there is a bite. See, the float is uneasy—makes little rings in the water. Now it moves slowly off—and dips a quarter of an inch—now it rises up, and lies on its side : that is sure symptom of a tench. Draw in your slack line, lest you hit your rod against an overhanging branch. Now, strike! Yes,

you have him. He is a fine fellow, too. See
how he rolls the water up with his tail, like
the blade of a revolving screw; down again,
head first! Give him play, but by all means
keep him in the midst of that clear spot:
Ah! he is yielding to the, to him, mysterious
power from above. Another last dive, and
then he can barely keep his head below the
surface. Be quick, but gentle, with the landing-
net; tow him within its open mouth. There;
he is safe—at least, in our view of his
position.

No, poor fellow, that muscular curving of
your strong back is of no use to you in the
new element to which you are transferred;
your slimy life among the weeds is over now;
you have swallowed your last mouthful, and
must play an altogether passive part throughout your next appearance at a feast.

Tench are best plain boiled; carp are only
vehicles for sauce.

I remember once, when the evenings were
warm, catching a number of tench long after
sunset. Every fish in the pond was awake;
you could hear them "kissing," for the tench
makes a small smacking noise with his coy
little mouth, just like that of a neat kiss—you
could hear them kissing in the weeds by the

dozen together. It was too dark to distinguish the float, so I shortened my line, let the bait hang about a foot beneath the surface, and landed a good basketful.

Though tench generally need careful fishing, they will sometimes bite in scenes of considerable publicity.

When a lad, I used to go every year along with a large party, all boys, old and young, to a big pond about twelve miles off, which was crowded with small perch. We fished from a boat that held about a score of us. O silent shade of Izaak Walton! the craft, when equipped, was a perfect scare-fish, combining every appearance and movement most likely to terrify the game. What with the rocking of the boat—the scrambling over the seats— the shouting and signalling to those on shore —the incessant splashing of fat floats, red, yellow, blue—and occasional recovery of the upper half of a rod flung bodily into the water—the paddling with our hands over the side, and the throwing in of scraps of sandwich-paper and empty bottles, the thing kept up as much disturbance as an eight-oar in a fit.

But still, if the weather proved very soft and propitious, we used to catch a number of eager little perch; and now and then, strange to say, a biggish tench. On those memorable occasions, all the rest took in their rods, and let the fortunate prize-holder play his fish; but, directly he was landed, or boated, in went the nineteen floats over the lucky spot at which he had been hooked. I need not say we never caught two running.

The carp is the shyest of all pond-fish, and requires both fine tackle and careful approach. Strange as it may seem, even in places where they are accustomed to human society—as in a moat around a farmhouse—they distinguish and suspect the angler. He must not only fish for them very early in the morning, but conceal himself while he does so. Creep up behind a bush; then with a short line and unobtrusive float, run your rod quietly out over the bank, and lower your bait without disturbance. There; your hook is neatly covered with a lump of tough, well-kneaded paste, and you have stuck a fresh gentle on its point. The float stands motionless up, reflected double, without any slack line hanging in the water.

It is a June morning, and very early, for the distant church-clock has just struck four. Man is asleep, breathing the loaded air of close chambers, his grimy chin and tumbled hair sunk deep in the suffocating pillow. Meanwhile, nature is awake; while you crouch behind your ambush on the moat's bank, or stand like a rifleman behind that pollard willow, you hear the lark singing as he mounts to meet the sun. See, there is a thrush with a snail in his bill; he is looking for a stone on which to crack his breakfast. Ah, that will suit! How he whacks the shell upon it! pausing every now and then to catch a tighter grip of its writhing inmate. Miserable snail! —your armour will soon be all chipped off, and you will have to slide, naked, down your captor's throat. Any one can find many of these sacrificial spots at the edge of a coppice where thrushes abound, shining as if smeared with gum, but with numerous fragments of snail-shell littered about, and bearing witness to the nature of the varnish with which the stone is covered.

Look, too, at the ants—hurrying about with lots of baggage, like railway-porters five minutes before the express starts : how those pupæ manage to survive such apparently rough and incessant shifting, always surprises me.

Look, too, at the swallows and martins,

breakfasting off the meadow, shaving the grass tops, and whipping up a mouthful at a time, thirty miles an hour.

The rooks, now—I always feel an especial respect for them, they have so much of the good old-fashioned country-gentleman air about them—see what a pleasant conversational meal they are making meanwhile in that soft, newly-ploughed field.

But we must be looking after our carp. Ah! I thought we had provided the right victual even for those dainty aristocratic palates, and they have not found us out,—not yet at least. Keep low behind the bush—watch your float—see how steadily it sweeps off—how steadily it dives. Yes, a fine fish, I declare. Bait again; you will have another before the homestead turns out, and the yard-man stumps up to see, but spoil your sport. Put up your rod; shoulder your fish; and when you get home, and join the lazy sleepers, who by this time have shaved, and come down smug and brisk, "perhaps you won't" break-fast yourself, as young Bailey says in *Martin Chuzzlewit*, "perhaps not; oh no."

I AM glad to see the cause of the little birds taken up as it is now, not only by naturalists, periodicals, and the like, but by the *Times.* The eagle pleads for the wren. It is well known that small birds are very scarce in some parts of the Continent; but their destruction is not so senseless there as it is with us. They are eaten in France and Italy. They are sold in the market· by scores. Monsieur brings home his pockets full, after a day's shooting, and Madame has them hung up in the larder. Signor makes, in some places, very ingenious arrangements for the capture of small birds : he spreads a net between two trees, and seats himself high up among the branches of one of them. When the "game" approaches, he flings a stick down at it; the poor little thing mistakes the missile for an enemy, perhaps a hawk, and, dodging down between the trees to avoid it, pops into Signor's net. This I

say, is intelligible. Signora plucks the wagtail, and it smokes upon the board; but our
English destructives kill under a stupid mistake. The farmer gives so much a dozen for
sparrows' heads, or eggs. A sparrow club is
formed, at which prizes are awarded to the
destroyers of the greatest number.

These thoughtless wholesale executioners are
not probably aware of the mischief done, not
by their victims, but by themselves. And
yet it seems strange, not only that they should
be so unobservant as to live in the country
and remain thus ignorant of the habits of
small birds, but that they should defy the
accumulated testimony of naturalists. It does
not speak much for the intelligence of our
middle country classes when so much popular
science is disseminated, and yet a number of
farmers can be found to join in a systematic
slaughter of some of their best friends. No
doubt sparrows eat corn in harvest—indeed,
more or less, when they can get it; but they
can be easily scared away during the short
time that the grain is ripe for their food in the
field.

I want, however, to ask the destroyers of
little birds, " What do you think they eat
during the greater part of the year, when

there is no grain? Above all, what do they feed their young with?" Look into a nest—see the chorus of yellow mouths wide open in blind faith. Observe their unfledged and well-filled, but most unpleasant-looking stomachs. How are they supplied? Upon what do these insatiable little gourmands live? Insects. All day long, from daybreak to dusk, papa and mamma are flitting backwards and forwards, from the field and the garden to the nest, and popping flies, grubs, &c., &c., into the half-dozen hungry mouths. There is no satisfying them. Their meal is day long. They take in at one mouthful as much in proportion as a man consumes during the whole of his dinner. Conceive a score of nests in the neighbourhood of a garden. Say that a hundred mouths are being filled for twelve or fourteen hours at a time,—filled, too, as fast as they can be,—and what a removal of pernicious insects does not this represent! Yet the countrymen kill these indefatigable scavengers, because they pick a little corn.

It is not, however, during the breeding time that they transfer mischievous insects from the plant to their young broods, but before and afterwards they themselves are incessantly on the alert for grubs, and other plagues of the

farmer and the gardener. Watch a lawn, or
a hedgerow, for half an hour, and see how
ceaseless is the consumption of insects. The
swallow snaps them up as he skims over the
grass, or threads the stream. The wagtail
runs right and left in a prompt, successful sort
of way. Every time he makes one of those
sudden little charges he has caught and disposed of his prey. See the thrush, with long
elastic hops, busy among the vegetables. He
is revelling in caterpillars, or, perhaps, he is
snail-hunting. See, he has got one, and trips on
one side to settle matters with him. He can't
swallow a snail, shell and all ; so the thrush
proceeds to get rid of this incumbrance.
Seizing the snail, by what we will call the nape
of the neck, he whacks him with all his might
on a stone. Off comes a great piece of shell.
Whack again. Poor snail ! it must be very
unpleasant for you ; we won't watch the whole
process. Presently, Mr. Thrush hops gaily
out into the world again, with a smile on his
countenance, and begins to look for another.
The appetite of these birds is prodigious; their
digestion powerful and rapid. Besides those
I have mentioned, think of the crowd of soft-
billed birds, all grub-hunting. What numbers,
whose very name is " Flycatchers ! " How

many are classed under the title of " Insecti-
voræ !"

There are some wild birds, which, I grant
you, must provoke the farmer immensely. A
flock of wood-pigeons in a field of ripe peas
really consume a valuable share of the expected
crop. But the rook is shamefully libelled. I
have read with the deepest indignation of their
destruction by poison. No doubt they like a
change of diet sometimes ; but if you want
to know what they love, look at a field being
ploughed. See how eagerly the rooks pounce
down upon the fresh-turned furrow. They
are then doing incalculable good to the farmer
—they are saving his crop from the wire-
worm ; and in return he poisons a rookery.
The birds fall from their familiar trees, where
they have bred and cawed in security for years.
One after another yields to the mysterious
influence. The many-wintered crow loses his
foothold, and comes writhing down. The
mother of the summer's brood drops beneath
her nest. The charm of a country house is
poisoned. Farmer Numskull has " sarved out
them there thieves of rooks at last," he says.
I'll tell you what : I wish somebody could
persuade him to make a pie of a few ; a little
uneasiness under that great waistcoat of his

would serve him right; and, if I had the
curing of him when thus disturbed, I would take
measures calculated to impress the recovery
upon him. No homœopathic infinitesimal doses
would I prescribe; but I would give him,
and repeat the dose, if he could be approached
a second time, let me see—I hardly know what
just now, but it should be something like a
horseball.

But seriously, this destruction of small birds
is a grave question. In France legal measures
have been taken to stop the mischief from pro-
ceeding, and to remedy the past. Here, in
England, the police could hardly interfere. The
common sense and common observation of
residents in the country must be aroused and
appealed to. Above all, let the farmer reflect
upon the questions, how do small birds live
during that great portion of the year in which
they can get no grain? how are their broods
fed? If you really believe, as you do, that
small birds affect your crop, is it not worth
while to look for yourselves, and see what they
and their families consume so busily during
the spring? Is it not worth while to calculate
what those grubs and insects would produce
and consume during the summer? And yet
you destroy those quick little eyes, which alone

can spy them out, and put poison in those nimble beaks which alone can reach them. In them you have living microscopes and tweezers, which hop about and manage themselves with inimitable accuracy and unwearied success. Do you think you could replace them with clumsy thumbs, hired at sixpence a-day?

THERE are few facts more perplexing than the migration of birds, especially of those which visit us in the summer. Some people who accept migration as a household word, and talk about "flitting" themselves, have never thought or asked about the number of birds that migrate, which they are, whence they come, when they go. They rest their ornithological consciousness upon the swallow, but have no idea that many of the little bustling songsters which delight us in the spring have just come from abroad as well as he. The swallow is conspicuous by his domesticity and swiftness of flight. We detect his arrival at once; he comes to our houses when he comes to our country. He is our summer guest, and sits in the chimney corner. But the crowd of his companions are to most as nameless as the chorus of a concert. The swallow is the master of the ceremonies. Everybody sees him whisking about in his tail-coat, which is a sure sign that the performance is at hand or in progress.

Again, there are people who perhaps would say that migratory birds visit us in the summer: so they do, but not in the summer alone. Huge, ponderous flocks of geese and ducks come over in the winter from the Arctic regions; Norway, Sweden, and the shores of the Baltic sending us large numbers of thrushes at the same season.

In fact, migration goes on throughout the whole of our year. One set comes to us in the winter, both to avoid the extreme cold of the north, and to find a sufficiency of food. Indeed, the severer the winter the larger the company—not because they like the frost, but are escaping from it. As soon as the winter moderates, this set returns to the north, whence it came, and another set arrives from the south not for warmth, although they sojourn with us during summer, but for comparative coolness. This last army is recruited over an immense area, from Guinea to France. When summer is over, they winter abroad like invalids.

One impulse seems to guide this great moving world of birds; they fly northward to breed. Although some remain, and rear their young with success, the mass breed at the northern

limit of their wanderings. Why, many thoughtful
naturalists are at a loss to say. There seems, for
example, to be no hindrance in the way of the
woodcocks' permanent residence here, for they
have built and bred successfully in our heaths
and desolate places; but the main body of
these birds retires to Norway about the latter
end of March. The redwing and the fieldfare,
too, leave us, while the thrush remains. These
are all birds of the same genus; but the former
breed far away in a distant northern home,
whilst the latter builds its nest in our gardens,
copses, and hedges; hopping actively about
our lawns, and eating our fruit with pleasant,
though irritating confidence. The apparent
preference of the redwing and fieldfare for
wintry weather is the more remarkable as
they are delicate birds, and are not unfrequently killed by hard frost, like their cousins
the thrushes. During one severe season, Bishop
Stanley tells us that he found dead redwings
in greater numbers than any other birds.
Sometimes they have come over to the north-
east coast of Britain, followed so suddenly by
hard weather, that it was evident that they
were escaping from its pressing severity. It
seems, however, a pity, that if they leave
Norway in the winter for warmth, some one

could not give them a hint of the warmer
weather to be found south of our country.
But, then, schoolboys and hedge-poppers in
general would lose their head winter-game.
Talking of this, I have often wondered at the
restless nervousness of fieldfares. They are
the most inaccessible of middle-class birds. You
see a dozen on a bare tree, and (I speak as a
boy) tucking your gun under your jacket, and
yourself under a hedge, crawl with a beating
heart, and triangular rents in your back, just
near enough to be out of shot, when they
cackle off. The Norwegians must be a fidgety
persecuting race, to make the winter visitors
from their woods so fearful of man. Perhaps, however, there may be some biography
popular among fieldfares, representing England
as peopled with crouching, bloodthirsty schoolboys.

These birds, Mr. Hewitson tells us, unlike
our English thrushes, make a community of
nests in the great pine-woods where they breed.
Redwings are stated to frequent the shores of
the Baltic during the summer.

Not only, however, does the great impulse
to move northward for the purposes of breeding
seem unaccountable when half the thrushes
only obey it, but the exception is observed in

the case of several other birds. The crow
may be considered an established resident.
The disappearance, however, of one species
from portions of England during the summer
continues to puzzle naturalists.

White of Selborne, who retains his character for honest observation, says : " Royston
or gray crows are winter birds that come much
about the same time with the woodcock; they,
like the fieldfare and redwing, have no apparent
reason for migration, for as they fare in the
winter like their congeners, so might they, in
all appearance, in the summer."

To this, Jesse adds a note, that "the Royston
crow breeds and is stationary on all the west
coast of Scotland; and it is probable that most
of those which visit England during winter
arrive from Sweden and Norway."

Here is a strange exception to the domestic
habits of a family. The swallow, again, affords
another instance of a seemingly needless deviation from a great rule. These birds come from
a warmer climate, but, as it would seem, not
necessarily because they cannot rear their
families elsewhere.

Bishop Stanley tells us of a person who
resided for seven years on the west coast of
Africa, whence some of our swallows visit us,

and who found that many remained there all
the year. Their numbers, he says, diminished
from spring to autumn, when they were supposed to be absent in Europe; but enough
remained to show that they were not obliged
to migrate by any imperative universal necessity. The great feature, however, of migration,
as observed in England, seems to be that birds
fly northward to breed. Wild ducks which
escape from the sharp, unbroken, wintry frosts
of Lapland to feed on our comparatively mild
coasts, return there in the spring, and form
huge breeding-colonies during the short Arctic
summer. Summer visitants leave various parts
of Africa, and probably some districts in Spain,
from May to September, more or less, to rear
their young in the cooler climate of Great
Britain.

There are about forty of these summer
visitants to some twenty-five of the others,
the swallow being, as I have noticed, the
best known; and yet he has caused more
perplexity and discussion than any other. It
is now established beyond doubt that swallows
migrate; but so accurate an observer as Mr.
White of Selborne seems to have often inclined
to the opinion that many of them remain here
in a torpid state during the winter. No one

can turn over his charming book without being struck with the doubt, and almost anxiety, he showed about the matter. The discovery of single or clustered swallows deliberately committed to a state of sleep, has, I believe, never been made certain. There seems always to have been an element of doubt in the evidence. Either they have turned out to be bats, or died so immediately after artificial reviving, as to suggest a suspicion of some unnatural weakness as the cause of their detention here. There is, indeed, an accepted anecdote of some martins who plastered up a late-born brood, which remained throughout the winter in the nest, coming out fresh and healthy in the spring; but nothing has been found to shake the evidence of their annual migration. No doubt it is strange that solitary birds should make their appearance sometimes on an unseasonably warm day in early spring, or even mid-winter. This must have been frequently noticed, or we should not have had the proverb, that "one swallow does not make a summer." Markwick says he once saw on the 8th of December two martins flying about very briskly, the weather being mild. He had not seen any considerable number either of swallows or martins for a good while before.

Still, swallows have been watched migrating. They have been observed setting off; numbers have been met with at sea. They have even been accused of weariness when newly alighted on their arrival here in the spring; but there can be no necessity for their fatigue, since they might come from Africa with only two short passages across the Straits of Gibraltar and the Channel. The matter of a hundred miles or so is nothing to a swallow. The martin who flashes by your window could whisk over half the county while you are eating your breakfast; but he has set his little chirping heart upon a particular spot under the eaves of your house; and by the time winter is gone, and you let the fire out in the middle of the day, and leave the great-coat hung up in the hall, he does not overshoot the mark of his home— not he; you hear his liquid sociable chirrup, as he rubs up his memory with a flitting inspection of the old nook.

Sand martins almost invariably come first, and apparently skim over the familiar pond as soon as they arrive with as easy an air of possession and facility of flight as if they had never left it. Perhaps, however, within the week they were whipping up insects off the swamps of Guinea, and taking a bird's-eye

view of the slave-trade.   The speed at which
some of this tribe fly is almost incredible.   It
has been calculated that the swift can get over
nearly 180 miles an hour; *i.e.*, he could cross
the Channel from Dover to Calais, and come
back again, while you were walking from Port-
land Place to Pall Mall.   What would not the
Geographical Society give for such powers of
locomotion?   The bird that twitters in the
chimney of their committee-room, knows quite
as much about the veritable Mumbo Jumbo as
he does about Sir Roderick Murchison; and
could tell the savants as much about the
Niger as about the Serpentine.

It has, I believe, never been ascertained
whether the old swallows lead their young
ones on their first long journey; if not, as is
likely enough, for these birds do not always
depart in a body, the instinct of migration
appears the more remarkable.   Still, I like to
fancy, that as troops are paraded before a
march, so the autumn gatherings of swallows
and martins on bare branches and roofs have
something to do with the coming event, and
that the old birds give public lectures on
geography before the season is over, and
society breaks up for its autumnal travels.

But the great question is, where do the

feebler birds of passage go?—the redstarts,
wagtails, blackcaps, &c. See what a business
they make of flying across a big field; how
they labour and jerk; how gladly they seem
to alight, pitching down into the opposite
hedge at the risk of sprained ankles. These
little creatures flit rather than fly. How do
they manage the long journeys of migration?
It has been computed that a sparrow could fly
three thousand miles in a fortnight, "at leisure,
and without the least fatigue." I fancy, however, that such a trip would take the "bounce"
out of him. In fact, he does not shift his
quarters, though he extends them. During
the last century, the sparrow has spread gradually over Asiatic Russia, towards the north and
east, always following the progress of cultivation. He is the farmer's bird. Where the
land is broken, there he comes, but he does not
migrate.

He does not throw light on the movements
of the warblers. One great assistance to the
delicate birds of passage which jerk about
our coppices and gardens is the wind; they
frequently come north with the south-east
wind in the spring. The change in the
weather which marks their advent facilitates
their flight. Once fairly off, with a good

breeze astern, even a blackcap can make very respectable way.

It is not probable, however, that the tender birds come far. It appears that some are found in Spain, and have only to cross the Channel; but it is likely enough that a portion of these have been taken or observed on their way to and from the north of Africa, the great winter retreat of the European summer visitants. White, who thinks that few of our tender birds leave our continent, was greatly pleased to see among the collection of birds from Gibraltar some of those short-winged English summer birds of passage concerning whose departure we have made so much inquiry.

"Now, if," he goes on to say, "these birds are found in Andalusia to migrate to and from Barbary, it may easily be supposed that those that come to us may migrate back to the continent, and spend their winters in some of the warmer parts of Europe. This is certain, that many soft-billed birds that come to Gibraltar appear there only in spring and autumn, seeming to advance in pairs towards the northward, for the sake of breeding during the summer months, and retiring in parties and broods towards the south at the decline of the year; so that the rock of Gibraltar is the great rendezvous and place of observation from whence they take their departure each way towards Europe or Africa."

In short, it seems that some of the delicate summer birds which flit, go a little further south than the others, but that none go beyond the north of Africa. Their migration is the more puzzling, as they are seldom seen on the move; they come and go unperceived. One spring-day we still feel the sting in the tail of winter; on the next, the wind shifts towards the south, and we hear the shrill but cheerful note of the wryneck, or cuckoo's leader.

Curiously enough, these small birds migrate in the dark. Jesse says that they not only traverse vast seas and continents—he is referring to those which shift from England to Africa—but they take their departure at night; for they have been found dead in light-houses, having flown against the strong light.

But what an estimate does this give us of the irresistible impulse of migration! We know how punctually and anxiously little birds put themselves to bed, and tuck themselves in, in the evening. Did you never stir the shrubs about the garden on a summer's night, and startle out bewildered little fellows, which slept till they were almost touched? And yet on some chilly autumn night we must believe that these domestic guests, which flit from hedge to hedge, and hop under the bushes out of our sight, rise up in a body, and make straight off, through the black wilderness of sky, for the north of Africa or south of Spain, without a compass or a map, in the dark, and guideless!

There is one thing which these little birds cannot stand, and that is a chain of mountains. The Alps appear to divide the migration of European birds. Moreover, the feebler sort are seriously influenced by the wind. As I have said, a fair wind brings over troops of them; but it has been noticed that when west or north-west winds have prevailed for some time in the spring, there are few arrivals of our immigrants; but that when the south-east wind blows, that corner of England, at all times the country of songsters, is full of them. I have wondered at some of the delicate songsters coming here, and with liquid defiance of sore throat, beginning their spring-notes in a shrewd east wind; but the wind really has brought them over.

It seems that summer birds do not go far inland on arriving; this accounts for their abundance in East Anglia. Some work their way north and west, but others give a constant preference to the first part of the island they meet with; the nightingale leaving many districts north and west unexplored, and being content to sing his song to the clodhoppers in the dull flat seaboard of Essex rather than the groves of Devonshire.

The cock-birds apparently come first: this is known to bird-catchers, who value their earliest captives accordingly. When the hens come, the cocks look out for their mates by singing. That excited inflation of the throat, those emotional quiverings of the body, are the natural fine airs of the early songster to win a bride. The female glow-worm hangs out her lamp, and the male, a dingy, unpoetical snob, crawls up to make his bow; but the singing bird challenges the admiration of the opposite sex, and the rivalry of his own, like a troubadour.

When one comes to think of it, what variety appears in the life of a migratory bird; nay, what a number of lives are crowded into his little existence. In the first place, he is a natural inhabitant of two quarters of the globe; he is at the same time an African and a European.   He is faithful in wedlock, and yet has the experience of a number of wives without widowhood, jealousy, or complaint. He rears his family with care, seeing his sons and daughters off in the world, and able to support themselves; then he reappears with all the glow of youth, and woos a coy and twittering mate with artless, virgin enthusiasm. In the autumn he is a fussy and experienced paterfamilias, somewhat the worse for wear, with children precocious and exacting, as big as himself.   Next spring he is a gay young bachelor, with freshened energies and vesture. He has indeed grown old, but he grows young again.   He casts his plumage, and loses his voice; but in the spring he begins the career of life again with all the labour and beauty of youth.   No wigs or false teeth for him.   It is as if an old man had found an intermittent elixir, and passed through the stages of thoughtless love and loving care again and again.

Besides the regular orthodox migrations from one country or continent to another, there are many movements among birds which can be accounted for only on similar grounds. There is the flocking of some species which remain with us the whole year. They change their whereabout, in company, for the sake of food. One remarkable feature of the winter flocking of these resident birds is the division of the sexes. Thus chaffinches separate, hens and cocks forming separate flocks. These migrate, too, partially, moving from one place in the same country to another. This takes place in the winter, when many of their summer associates have left their shores for warmer weather. This separation of the sexes, and, indeed, change from a married to a single life, would probably, in the opinion of selfish old bachelors, be a great recommendation to bird-society. Sometimes we see a young couple wholly wrapped up in one another. Edwin cares for no society but Angelina's; Angelina despises all balls since she danced with Edwin; the dear couple marry, and decline society. After a while they would be glad to accept the invitations, &c., which at first they refused. Of course this is very exceptionable and wrong; but the chaffinches provide against it. Through the wooing and the wedding, the bird-world is to them taste-less and flat. They bill and coo; they eat caterpillars and grubs off the same twig; they flutter through the garden in dual delight;

but they grow tired of it. Edwin ceases singing; Angelina ceases to reciprocate. All at once they separate on the best of terms. Edwin joins a party of gentlemen like himself, who club together; Angelina consorts with her sex, till they all get tired of the change itself in turn, and pair again. The only thing like it in human life is the separation of the sexes after dinner.

There is another semi-migration among birds : I mean the retreat from the homestead to the wood during the summer months. Summer is not the time for robins—we seldom see them ; but other birds seek the quiet of the forest more utterly than they. There is also a suspected migration of some birds during the summer from one part of England to another. On the whole, it seems as if all who had the means of locomotion, whether in the shape of wings or railway tickets, took a change in the autumn ; showing surely that constant residence in the same spot is not only unpleasant, but unnatural.

HE starling is a common but a peculiar bird; it is at the same time sociable and reserved. Some of our feathered friends live near man; but, though we are pleased to watch and welcome them, their familiarity is not always essentially amiable. The robin, for instance, which draws so close to us in winter, and will sit on the snow-powdered window-sill, and look steadily into the room with a half-remonstrant air, as if surprised at our not having already thrown some crumbs out for him, is a fierce, quarrelsome little gentleman. He will fight his fellows, friends and strangers alike. His very confidence has a dash of audacity about it. The sparrow, too, who makes himself so free about our yards, is an uncourteous, impudent fellow at times. He is dirty and rude. Indeed, he is altogether too bold and coarse to become much of a favourite; besides, he can't sing. Thus his audacity is not, like the

robin's, tempered by any accomplishment.
The starling, on the contrary, is often very
confiding, and is easily domesticated; but his
sociability is not marred by rudeness. He is
very playful with his own kind, and lives
on excellent terms with several other birds.
When he makes friends with man, he approaches with a gentle reserve. He trusts
us, but he will not intrude. He never insists
on attention, like the robin, or commits any
breach of good manners, like the greedy
vulgar sparrow. He is clean and civil; when
other birds quarrel on a muck-heap, or rob
our fruit-trees, he will walk about our lawns
with a quiet, business-like air, looking for
insects, larvæ, and worms, interfering with
no one.

His very gait is quiet. The starling does
not hop, nor does he run about like the wagtail, but walks with a swift easy motion. No
doubt there is a good reason for this : probably
he moves about thus because his prey is small,
and might be missed if he took such bounds
as the thrush, which seems to prefer snails and
slugs. These last are large objects, and not
easily overlooked. The starling, however,
would gain nothing by bouncing over his
feeding-ground. Probably, too, being a much

heavier bird than the robin, for instance, if he were to hop, he would give warning of his approach to worms, which are very quick in detecting any vibration of the ground. Depend upon it, there is a reason for everything, whether we can detect it or not.

The starling has been accused of sucking pigeons' eggs; but I fully believe this to be a slander. He has been seen flying out of dovecots in the laying season; but this is because he sometimes builds his nest there, and is looking after the business of his own eggs alone. We had a very large pigeon-house near our own, with breeding-holes for many hundred pigeons, and yet, though the starlings used to frequent it, I never found a pigeon's egg injured. I can't help fancying, too, that such shrewd jealous birds as rooks would never allow starlings to associate with them, and even build under their nests, if they were thus mischievous. Rooks punish thieves in their own society, and would hardly tolerate them among such near neighbours as starlings. Rooks can be very disagreeable to strangers, and will hurl themselves at suspicious characters—the swell-mob of the bird-world—with a rush in the air which you can hear from a distance. I don't think the starlings

K

would fare well with them if they behaved
amiss.

Many people who fancy that they know the
starling, have no idea of its beauty. At a
distance it appears black, but when seen near,
reveals the most exquisite coat of shifting
colours—green, purple, copper, which glance
off the feathers with a lustre which is almost
metallic. Unlike pretentious beauties, the
starling will bear examination. It does not
care to show off; but the closer you look,
the more you will find to admire. The
plumage of the adult alone, however, is thus
beautiful; the young starling, even when full-
sized, in the autumn of its first year, is of
a dingy, unpromising brown—so unlike its
parent as to have been taken by some naturalists as another variety of the same bird.
Indeed, it has been drawn and described as
the brown starling, and has been called the
"solitary thrush."

Starlings are remarkably sociable; not only
do they frequent the dwellings of man, and live
amicably with rooks and jackdaws, but they
agree so well among themselves during the
breeding season as to have been accused of
polygamy. There is no doubt, however, but
that they pair like other birds, although they

either do not feel, or manage to conceal, any jealousy. Their unanimity is wonderful. A flock of starlings on the wing seems to possess but one mind. When large numbers fly together, they show at a distance like a cloud. In an instant—while you are watching it—it becomes invisible. Every individual in the whole flock—containing perhaps thousands —has checked itself in mid-flight, and turned edgeways at the same moment. The movement is so simultaneous, and is executed so suddenly, that it cannot be the result of a signal. You watch the moving cloud—phit! it is gone! not a single bird is visible. In a minute more it reappears completely; the starlings have all turned again, and presented the full surface of their wings to the spectator. Of course, this phenomenon appears only when the flock is so far off that the form of each bird is indistinguishable. At fullest it is only a flat dot; but when turned with its edge towards you, it disappears. The whole flock turns thus with a flash like the thin parallel boards of a Venetian blind. Not one hesitates or forgets himself. This perfect drill—if such it may be called—is seen best in the neighbourhood of the fens, when the birds are about to settle down to roost among the reeds in late autumn. They often fly round for some time—as if to see that all is safe—and when they do pitch down, every tongue is loosened. None but those who have heard it, can conceive the babel of chatter which then breaks out. It generally takes some time, however, for them to settle down. Half a dozen will alight together on the same reed, which breaks under their weight, and compels them to take to the wing again, though not to rise high. Thus, there is a sort of surf or spray of birds for awhile, after the whole living torrent has poured itself down. At last they all get secure foot-hold, but not till they have destroyed many reeds, which are valuable for thatching and other purposes.

When they rise, they do so at once, with a rush like a storm. If you can creep up near enough, and then snap a cap or fire a pistol, the air, without exaggeration, is darkened in a moment. It seems as if every starling were a sentry. Large numbers are then sometimes killed at one shot. Colonel Hawker, in his book on shooting, tells how, with his large double-barrelled punt-gun, he once brought down five hundred at one discharge. He adds, at the same time, as

if in excuse for such wholesale slaughter,
that starlings are very good eating when
stewed with rice, but that you must pull
their heads off directly they are killed, otherwise they will have a bitter taste. I have
found cats unwilling to touch them, though
they will eat other birds greedily. Their
dislike may arise from this same posthumous
protest on the part of the starlings against
being killed.

The starling is an imitative animal. It has
been said by some to mock the notes of
other birds even when in the wild state.
We all know that it may be taught to pipe
tunes and speak when in captivity; the
practice of splitting its tongue to facilitate
its learning is, however, as useless as it is
cruel.

There is a sociable variety in its language
at all times. When starlings appear in the
spring, after their partial migration, or revisit
their breeding-places for a week or so before
shifting their quarters for the winter, their
pipe is very plaintive and pleasant. When
building and breeding, I have noticed, beside
the sound of love-making, a peculiar anxious
cry of alarm at being disturbed, which they
utter while on the wing; otherwise they

seldom speak, except when perched. Thus
they are unlike their companions, the rooks
and jackdaws, which converse incessantly
with solemn caw and pert " jackle " during
flight.

The starling does not build in trees, except
sometimes in holes and under the nests of
rooks. It loves above all places the ruin and
old church-tower. There, deep in holes,
cracks, and hollows, it makes a large, loose,
artless nest with straw, grass, and feathers, and
lays several very pale-blue eggs.

Many and many a time have I, when a boy,
found a starling nest, or rather the hole which
led to it, up in the airy bell-chamber of our old
church, but have been quite unable to touch
the coveted eggs. Either the entrance was
too small even for a boy's hand, or the nest
made so deep in that I could not reach it,
though at the sacrifice of knuckle-skin and
jacket-sleeve.

Since I used not to "harry" nests, but
only carry away two or three eggs, soon
replaced by the birds, I considered this rather
hard after a nasty scramble among the timbers
and wheels of the woodwork in which the
bells were hung. No doubt, however, a pretty
piece of sentiment might be founded on this

triumph of the starling, who had sought sanctuary, over the profane invader.

When the starlings have done breeding, they take to the meadows, especially the low grounds, for the remainder of the summer, associating in small flocks. In November they congregate in much larger numbers. It is difficult to say where they go during the winter—probably to the warmest, moistest spots they can find in the British Islands. In the spring they make an early appearance at the old breeding-spots, just one and then another showing himself on the favourite tower or tree, for a hasty inspection and a few reflective pipings, as if he were brushing up his memory of the whereabouts. Then he skims off, and in a few days half a dozen more come, till by degrees the whole colony arrives, and, after comparing notes, sets itself to work for the great annual business of rearing families. Then the starlings bustle about, building nests and making love with incessant industrious affection; for birds, above all animals, teach us that young married couples may be thoroughly happy, even if they have to work hard.

Mother Nature knows well that the future of a home depends upon thrift of the newly-made pair, quite as much as upon their mutual love; and therefore, where she bears rule, ordains that there shall be no billing and cooing without at the same time an assiduous building of the nest.

HEN Swift made Gulliver superintend the Lilliputian wars, and
therein convey or kindle sarcastic
thoughts about the events of his own day and
the doings of his fellow-men, he might have
saved himself a severe strain on the inventive
powers by looking into the insect-world, the
naturalized Lilliput. Every man has in his
garden, or at least within half a mile of his
house, a system of tactics and military operations in practice, not excluding the effect and
influence of uniform and drill, which affords a
minute but apt parallel to the " Army and
Navy Intelligence" column in the *Times.* I
refer to my friends the earwigs, beetles, &c.,
of creation. " Go to the ant," said a great
authority—" Go to the ant, thou sluggard, consider her ways and be wise." Now, I cannot
believe that this referred only to a selfish
anticipation of necessities. I cannot believe
that this was left to stand in apparent con-

tradiction to other revered advice against
being careful for the morrow. I believe that
it involved a general, not specific, reference
to the ways of the insect-world. I believe that
man may find himself more accurately reflected
there than he is prepared to expect, and, for
this time, I propose a short reflection about
" Insect Warfare."

When you smoke serenely in the garden
on a summer's day, you are surrounded by a
world of strife. How much size influences
the effect of a quarrel! Could the myriads
around you be suddenly magnified, you would
swoon at the crowd of monsters gobbling,
crunching, butting, stabbing, and generally
making at, dodging, circumventing, murdering,
and eating one another. Every lawn is a
battle-field; every flower-bed a grave; every
shrub a barrack. But it is Lilliput, and you
smoke the pipe of peace. Did you ever see
a drop of water—they said it was water—by
the help of the solar microscope at the Polytechnic, or elsewhere? I remember the sight
when a little boy. A great circle of light
suddenly appeared, about the size, apparently,
of Astley's amphitheatre, wherein a parcel of
little sprites were hopping about and sidling
out of the way of two dragons, as big as bulls,

who suddenly navigated the arena. All at
once one of the dragons flew upon the other
with open mouth, and ate him before the
audience. How they wrestled and smacked
their tails about; but one ate the other at last,
growing perceptibly bigger as the victim
expired and shrank to his skin! Had they
been dogs it would have been a brutal
exhibition, notwithstanding the delight they
take in barking and biting. As it was, the
cruel conqueror enjoyed himself without any
cries of shame; indeed, I have no doubt the
pair were confined in that drop in hopes of a
resultant tussle. The exhibitor and audience
were charmed. I know that I, as a little boy,
had some precocious questionings within my
Sunday waistcoat about the loveliness of
nature. Since then I have come to the conclusion that we are not the most bloodthirsty
and ferocious of living creatures; that it is all
very pretty to say that " every prospect
pleases, but only man is vile," but that the
first clause of the sentence is questionable, to
say the best of it. Nowhere will you find a
more fierce, vindictive society, than among
insects. Nowhere does it seem that natural
appetite is indulged with more permitted pain.
No animals are furnished (for their size) with

more tormenting weapons of defence and
attack.   You have seen a big-bellied spider,
who already looks as if he had had dinner
enough to last a week, eat an inquisitive
morning visitor of a fly, alive.   I always feel
for the fly ; how it shrieks and writhes in the
monster's clutch ; how slowly its cries die out,
how it wriggles and kicks !   I feel quite glad
when the glutton pounces on the wasp by mistake, and meets his match ; how he, in his
turn, skips out of the way of the bare dagger,
and sometimes bolts back into his hole, leaving
the angry visitor to demolish the premises in
his retreat.   I believe I have even put a bee
in the web of some gluttonous tyrant, just to
teach him fair play, and restore the balance of
power for a minute ; but I suppose it would
hardly be right to turn Mr. Giblets, the
butcher, into a paddock with a mad bull, for
the same purpose.   Butchers are bigger, and
beef must be had.   The bee generally wins,
though at first surprised and emphatic in his
demonstrations ; the spider clambers about in
a threatening business-like sort of way, but
ends with sulks and retirement.   Talking of
insect retribution, you will be glad to know
that there is a kind of bug which devours its
familiar relation.   It is known to entomolo-

gists by the grand name of " Reduvius per-
sonatus." This classical gentleman is a dirty
fellow to look at, but takes the side of man in
the domestic battle-field, and deserves as fine
a title as he pleases.

Insects do not rely entirely on the sting and
the jaw for the purposes of warfare. Some
wear, as we know, armour; but it is supposed
that others dazzle the eyes of their enemies or
prey with the brilliancy of their colours : certainly, some scare away children and nurse-
maids by their ugliness. Others imitate death
when touched, with such perfect success as to
deceive both the collector and the bird.
Others elude capture by the fitness of their
colour to the place they live in, or to the
peculiarity of their shape, which makes them
resemble leaves, twigs, or pebbles. The dung-
beetle will sham dead capitally. It is said
that rooks will not eat them unless alive; the
presence of mind of these insects is thus
remarkable, which leads them to stick out
their legs and stiffen themselves when their
great black enemy hops up and investigates.
But some beetles show fight, and struggle
hard. Any one who has caught a cockchafer
knows how it fights and wrestles in the hand,
and with what tremendous strength it will

force itself out between the fingers. The earwig, too, makes a great display of the nippers at the end of his tail, but they are more formidable than effective, the nip from them being anything but severe, for an insect. But about beetles, commend me for military effect to the famous "Bombardier," as it is called, which defends itself with a report and little puff of smoke, banging away at its enemy like a gunboat, up to twenty rounds. It is true that there is "vox et præterea nihil," unless you except the smell of the engagement, for his piece is not shotted. A full account of this natural artillery is given in Kirby and Spence.

It is well known how poisonous are the wounds inflicted by some insects, some with the sting, others by biting, the latter mode being most familiarly exemplified by ants, the former by bees or wasps. These last are the most formidable and provoking. They seem to be conscious of their powers of insult. I cannot conceive anything more gratifying to the malice of a wasp than a congregation perforce restrained in their attempts at resistance or escape on a hot Sunday afternoon, when the church window is left open. The brute exults in keeping an aisle in terror, and evades the furtive blow of an hymn-book with agile vindictiveness. Sometimes, however, he falls before the sudden skill of an attentive treacherous schoolboy.

Bees, on the contrary, seldom seem to use their weapons except in retaliation. I never shall forget a scene I once witnessed in a parsonage garden. The rector had come out in spectacles to watch his servant take the honey from some patent hives, but had armed himself, as a precaution, with a battledore belonging to one of his children. The bees resented the robbery, and made at the divine. I was looking over the hedge, and must confess, boy-like, enjoyed the scene amazingly. Had they known that he, good man, had introduced these hives for the express purpose of sparing their lives in the inevitable appropriation of their honey, perhaps they would not have charged him so fiercely. But so it is, we must all of us be prepared to miss appreciation, even when we do our best to save people an annoyance which others inflict without apology.

It has often struck me that bees defend themselves blindly: rushing at their intruders with more bravery than discrimination. They charge with the courage of the Light Brigade, and suffer as much. We know what the

French general said, as he looked down from the heights on the gallant six hundred :—"This is magnificent, but it is not war." So with insects which attack an animal immensely superior in strength and cunning. Instinct does not tell them when they have no chance—at least not always—nor how to use the opportunities they possess. I remember, when a boy, getting some twenty pounds of honey out of a space between two timbers in a lath-and-plaster house. We took no means to stupefy the bees; indeed, it would have been dangerous to burn anything under them. When, therefore, I opened a hole in the wall, out came the bees, highly choleric. Of course I knew that I was taking a liberty, and had tied a veil over my head, and put on thick gloves. But all the bees could think of was to fly at me full butt, though a little judicious crawling would have discovered some weak place, and gratified their resentment. Poor bees! they only took little tours in the air, as if they were appealing to the world, and then came back at me with all the malignancy of disappointment. I got twenty pounds of honey out of their hole, and we made mead of it, which all turned sour.

But whether bees are clever in warfare or

not, there is one great lesson to be learnt from them—that little fellows will be treated with great respect if they are ready to defend themselves when attacked, though they may go about their business at other times with all the patience expected in a civilised community.

HE man who wished he had a throat a mile long, and a palate all the way, might envy the feats performed in the world of insignificance. Some insects are endowed with an appetite so keen, and a digestion so rapid, that they eat incessantly throughout the whole of their lives. They begin as soon as they are born, and go steadily on till they die. Their existence is a feast, without a change of plates, or a pause between the courses. Morning, noon, and night, their mouths are full, and an endless procession of favourite food gratifies the unwearied palate. They know not the names of meals. Breakfast commences with infancy, and their only after-dinner nap is a passage to another state of existence.

This is generally the case with grubs, where the eggs from which they are produced are laid in the food on which they live. Thus they lose no time when they come into

the world. Everything is prepared for them.
Their work is to eat. They have no other
calling, amusement, or pursuit. Talk of a pig!
In a natural state, he has to think and bestir
himself to get victuals. His intellect is exer-
cised in searching for the whereabouts of
acorns, snails, and what not. Besides, society
expects him, occasionally, to lie in the sun
and grunt. Many hours of his youth are
spent in spasmodic gambols with his little
brothers and sisters. Unless shut up, and
supplied by man, he never grows fat. A cow,
certainly, contrives to fill up a good deal of
her time in gratifying the sense of taste.
What with *bonâ-fide* eating, and then
a material review of that process, with
her eyes shut, she makes the most of a
mouthful.

But for steady consistent application commend me to a grub. While in that state,
the quantity of food consumed by insects is
vastly greater, in proportion to their bulk,
than that required by larger animals. Some
caterpillars eat twice their weight of leaves
daily—which is, as if a man of twelve stone
were to get through something over two
hundred legs of mutton in the course of a
week. There are larvæ, however, who dis-

tance the caterpillars. The maggots of flesh
flies have been said actually to treble their
weight in half an hour.

As might possibly be expected, these animals
in the next stage of their existence, which is
as sublimated as before it was gross, eat very
little. The greedy caterpillar, when become
a butterfly, dips the tip of its tongue in honey;
and the maggot itself, when transformed into
a fly, is content with an occasional whet of its
proboscis.

But there are many insects in a state higher
than that of vulgar larvæ who distinguish
themselves at table. The ant-lion will devour
daily an animal of its own size. Fancy
the Fusileer Guards eating up the London
Scottish at a meal. But though these little
Heliogabali are so greedy, their powers of
abstinence are equal to their appetite.

Instances are given in that charming book,
" Entomology," by Kirby & Spence, of a spider
being made to fast, without injury, for ten
months, and of a beetle kept alive for
three years without food. Another writer, a
foreigner, tells us of a mite, which he gummed
alive to the point of a needle, and placed
before his microscope, and adds that it took
eleven weeks to die. Horrible!

The quality of animal food is also as remarkable as the quantity they consume. There is hardly anything which some one or other of this extensive family of living creatures will not eat. Man, indeed, is almost omnivorous; by artificial means he is enabled to prepare food from a vast variety of animal and vegetable matter; but the other large animals are generally confined to the leaves, fruit, and seeds of plants. Not so insects. Some live upon the leaf, some eat their way into the heart of the solid wood, others prefer the pith, while a few will touch nothing but bark. The bee selects honey, but there are little creatures who get their living head over ears in vinegar.

Of those which feed upon flesh, some wait until it has begun to decay, while others feast upon it before it is dead. The gadfly gets beneath the skin of an ox, where it sets up an action like a seton, and feeds upon the result. The ichneumon, too, is lodged and boarded in the living body of a caterpillar, and eats up his apartments at last so thoroughly, that on the cocoon which the caterpillar spins being opened, an ichneumon steps out, instead of a butterfly or a moth.

It is questioned whether the power of

"eating dirt" be not a prerogative of man ; but some insects have tastes more gross even than such a diet suggests.

There is a race of them, much persecuted, but very useful : I mean cockroaches, who are kitchen scavengers. They come out of their holes when the sleepy cook has gone to bed, and clear up every little scrap of grease and fat she has dropped upon the floor around the grate. When shut out of the places where food is kept they do positive good, though it must be confessed they are rather unprepossessing scullery-maids, and their fear of the light makes one naturally suspect their motives.

Other insects, however, which attach themselves to our household, are unequivocal nuisances. Still it is curious to see animals finding a relish in such dry victuals as cloth, hair, and the like. There is one kind, too, which not only manages to fill its belly with horn, but thinks it quite a prime dish.

Others, like the rover or wandering beetle, kill and eat their prey outright, while the flea and his cousins cut and come again.

But about these beetles, the following anecdote rests upon the authority of a reverend doctor, who gave it in perfect faith.

A friend of his, after a beetle hunt, brought home twelve, one considerably larger than the others. Having, as he believed, killed, he pinned them to the bottom of a tray in his cabinet, turned the key, and presently went to bed.

Next morning, on looking at his specimens, he was surprised to find eleven of the pins standing empty. It turned out that the big beetle, recovering himself, and feeling very hungry, had struggled up, and, though still transfixed, had gone round and eaten his fellow-captives clean off their pins. There he was, sitting in the corner, looking very guilty, and tight about the waist.

The times at which insects feed are different. It is quite a mistake to suppose that the sun calls the whole world into life. A very large number of small animals, as well as great, go forth only by night; lie a-bed all day, and, as soon as it begins to grow dark, set about foraging for food.

Our friend the grub, indeed, knows no repose, but munches away perseveringly, let the world make what arrangements it likes about the division of time. He knows no failure of appetite, and fears no nemesis of dyspepsia. With the best larder, the most

cunning cook, the strongest digestion, or the
most successful antibilious pills, the greatest,
richest gourmand among men is no match
whatever for a merry maggot.

HOPE you like dogs; if you don't, skip this paper, and improve yourself farther on; I dislike having an unsympathising reader to sneer at my honest affection for them. They were among my earliest friends. I remember—and it's one of the first essays I can call to my remembrance —trying to write the news to an absent friend, and putting it down thus :—" Bo is well ;" nor did I quite believe my meddlesome informant, who told me my dear dog-friend always spelled his name " Beau." However, the public continued to call him " Bo," without correction, and I therefore very fairly thought myself right throughout. He was red and white—

* This paper was written long before I saw Dr. John Brown's delightful book, and therefore is no attempt at an imitation of his chapter on " Our Dogs." I cannot rival him : I wish I could. If he, however, should read this, he will see in it, I am sure, the heart of one who loves dogs and himself.

rather ignorant, now that I come to look back
on him by the light of experience gained in
the society of clever dogs; but then he liked
me, and does not that atone for many defi-
ciencies? He had sense enough to discern
attractions in me. Just fancy if our friends
could not like or love us without giving good
reason to the world for their predilection, or
suppose we felt uncomfortable and suspicious
at the consciousness of being liked by dull,
unaccomplished people! Not that Beau was
dull; anything but that : he barked and
capered incessantly; so fond was he of lively
exercise, that he made quite a beaten path in
the shrubs all round a largish garden; and, as
soon as he was let out of the house for a walk,
he would make the round of the premises
before beginning to frisk. In this tour he
generally surprised thrushes and blackbirds,
which flew out, making a great noise among
the laurel-leaves with their opening wings.
When he returned from the home-circuit, he
cut a caper, and was then ready to walk out, as
a sober dog should. He never learned any
tricks, or did anything wise or mischievous.
Beau lived till I got into the first Latin exercise-
book; then my brother and I buried him
under a yew-tree, and set up a whitewashed

tile as a grave-stone, with an appropriate dog-Latin epitaph upon it.

Brisk was another of my early friends; he got the name because he succeeded to a predecessor so called; but he never deserved it. He was very corpulent and bilious; and this made him cross and exacting. As with some people whom, I have known, his testiness brought him considerable respect; he was less put upon, more humoured and consulted than any dog I knew. We all called him Mr. Brisk; and sometimes, when out walking, had to wait for him to keep up with us, he was so fat and slow. I see him now, bringing up the rear in the middle of the road, or ungraciously offering himself to be helped over a stile, without so much as a whine or a wag. Another Brisk, his immediate predecessor, killed himself with eating—not at once, but slowly, like a man. Besides having ground down all his teeth, gnawing stones in a persistent, aimless sort of way, his taste in old age became so vitiated that he would eat most unlikely victual. I remember a dish of curry so hot, that, though we were rather famous for hot curry, none of the party could swallow more than a mouthful. But Mr. Brisk ate it all up at one go, without so much as winking. He was a humorous dog enough, and used to submit to a pair of spectacles, sit up on his end, and learn German; but he could not endure Sunday, and always howled when the church-bells began. Except to church, he accompanied his master everywhere.

Talking of inseparable dogs, I knew a bloodhound, in Scotland, who, one day, being late and not sure which road his master had taken, ran up stairs and looked out of a window to see. This was more reasonable than a trick he had of chewing the buttons off the coats of the laird's guests while they were at dinner. Bloodhounds, however, are rather dangerous pets; sometimes they justify their name by sudden fits of savageness. I remember one, a magnificent fellow, who got into sad disgrace with his owner by frightening the butcher's boy into fits. He was given away, and, I heard, hanged at last for trying to eat a sweep—a dirty piece of business, to say the least of it.

Sometimes, of course, house-dogs are of use; we had one, however, who always wagged his tail with catholic hospitality to every comer. His kennel was close by the front door. Generally, Jupiter—that was his name—lay outside it, unchained, waiting to do the honours.

One day, while there were painters about the premises, we boys got a brush, and printed· in big letters on the kennel, " Beware of the dog." Lo ! the power of simple assertion ! Presently Captain H—— called in a gig ; Jupiter advanced with a smile, as usual, and we received unbounded gratification at perceiving the captain remain sitting in his vehicle for more than five minutes, ashamed to retreat, but not daring to get down ; he had to hollo for the gardener to hold the dog, whose forward civility he thought only designing.

I should tell you we had a race of Jupiters, as we had a brace of Brisks. One of them was a very fierce brute ; he was always chained up strongly, and his kennel pinned down. He loosened it, however, on several occasions, and gave chase to terrified beggars, thundering after them, house and all. Fox was another house-dog we had ; he never barked, but pounced on his game silently. Once he brought down a vagabond merchant with a great basket of yellow crockery on his head ; he seized him behind, and seated him with a jerk in the middle of the carriage road. Both of the pedlar's hands being raised up to hold his load, he could not defend himself, and so got unequivocally bitten. We brought him into the kitchen, and purchased some of his wares to atone for this, besides giving him a hunch of bread and meat, with a mug of beer, to make things pleasant. I was quite a little boy then, but at this moment I distinctly see him depart down the avenue bolt upright, steadying his crate on his head with his left hand, while he rubs the injured, but to him invisible part, with his right. The dog who bit him was a white terrier, not very refined, though useful in his calling.

The most gentlemanly, well-educated dogs I ever knew have been large brown retrievers. I have had several. Their business demands much sagacity and self-command. They must not only trace the wounded animal, without being puzzled or led astray by the scent or sight of any number of unhurt ones among which it may retreat, but they must bring it back alive. A dog who bites the winged bird is considered worthless, for from biting he will probably proceed to eating. I remember a friend of mine taking out a dog one day, who got the first bird down his throat before the sportsman could reload his gun. The keeper shot the greedy brute on the spot. Generally, however, these " red " retrievers are tender-mouthed. I had one who would

bring a cat out of a corner, or a duck from off
a pond, loudly remonstrant, indeed, and probably alarmed, but unhurt. Poor Busy was
both clever and affectionate, though artful. No
one knew better than herself when she had
done wrong. When she felt the offence could
only be atoned for in person, she would, being
so desired, bring the whip herself. Hers,
however, was a very conscientious family.
Two of her grandchildren, while pups, had
been mischievously eating the heads off some
carnations. I spoke to them both seriously,
and they appeared penitent. Next morning,
while I was getting up, I saw the young dogs
walk into the garden from the stable-yard;
presently, finding no one near, they nudged
each other, and made for the carnation-bed.
Just as they were about to begin their mischief,
I threw up my dressing-room window, when,
before I could say a word, they both scampered
off shrieking, though smitten and stung in
their consciences alone. Their father, Busy's
son, went mad. In the early stages of the
malady, he walked round and round for hours.
Not feeling certain what was the matter with
him, I had him chained up in the stable and
watched. Presently my groom came running
to me into the garden, crying out that Ranger

was loose and raging round the stable. I had
on a thick pair of hedger's gloves, and went
straight into the place to catch him. He flew
at me like a wild beast, and I had to strike
him fairly to the ground, poor fellow, with my
fist, before I could get hold of him. This
done, I put him into an outhouse; and finding
the symptoms he showed too clear to leave me
any reason to doubt his madness, shot him
before he did any harm, through a little hole
in the door, which I cut with my garden
axe.

The old rhyme says—

A wife, a spaniel, and a walnut-tree,
The more you beat them, the better they be.

Now, I am not going to question the effect
of correction on the other subjects of this
verse, but a spaniel I knew—who was more
flogged than any dog of my acquaintance—got
rather worse than better under the treatment.
He was not mine; he belonged to a friend of
ours, who lived on the other side of a shallow
valley, about half a mile, by the road, from
our house. We used to remonstrate sometimes, for the punishments were quite audible
to us at home on still days. I have even
heard, or felt almost sure that I heard, across

the valley, the whacks upon Cæsar's back. Cæsar, though a high-spirited dog, used to yell horribly under the stick or lash, though, the moment he was let go, he would caper round his master, and not unfrequently consider himself entitled to begin running up a fresh score of offences immediately. The way that dog heaped one transgression upon another showed a disobedience almost human. His master once went to Wales to fish, and took him with him. Part of the journey was performed by rail, part by steamboat. While in the train, Cæsar ate a hole through the side of the box he was put in; on board the steamer he slipped his collar, and did fatal damage among the luggage, especially crushing and flinging about some bandboxes. When his master landed, he gave directions to have him carefully tied up in the stable of the hotel where he slept, but there was some harness within reach, which Cæsar spoiled. The next morning, being taken out fishing, he killed a sheep.

To pass from spaniels to terriers. I have had many friends among the latter. One of the first was Mungo, an uncertain beast, but with rather a predominantly vindictive character. One instance of calculating revenge must

suffice to describe him. He fell out on many
occasions with a fierce cat we had ; Pussy,
somehow or another, managed to hold her
own in several disputes. She scratched his
face, and cuffed him about the chaps—he was
but a little dog—with such vehemence, that
he generally drew off, and expected society
to consider it a drawn battle. Once, however,
when she had kittens, or rather a kitten, for
all the litter was drowned but one, he attempted
to molest her, thinking, most probably, that
her attention being drawn towards her young
one, she might be approached with less risk.
But Pussy slapped and spat at him, if possible,
with more virulence and success than ever :
so Mungo swallowed his anger, and waited
his time. One day she took a little walk,
leaving the kitten at home, when, I am
sorry to say, he killed it with malicious
satisfaction. He was a smooth black-and-tan
terrier.

Another we had, a rough Skye, atoned for
the treachery of his kinsman. A cat of ours
having borne kittens, deceased, Shock took
them under his especial protection, lying with
them in their basket, suffering no suspicious
interference, and tenderly bringing them back
to the crib, when anybody tested his affection

by removing one and setting it down at some distance on the floor.

One peculiarity of these Scotch terriers is their tendency to be lost; you can never read the second column of the *Times* without seeing several advertised as strayed. They lose themselves like bunches of keys. I kept one for some time once in London; but I should not have done so, unless I had kept him at home. Whenever he went out for a walk with me he managed to half-lose himself. What with the inspection of areas for promiscuous cats, and a catholic interest in everything going on the streets, he was always getting out of sight or loitering behind; then missing me, he would consult anybody's countenance for directions or identification. Hence, he gave me so much trouble that I left him at home, where he grew fat and irritable. Often he sat half the day at the top of the area steps, barking at our neighbour's cat, or making violent efforts to get at some offensive street boy, who mocked him safely through the railings.

His father was never in town, but died as he had lived—in the country. Poor Curry was a mighty hunter, especially of mice and cats; a common enemy to two inveterate foes. I

remember on one occasion—it was the disturbance of a stack, I think—he not only killed,
but swallowed twenty-seven mice, for (I desire
to record my test as delicately as I can) he
reproduced them after the sport.   I can
imagine twenty-seven mice, imperfectly killed,
or at least swallowed before the agitation of
their muscles, consequent on sudden death,
had subsided, might well have disagreed with
him.   He was an insatiable enemy of cats.
The parson of our parish, with whom he was
great friends, once took him a round of paro-
chial visitation.   The first cottage he entered
to see a sick man, Curry entered too, and all
went on well for some few minutes, until the
pastor was suddenly interrupted in the midst
of a serious interview by a battle-royal under
the bed.   Curry had found the cat, and, with
all forgetfulness of the command of temper
generally displayed at theological discussions,
pitched into his enemy at once in the most
personal and offensive manner.   Before he
died, he had one of his eyes nearly scratched
out.   Coming unexpectedly on a cat with
kittens, she slapped him in the face with such
effect, that henceforward his left eye was white
and blind.   He grew quite grey in his old age,
but was a favourite to the last.   He was a

desperate fighter, and would tackle a dog twice his size. I remember, in one of his duels, when he fought a big dog of mine in the porch of our house, and got his teeth fixed deep in his enemy's throat, taking the big dog up, and loosening Curry's hold by knocking him (he was as tough as india-rubber) against the door-post.

I never had much to do with shepherds' and drovers' dogs, but have always considered them, intellectually, an ornament to their race. I suppose my reader knows the theory which accounts for some sheep-dogs having no tails : they take it out, or absorb it, at the other end, in brains. By the way, what an odd thing that same wagging of the tail is ! I have several times tried whether the sensation could be reversed, and the dog made happy by having his tail wagged for him ; but, like most forced attempts at fun, the experiment always failed.

I have heard it said of some dogs, that they could do everything but talk. I knew two or three who did even that—not that I could always understand them, but there was a rude attempt at speech in the modulation of their whines, quite distinct from barking or growling. They evidently had something particular to say, and were giving it, as they thought, an intelligible utterance. But whether dogs can speak or not, be sure they understand what is spoken. Would they be companions if this were not so? As it is, they are sometimes the safest. When I have told my troubles to Smith, how do I know that at some unguarded moment he may not repeat what I am sure he intended to have kept sacredly to himself? Now, doggie may be utterly trusted; you may tell him all you think about any one, and he will not only take the liveliest interest in the communication, but never peach. In Hood's *Bachelor's Dream*, we see the gradual confession of the master expand in the discreet sympathetic society of his dumb friends, beginning thus :—

> My pipe is lit, my grog is mixed,
>   My curtain drawn, and all is snug ;
> Old Puss is in her elbow-chair,
>   And Tray is sitting on the rug.
> Last night I had a curious dream,
>   Miss Susan Bates was Mrs. Mogg ;
> What d'ye think of that, my cat ?
>   What d'ye think of that, my dog ?

I have, however, met with inconsiderate people —grown-up people, I mean—who have laughed at the animal pets of old maids. Poor ladies! depend upon it, in many a case their seemingly excessive care and affection for a dumb brute is but the outpouring of love turned back upon themselves, or never led in the right human direction. They must have something to caress and fondle. Mateless, childless, brought up in a prim artificial way, and yet withal conscious of affection, yearning for some living thing of their own they can care for, what wonder they dote upon a poodle, being denied all else! To them a dog is a merciful safety-valve; and, so far from thinking an old maid with a pet spaniel indifferent to the graver, truer ties of love, I believe she is just the person to do good to others, if only she could be shown how to do it.

Love for dumb animals by no means excludes that for our kin, while a man whom no animal can be brought to like, will always, in my eyes at least, be a suspicious character. Generally, if disliked by dogs, he is disliked by children too, which is horrible.

Of course there are persons who can see nothing to admire in dogs. I knew of one old gentleman who persistently refused ever to pat one, because they are never spoken well of in Scripture. The dogs there mentioned are mostly, perhaps entirely, the wild animals of the street, which indeed produce anything but a pleasing impression. They grin and run about through the city. But they are very useful for all that, and act as scavengers where sanitary laws are despised. Indeed, dogs are such foul feeders that house-pets have often to be watched and dieted, lest their coats at last should betray the coarseness of their victual.

Dogs bolt their food without more mastication than is needed to get bones and pieces small enough to pass down the throat. Instinct does not always tell them when they have had enough. As pike have been known to swallow fish nearly as long as themselves, and indeed sometimes show the tail of a dinner sticking out of their mouths, so I have heard of dogs obliged to let a remnant of some long tough piece they have swallowed hang from their lips. We had, so our gardener told me, a horrible illustration of this one day. A little dog of ours in the country got and nearly swallowed a meal in one dainty strip, which, however, he could not bite through : this was unfortunate, as he hadn't room enough for it all, and so was obliged to leave off with a pendant of about four inches from his chaps. Up came a big roomy dog, and laying hold of this, succeeded in securing the whole slippery meal himself, little dog growing meanwhile perceptibly lank ! What a situation ! to realize the gradual return of hunger, and see your enemy, nose to nose, absorb the late-won prize.

Every one knows anecdotes recording the dog's special excellence over many other animals; we have, however, yet to hear of one dog teaching another; when that comes to pass, we may expect the strangest progress in the world of brutes. Hitherto, animals have only learned; teaching is of man.

But there are some things, such as patience, attachment, and courage, in which some men might take a lesson even from my friends the dogs.

ON'T tell me that the days of steam bring places closer together than they were. I doubt it; I disbelieve it utterly. In the old coaching days—I knew them well—a journey of a hundred miles into the country took the edge off the sensation of change which a Londoner feels at walking in the meadows, or sitting out on the lawn, after a long period in town. The streets melted into the roads, the suburbs into the country, as you drove pleasantly along. The coachman stopped at wayside inns, remarked on the change of farmers, the progress of the hay or the corn. By the time you had got to your journey's end you were familiar with the stage of the seasons and the gossip of the country-side. Now, the train whisks you at once into your friend's garden. No rural sensations enter the window of your carriage. If you do get out you encounter buttoned-up-officials, and see metropolitan advertisements.

The guard of the train, and Heal's Family Bedstead, to be had in Tottenham Court Road, form no preparative for the country. When you deliver up the ticket, and leave the station, you appreciate, in a way no coach ever would have enabled you to do, the distance you have travelled. Your friend's house is incalculably remote from your own. Steam has not brought them together; they are set apart as unconnected places. You leave the world of London, and enter that of green things with a sense of contrast which, to me, does not wear out. Every time I find the change from town to country more striking than I did before. If you let me ramble on about my doings down here, though they hardly deserve so active a name, I may possibly kindle the sense of faded garden memories in some tired town-brain, or give some country idler a hint of much enjoyable but unnoticed life which goes on round his home.

Yesterday at four o'clock I left the city. To-night, I am sitting in my friend's kitchen, where I may smoke and jot down the journal of a day. After breakfast I carried one of the hall-chairs into the greenhouse, and settled myself down with a pipe and a book. I was surrounded with bloom. Great humble-bees wandered in through the open door, and after rummaging among the flowers, tried with failures and wrath to fly out through the glass. Insects, green as the leaves on which they lived, pitched upon my page. An inquisitive spider let himself cautiously down to my level by a single line, up which a puff of smoke sent him back, hand-over-hand, far more surprised than satisfied. Birds hopped past the entrance, sometimes pausing for a steady side-look, and then, with a sudden duck of the head, as if they had made up their minds about me, flapping off.

Presently the gardener routed me out. Why are these men so fond of pursuing and interrupting visitors? On this occasion, "he would not disturb me in the least, but he wanted to water the plants." There is no privacy in a garden with a gardener. Give me a nook where I shall see no labelled flowers, and where no man at work shall rebuke my repose by his restlessness.

From the greenhouse I went on the lawn, and lay down under a tree. What a world of life is discovered on a nearer inspection of the grass! If the meanest insect feels a pang as keenly as a giant, I can conceive no spot on the face of the whole earth more full of pain and misery than a well-kept lawn which is rolled, mown, and swept daily. There is no cessation in the torture; every blade of grass which is kept down represents continual death, dismemberment, and mutilation. I can't sing in tune with those kind people who extol the beneficence of Nature. Beneath her smile, countless thousands are wriggling in pain; they are maimed, eaten alive, drowned, starved. Nature lives by change—that is, by death. When she seems still and gloomy, as in winter, she is in reality less prodigal of life. It is in summer, through the bright blue days, when her face is gay, that most perish in the struggle for existence, and perish with remonstrance too. Did you ever see a bird eat a worm? Have you not noticed the twistings, frantic tumbling, and knottings-up of the captive? Have you seen an ox put its foot in an ant's nest? Have you seen a thrush, by the hour together, stripping caterpillars off the vegetables? Conceive the squeeze of that hard bill, and, if you fancy that the caterpillars don't mind it, just lay hold of one with a pair of tweezers. It is all right, I know, and caterpillars have no business to eat our salads; but still, don't make too much of the contrast between gloomy, grumbling man, torn by his passions,

full of envy, ambition, and guilt, and the
happy twittering world through which he
frowns. It is my belief that man has much
the best of it, and that even a bad man, who
ought to be ashamed of himself, has more
enjoyment than the merriest brute, be it big
or small.

While I was lying on the lawn, looking close
at the commotion among its inhabitants which
the grass-cutting machine had made in its
passage, I heard a "tinning" begin. Bees,
thought I, looking round. Yes, there was a
swarm settling on one of the boughs of the
lime-tree under which I was, and on the other
side of the wall my friend's man-servant, who,
with apron on, had rushed out from his pantry,
and catching up a bill-hook and a fire-shovel,
was hammering away, as a sedative to the
bees. Scientific bee-fanciers say that this din
tends to irritate and drive away the swarm, but
still the custom holds its ground. In this case
the swarm gradually shrunk down from a
buzzing cloud into a living lump of bees walking over one another's backs, and congratulating
one another, on having the queen safe beneath
their feet in the middle of this solid mob. It
hung on a branch about five feet above the
ridge-tiles of an outhouse. "An awkward

place," the gardener remarked, "to stand on,
for cutting them down."

What a curious thing that bees will not
sting some persons! I know a man who will
shake a swarm into a cloth, and then stir the
bees about like seed, and pick out their queen;
deprived of her, they return to the hive
from whence they came out. Let another
man but approach them, and they fly at him
angrily. But about the bees on the lime-tree.
No one would meddle with them in the absence
of the coachman, who had gone to the station;
so I volunteered, and was just putting a cloth
over my head, and buttoning on my gloves,
when the coachman made his appearance, in
his shirt-sleeves, bare-necked, and with only a
little cap above his ears.

Bees must be very tolerant. It is said they
hate noise and dirt. You must be quiet when
they swarm, and put them into a clean hive.
In our case, the footman made the air hideous
with his bill-hook and shovel. The coachman
fetched a hive and small table; then he mixed
a yellow basin of beer and sugar, and taking
a succession of mouthfuls, squirted it all over
the inside of the hive, till there seemed hardly
an inch on which a delicate bee would care
to step; then setting a ladder against the

tiles, he went up whistling, in a pointed way,
Whee-μ-ugh — whew, whew, whew, whew,
whew, and quietly cut the branch on which
the swarm hung to the same stable accompaniment. Then carrying it down, like a great
bunch of grapes, still whistling, he shook it
into the beery hive, which he set upon the
table, and covered with a white cloth and some
leaves.

There was, however, a mystery throughout
the whole process. The people in this part
of the world are very superstitious about bees.
My interest and assistance in this case were
received coldly. I am afraid now that I did
some unlucky thing. The performance on the
shovel was perfectly sincere; so was the nasty
squirting into the hive; so was the whistling;
and yet I fully believe, on good authority,
that they were all far more likely to hinder
than to assist the work. It was, though, and
will continue to be, done in spite of them.
Indeed, I suspect that most of our manipulation, I don't mean only in connection with
bees, is mere pedantry.

People don't like to see an important thing
done simply. "Wash, and be clean," is generally offensive advice. Is that all? say the
million. We love mystery. Don't, pray don't

give us nothing but simple methods and naked truth. Don't insist on cutting down our belongings and appliances to the skeleton of necessity? Is there to be no regard for appearance? Must everything be obviously useful? Has not ornament a tinge of the divine? Is not ceremony natural? Why should the rose propagate its kind, or ripen its seed, through the stages of the bud, the blossom, and the full-blown flower? Why spend colours and sweet perfume in the process? Think of the display through which a chestnut has passed before the pig crunches it at the foot of the tree!

Let us weave our harmless web of mystery, ceremonial, or ornament, about the common things of life, and not always think ourselves bound to strip our work quite bare, when we see Nature loving to adorn and complicate hers.

When the bees were hived, I went back to the greenhouse. At the entrance is an underground tank, with smooth hard sides and a trap-door, which uncovers about one quarter of it, and permits the gardener to dip for water. It was then being replenished. I peeped in, and met what I may call a chorus of appealing looks. A number of frogs had jumped in, but could not get out. In exploring the garden, they had come to this tank, and seeing water, hopped in. When one had done so, another had less hesitation; but at last, when Mr. Froggy had taken his bath, he found to his dismay that there was no way out. You may be a good swimmer, but it is no joke to swim for a month.

Some of the frogs were very tired; they had swum round and round the tank to find everywhere the same smooth, upright wall. Sometimes, by getting in a corner, and thus touching two sides, a fresh comer, less weary than the rest, could support himself for a few moments; but he soon slipped down, especially as, the instant he succeeded in getting a little purchase, a companion would climb upon his neck, and weigh him down.

When, therefore, I stooped down and peeped in, I was met by an appealing look from the whole party, who swam together under the opening, and begged to be let out. Some pawed at the slippery wall, some let their legs drop, as if worn out, and simply held their chins above water in ungraceful but pathetic attitudes. One had found a little raft of four rooks' feathers placed crosswise, on which he squatted. All were fearless from fatigue.

Every now and then, the expectant little crowd beneath the trap-door was dispersed by the emptying of a pail of water, for the tank was being replenished, and a boy went incessantly during the whole morning, with a hoop and two pails, to a neighbouring pump for the supply ; but as soon as the disturbance made by the pouring in of each pailful was over, the frogs were there again, buoyant but piteous.

Having found a board a foot and a half long, and six inches wide, I let it down into the tank by four strings, so that I might haul it up steadily in case the frogs really meant what they looked. As soon as my raft touched the water, several of the most tired swimmers made at it, and clambered up slowly, like lame old gentlemen getting back into a bathing-machine. Once on board, they neither hopped nor stirred, but remained squatting at the edge, grateful though distressed. When I pulled up my raft, they sat quite still. Thus I drew six-and-thirty out of the pit. When I set the raft down on the grass-plat—after a moment's hesitation, as if to feel quite sure the thing had grounded—away they all jumped, and in a short time there was not a frog to be seen. I believe that frogs are far from useless in a

garden; at least, I secured the immediate
safety of these thirty-six by assuming to the
gardener that they were his friends rather than
enemies.

One or two frogs remained in the tank.   I
suppose they had just jumped in, and had not
found out the drawbacks of the place.   Confident fools! they came up to look at me, and
then dived as soon as I let down the raft.
Nothing would induce them to mount it.
They could swim, thank you, and away they
struck off into the obscure places of the tank.
In a month, they will repent.   Then I shall
have long ago returned to town, the weather
will be wet, the tank-door unopened, and the
thin, weary frogs feeling round the hard, slippery, upright edge for some support, some
change of gait, in vain.

Finding the late brisk offenders inaccessible
to my material offers and remonstrance, I shut
the tank-lid down, and went to feed the pigs.
I like feeding pigs; I like being appreciated.
There were seven pigs, quite new to me, in
the yard.   I found some Swedes in the barn,
and cutting one of them into strips, sat down
on the threshold, and held them out.   They
were eaten out of my hand, after a careful,
cunning approach.   The pigs were, of course,

querulous and greedy, but civil enough to me.
They appeared all of the same size and age,
were all black, and exactly alike. I found,
however, at once, varieties of temper and confidence in the distribution of the first Swede.
Now, thought I, "I'll be bound some one pig
is sole master here, has some mental ascend-
ency over the rest. Wishing to try this, I
threw a whole Swede among the party. The
nearest whipped it up, and jogged off; most
of the others yielded ; but one, no bigger than
his fellows, walked after the fortunate possessor, bit his hind-leg, and made · him drop
the turnip, which he then himself picked
up and ate publicly, without haste or hindrance.

The rain has begun to fall; I hear it on the
roof of the verandah. The tank will not be
opened again for weeks. The soft summer
rain is coming steadily down, and the air—for
I have laid down my pen to put my head out
at the door—is loaded with the scent of earth
and blossom. The clock has struck eleven.
I must be off to bed, but I shall leave my
window open. Good-night !

HAVING once executed a commission for a country friend at one of the great London flower seed shops, the seasons have ever since been marked to me by catalogues of floral novelties and garden stuff. My address, and the sum I was charged to disburse, were planted in the books of the establishment, and have produced this regular crop:—I have never bought anything from the advertiser since. I can never get anything to grow at my dingy window; but as sure as the almanac divides the year, an appropriate choice of unattainable beauty is pitched head first into my letter-box, and I read at leisure the gorgeous proposals of Messrs. Germen & Bulb. They are made in a closely-printed 8vo. of 120 pages. I see on the outside that "immediate proceedings in Chancery will be taken against all infringements of the copyright of this work. 1st edition, 1500." Hoping that I have not committed myself by pirating this

information, I turn timidly over the leaves till
my teeth ache. I don't pretend to understand
them all. I don't believe Max Müller could.
It is true that there is a list of "flowers having
popular names," but before this come 2,142
terrible plants. Can you picture to yourself a
man going a wooing with a "Delphinium Don-
kelærii" in his button-hole? Don't you think
Snapdragon hardly an august enough translation of "Antirrhinum caryophylloides?" No
humble-bee would venture to show its nose in
an "Indigofera-coccinea endecaphylla," and I
should like you to tell me, off-hand, what a
"Guiterezia gymnospermoides" smells like, or
a "Cucumis aradac."

Here is a plant which Germen & Bulb
say must not be crowded with others, otherwise it will not succeed well. Its name is
certainly unsocial. One in a garden would be
enough. Who would like a bed filled with
"Tropæolum Scheunermannianum?" I find
that this is better known as a variety of the
tall nasturtion, and is, I dare say, not a bad
substitute for capers in the making of sauce
for boiled mutton. Here is another, strongly
recommended :—"Pentstemon Hartwegi gen-
tianoides." The next I pitch upon is called a
"dwarf" in the catalogue. Its pretensions

are large enough :—the " Mesembryanthemum
pomeridianum." It would take a slow man a
quarter of an hour to pluck this. There is
no explanation whatever given about the
" Leptorhynchus squamatus," except that it
costs sixpence. I can't tell why, but by one
of those rapid, positive, inscrutable processes
of mind which despise thought, I must associate this item with something between a duck
and an armadillo. Not a few of the plants
advertised by Germen & Bulb repel us by
their names. Who would present a lady with
a bouquet of " Anagyris fœtida?" Some,
again, have a medical smack about them.
Thus, I should not wonder at a surgeon
taking an interest in " Cathartocarpus fistula."
Others, like prescriptions, appear in that ellip-
tical language which conceals the terminations
of our physic, such as the " Datura—alba
fl. pl."

There are some plants to which I can
hardly be sure of giving their right names,
the nomenclature of the catalogue apparently
requiring some skill in the accumulation of
titles. Here is one which would delight a
Spaniard. I believe I have extracted it
rightly:—" Ipomœa hederacea superba atro-
violacea." The next looks as if it ought to

be scanned rather than smelt, and reads like
a bad "nonsense verse"—really a "carna-
tion :"—"Dianthus Chinensis nanus rubro
striatus." The uneducated intellect, to which
a yellow primrose on a bank is a primrose
and "nothing more," is rather to be envied
than pitied.

This rage for long names may be very
acceptable to the printer, but it drives the
genuine lover of an honest good old flower
garden into a general dislike of science. Latin
and Greek are dead languages, and ought not
to be chopped up and sown in this barbarous
way; but it is the fashion, and "Germen &
Bulb" are only one firm of many.

I see, by reference to the "London Post-
office Directory," now lying open before me,
that there are 45 "seedsmen," 126 "nursery
and seedsmen," besides market gardeners,
herbalists, seed merchants, and, may we add,
more than 200 artificial flower makers. What
a scene of floral tyranny does not this suggest !
Reflect, too, that this gardeners' language, this
crackjaw conglomeration of classical disguises,
is spoken principally by Scotchmen, who are
the despots of the greenhouse. I pluck a
pretty little annual, and ask a raw-boned, red-
haired man in a blue apron and a flower-pot

what it is.   He takes it in his great freckled
hand, and in the conscientious malignity of his
own dialect, describes it as a " Podelepis affinis
chrysanthemoides."

If you want to enjoy Nature, fly from the
modern garden; pluck the cowslip in the
meadow, and the violet on the bank; rub the
sweet-briar shoot in your hand, and lean on
the gate of the bean-field in full bloom, or
of the clover buzzing with a million honey-
bees.

No doubt, the construction of new scientific
names is necessary to botanists in some
instances; but surely it is high time to protest
against the pedantry of illiterate gardeners,
who insist on thrusting classical polysyllables
upon you, which half of them cannot translate,
and which might, without contempt of science,
be replaced by some simple familiar name
recalling the scents and colours of childhood.

Under the " Flowers having popular names "
of the " work " before me, I cannot find a
daisy.   At last, through the "general observations," I discover the " Swan river," the
" African," and the " double " daisy as, respectively, the " Brachycome iberidifolium,"
" Athanasia annua," and the " Bellis perennis."

Why not put these down under the common names first, and then, if you will, the scientific? It looks as if these pretty plants were now best known to gardeners under the latter descriptions, and that the diseased vanity which converts a curling comb into a " Bostrochyzor" had invaded the garden as well as the barber's shop. If we go on at the present rate, we shall need a special Lexicon to construe the Language of Flowers.

D O not suppose, my friend and reader, that I am going to teach you anything new, or give you any fresh directions about the old. I have not invented a lawn balloon, and I avoid any reference to the rules of particular games. There must be rules, of course, but for them I depend upon my neighbours. I wish merely to have a chat with any one who reads this about garden games and their belongings in general.

First, I suppose, in the present day comes "Croquet." Is this a revival or an invention? It sounds, or is pronounced, as if it came from France; but I doubt this. French lawns are not smooth enough for it—the grass is too coarse, the worm-casts are too big throughout the whole of that country, to admit a supposition that croquet ever could have been general there. Besides, it is fundamentally opposed to the national sentiment, which has billiard-tables without pockets. Croquet mainly consists in striking balls through hoops; there is hardly ever a true cannon made throughout a game.

However, the game is here. It is adopted universally. There is hardly a lawn in England fit for the purpose without a set of little wire arches, which look like human springes and toe-traps for the unwary. The game is here; and it is a pleasant, tapping, chattering, respectable, flirting game too. Men, women, and children can play at it. Reverend dignitaries and fashionable dandies, crinoline and knickerbockers, can all play it at once. It is easy to learn, and yet admits many degrees of skill. It gives fresh air, and does not make you hot. It is clean. Unlike archery, it can be played on a small space. It is not dangerous—no one was ever mortally wounded at croquet. It is cheap. If not independent of the weather, it is not affected by the wind or sun—no one need complain of the glare of light in taking aim, or of the disturbing breeze which turns aside the arrow. It can be played by ladies and gentlemen on equal terms and with the same tackle. And it is the very chief provocative of small talk and garden gossip. Upon my word, I had no idea of the number of recommendations which it possesses. I had dipped my pen rather with the intention of blackening croquet than otherwise, and now its dissection has converted me.

I do not wonder at the polite rural world playing croquet. It conceals the age of the old, and displays the grace of the young.

Grandpapa, in whose hands a bow would look absurd, whose lumbago would interfere with the exercise of quoits or bowls, can and does often play a very close game at croquet. He need not bend his back; thus it is a good pastime for those who are getting rather stiffish. And for those full of ease and grace, what better?

A girl with neat ankles will play at croquet all day long—it is made for pretty feet and well-shaped boots. And yet, with all these social and coquettish recommendations, it is a game within the pale of the most strict and straitlaced society.

A Quaker might play at croquet with drab balls. Papas and mammas who would not endure seeing their daughters whisked about in the waltz by the young gentlemen of their acquaintance, permit them to tread the mazes of croquet, and see their interests represented in the osculating balls.

If I were a young man in the country, with

an average appreciation of young ladies'
society, I should probably affect to underrate
croquet. As it is, being a grave townsman, with
only an occasional glimpse, by return ticket,
of the green grass carpet with its checkered
shade and moving group of playful tapping
nymphs, I can only say that young men have
now opportunities which we ancients knew
not.

But let us have done with this croquet.
The original prejudice against it, with which I
began to write, is coming back again, and if
I don't get out of the subject soon, shall catch
myself sneering at the game as a dawdling,
effeminate——

There, now, I've cut the thread, and turn
to quoits. Lawn billiards are too like croquet
for me to venture on them. Let us to quoits.
Here we are at once in another atmosphere,
though at a garden game. The history of
quoits would lead us back into the twilight of
the past. It was a national Greek game in the
time of Homer; it was still popular and manly
at the height of Roman civilization. With
modifications, it has survived till now; and
though it has in some places a tendency to
associate itself with skittles, it is considered
both classical and manly, affording wholesome

exercise, and considerable opportunity for skill. The main difference between it as played by the ancients and moderns, is this—the latter pitch at a mark, the trial with the former was only who could pitch the quoit farthest. There is a difference, too, in the shape of the old and new quoit—the old was larger, flatter, and without a hole in the middle.

Leaving now the contrast, let us look at the game as played in the present day. It is a fair; manly game; there are no patterns, or colours, or devices about it. It has no paraphernalia; it wants only a couple of feathers, the quoit itself, and a cunning hand. I say feathers, for they are soft and visible, and far better than iron pins to pitch at. A good rook's wing-feather marks the goal, provides a stiff centre to measure from, and does not spoil a good throw. Sometimes an iron pin flings off the best quoit of the whole flight when it pitches upon it. Moreover, the feather, when cut down, is capable of being set up again, and serves as well as ever.

The two feathers ought to be twenty-one yards apart; this is a good distance to pitch. A string tied loosely round the quill serves to measure the nearness of the rival quoits. No quoit ought to be counted unless it sticks in

the ground; this affords a severe test of the
accuracy of the aim. It is not usual, I know,
under any circumstances, to reckon those quoits
which turn up and rest finally on their backs;
but even a flat quoit, which some players recog-
nise, will sometimes pitch at a distance from
the feather, and then hop or bowl close up to
it, cutting out others which have been better
directed. Unless you make a strict rule that
none but stickers shall count, there will be more
flukes made in this game than any other. · I
have many times seen a quoit which pitched
three yards wide of the mark, and didn't stick,
roll quietly in sideways, and lie down close to
the feather. You know the wonderful gift of
locomotion possessed by a shilling : you drop
it on the floor and it bowls off on its own
account, at no great pace, but with surprising
perseverance. Just so, a badly-thrown quoit
will occasionally travel up to the goal, and take
its place among the winners.

But if you play " stickers " the disc may
wander in with no worse mischief to the
skilful player than arises from the chance of its
getting in the way, and preventing a good
quoit which would have stuck.

A quoit ought to enter the ground at an
angle of forty-five degrees, and make a cut in

the clay or grass at right angles to the straight
line between the two feathers. If well thrown
it moves parallel to itself throughout its whole
flight, the greatest height of its trajectory being
about two-thirds of the distance from the end
it is thrown from. In delivering it you must
be careful not to let it go off out of your hand
too flat, otherwise it will be a " flopper," or
barely stick. Its claim to be a sticker is
decided by drawing back the lip of the cut it
makes in the ground; if the quoit drops in the
least, it is a " sticker."

A " flopper " is a demonstrative, deceptive
pitch. The quoit often looks well as it is
going, flies steadily, but comes down flat upon
its face with a smack, and not the ghost of a
" stick " in it. A " wabbler," on the contrary,
often sticks; it is an unsteady quoit, and a
most unpromising one in its flight, but very
often pops down in the right place, half burying
itself in the soil, and therefore all the less
likely to be knocked out by another. But no
good player can bear to see his quoits wabble.

You should not walk, much less run, up to
the place from which you deliver your quoit:
do it standing, quietly. The twist of the hand
which gives the quoit its steady flight can be
gained only by practice. The main thing in

delivering it is to swing and let it go without any slope to the right or left—let it meet the air full.

There are many pleasant recommendations to quoits. It is a fine appetising game; it is terribly destructive of luncheons. It exercises without fatiguing the player. Moreover, every one has his full turn; the worst player has an innings as long as the best. Nobody is kept waiting about. Each delivers his quoit in turn, and then walks towards the other end, but not in the direct line, unless he wishes to have the back of his head cut open by the rest of the flight. A blow from a quoit is no joke, but accidents are very rare in this game.

When I walk down Oxford Street, and see, near the bottom, chains and clusters of beautiful new polished quoits in one of the shop-windows, I always think of the paddock where I have played so many hundred games, or the bottom down in the low meadows by the slow stream where the ground was moist even in the height of summer, and where the dogs used to snuff about for inaccessible water-rats while we played. The only drawback to the spot was a beast of a bull, who used some-times to come up with a suspicious air of interest in our gestures. The best place was the paddock, where the turf was bitten short, and feathers could be picked up beneath the neighbouring rookery. Ah me! those old garden games! I like you better than croquet. Think of bowls! What skill, what philosophical accuracy are here needed! Bah! I'll stop. My window looks out into a mews, and there is a fellow swearing at his horses enough to turn the hair of my clothes-brush gray.

Yet a word. I don't call trap-bat or archery garden games. I see others represented by "les Grâces" (the shooting of a worsted hoop off two sticks), but I don't care to stop over them. I can't either believe that any one could keep up a very long interest in Knock-em-downs or Aunt Sally. I should not weep to see them die out. The young ladies who play at them are sometimes fond of slang; and, though men will often maliciously provoke it, there is nothing which sets them more against a woman than this.

Commend me, however, to swings. I hate them, and yet the enjoyment they cause to children is endless. Those great double ones which carry two, face to face, are horrible, most especially if your *vis-à-vis* should, as not unfrequently is the case, turn white, and be taken poorly while uppermost. There is no escape. But if you have a garden and a convenient branch, set up a swing for the young folks ; and if you want a delightful couch, combining in itself every conceivable phase of adaptability to the most yawning, lounging, leg-stretching idler you ever imagined, hang up an Indian grass hammock for yourself in the shade, and bless the giver of this hint.

DREAMS.

REAMS are the accompaniment of both idleness and work. They "come through the multitude of business," and occupy the lazy brain; they are associated with the sluggard and the enthusiast; they are honoured as channels of supernatural advice, and blamed as the offspring of sheer sensuality. We dream with our eyes open as well as shut—by day as well as by night. But the phenomena of dreams have defied scientific experiments and metaphysical inquiries. Now and then it seems as if some law were discovered, but the investigator is soon baulked. You fancy you can account for a dream, but you can't make one. It may sometimes be analysed, but I believe has never been composed. You do not know how it will turn out. Impress your mind strongly with this and that set of ideas, and lo, the whole slips out of the place where you put it, and another occupies

your sleeping thoughts. You can't cook a
dream. The skilful speaker can count, with
tolerable certainty, upon producing an impression something like that which he wishes upon
the waking mind; but, when we sleep, we
move out of the reach of his persuasive
machinery. But although we cannot construct
a dream, or order it beforehand, it may sometimes be directed while in progress with ludicrous effect.

Many accounts are published of the way in
which the thoughts of a dreamer, once fairly
committed to the dream, may be effected. He
is played with helplessly. An encyclopædia
will give anecdotes and references to books
about dreaming, in which most absurd results
have been obtained by dictating to the sleeper.
A man has been made to dive from his bed
under the persuasion that he was in the water,
and being pursued by a shark. But this sleeping obedience is happily rare. With far the
most of us—indeed, with very few exceptions
—the land of dreams is a strange independent
land, and our sleeping life unaccountably cut
off from our waking one.

Words may waken, but they seldom influence us. We hear, and do not understand;
there is a break between the minds of the

speaker and the sleeper; the sounds are not interpreted by the brain. This is the more curious, as many persons talk in their sleep; the tongue obeys the thought, although the ear will not convey it, except, as I have said, in very rare instances.

Perhaps the most curious thing connected with dreams is that experience does not correct them. People who, when their eyes are open, go about quietly on the face of the earth ordering their carriages, paying their cab fare, or trudging in the dust, fly in their dreams. Some even lead not only a distinct but a continued life in their dreams. They take the thread up, for several consecutive nights, with a consciousness that they are dreaming. Most dreams, however, are distinct. They may be repeated, but are without connection.

The most frequently remarked characteristic of dreams is the long series of incidents which are got through in a short time. We do a deliberate dream in several acts, and find we have been asleep for only five minutes. But this is one of the most easily explained phenomena. In dreams we lose our measure of time; while awake we are called to a sense of its passage by the sun, the clock, the appetite, the routine of the day; yet, with all these checks and reminders, we sometimes even find that hours slip by almost without notice : on the other hand, while we are waiting, counting the moments, Time drags along as if he meant to stop, and yet he moves on, as we say, "equally," whether we notice his progress or not. The clock strikes with a steady pulse, though sometimes it seems in a fever, sometimes in a fit. At any rate we have some fixed standard to correct the calculation of our waking time ; but in dreams the standard itself is visionary. We measure the succession of fleeting thoughts by a test which is purely fanciful, and thus can shorten or lengthen the dream without violence to our senses. You can think of heaps of things in two minutes, of the sun's rising and setting, for instance. Do that in a dream, and you have "a day," with its proportionate number and succession of incidents.

There is only one thing more I must notice before I go on to say why I mainly took up my pen to write about dreams. There are few who have not found themselves, in dreams, uncomfortably scant of clothing. Probably the Lord Chancellor has dreamt of sitting on the woolsack in his shirt. This comes of undressing before going to bed. The touch of the sheets suggest that we are unclothed; in fact, they are the only remaining test of the outer world. We move about in our dreams, and the bed-clothes hint that our own are put off.

I will not, however, dwell over our sleeping dreams; but I must say, by the way, that I pity the man who does not know when he is "dropping off." The consciousness of standing on the threshold of sleep when you are at liberty to indulge in it, is delicious. You are awake and not awake. The dream god has his hand upon you, though he has not yet led you away. You feel his magic presence, and the gentle dissolution of your waking thoughts under his touch. To you it is a private setting of the day. The sun goes his own road and at his own time, but you sink in a twilight of your own. You do not really "fall off," nor is it a steady descending slide into the night; the border land is broken, and you don't reach the level plain of sleep without some retrospective glimpses of the weary track along which you have passed. I pity the man who tumbles into his bed and sprawls away into a dream before the bed-curtains have done swinging at the shock of his plunge. No, it is better far to wait a minute at the palace-gate and let the proper ministers close your eyes and carry you in with irresistible but kindly touch.

A man who bursts into the mysterious land like a mad bull through a hedge, with a snore for a bellow, deserves to have a nightmare let loose at him, and be ridden out of the place of dreams with a shriek. Mind, I don't mean to advocate a passage to sleep which has to be assisted by mental arithmetic, the conception of a windmill, or the fixing of the mind's eye upon some endless procession of sheep. This is distressing. No: given a natural proclivity, let me neither fall headlong from day to night, nor attempt to help the busy ministers of dreamland. Let me lie down—feel them gather round me—lift me up and float me off with their own considerate, inimitable skill.

There is another faculty, which, next to that of tracing one's own progress to sleep proper, is much abused, but grateful, and, under some circumstances, wholesome. I refer to day-dreaming—not going to sleep by day, but dreaming with your eyes open. Of course, if deeply indulged in, this enervates the brain, but, to an over-worked or tired one, it is refreshing. It is like sleep without the stifling embrace of the blankets and the feather-bed. It is like dreaming without danger of a sudden apparition, or that spell-bound helplessness which is the paralysis of dream-life, when you cannot stir, and yet feel the breath of the unseen terror behind you.   Now, day-dreaming is free from these possibilities : you sit apart, and let the thinking apparatus play, like a fountain, by itself.   You don't tax or catechise it,—you turn the peg and see what it will do.   You have no more idea of what is coming than your shoe has.   You watch with something like the interest an old bird on a bough might feel in the frolics of its full-feathered young, and yet you can recall the whole brood with a "cluck."

Now, I mean to say that this day-dreaming is sometimes desirable and healthy.   We thus occasionally come across thoughts which we should never start by deliberate hunting.   We air the mind ; we get out of the little world in which we commonly move, and go back to it refreshed.

Day-dreaming is all very well, now and then, on a holiday ; but a woman who gushes with moonshine and romance is seldom a good judge of butcher's meat, or a skilful interpreter of accounts ; and a man who aspires at an angel deserves to dine off stringy mutton and underdone potatoes, on cold plates, for the rest of his life.

Young man, think twice before you commit
yourself to the romantic young lady, whose
impulsive ideal of faithfulness and devotion
will never enable her to protect you from short
weight, domestic pilferings, and frayed, button-
less linen.

ERHAPS no subject offers more metaphysical difficulties, and at the same time finds more incessant illustration in the commonest, most thoughtless life, than that of Association. Association is the belt of the world—it embraces heaven and earth, God and man; life and death are contained within its bounds. It is the mystery of the past, the present, and the future.

After a glimpse, we must be touched with a sense of its immensity; we may therefore more freely handle a few little tags in the fringe which borders it. Some subjects may well dismay us, for they appear to be within compass, and to expect an exhaustive examination, if they are examined at all; others are so large that the philosopher can really make little more impression upon them than the fool, and it is no more pretentious in the one than in the other to approach them. Here we are, then, by the brink of the great sea of

Association, without horizon, sounding, or end;
let us dip our little mug in and sip upon the
beach.

Events widely severed are joined and meet
together in some familiar scene. Take, for
instance, the story of the groom and the eggs.
A gentleman was driving, on a moonlight
night in September, over a bridge, in a one-
horse phaeton. He wore a white coat, and
his servant sat behind him. Just beyond the
bridge, on the right, was a windmill, and on
the left, a church. The clock struck eleven.
The gentleman turning round suddenly to the
groom, said : " John, do you like eggs ? "
" Yes, sir," said John, touching his hat.

Exactly twelve months afterwards, he was
driving the same vehicle over the same bridge
at eleven o'clock by moonlight, in a white
coat. The clock struck. The gentleman
turned round suddenly to the groom, and
said: " How ? " " Poached, sir," replied John,
touching his hat.

The eye and the ear annihilate space and
time. An unexpected familiar sound trans-
ports us in a moment. When we hear the
whetting of a scythe, there is a vision of the
hayfield, the harvest, or the lawn. If we were
to hear it in Piccadilly, we should still see cabs

and granite with the outward eye, but swaths of grass or bending barley would be immediately present to the true or inward seeing power.

A passer-by says, " Tlck," and horses come into the field of vision. The hiss of the groom recalls the stable-door, the bucket, the sponge, and ammonia. The bleat of the lamb carries us another way. The tom-tom of the Hindu beggar strikes the contrast between the East and the West. The peal from the steeple rekindles a mixed memory of weddings, victories, and elections.

There are, of course, catholic sounds which suggest the same ideas to different minds with approximate certainty. The passing bell has one message to all. But each associates some private scene with some particular sight, or sound, or smell.

I can never see a knife laid with its edge upwards without thinking of a particular picnic. There was a pause, and I suppose a moment of unusual receptivity in my brain; we talked about accidents in carving, danger of carelessness with knives, &c., when a gentleman, with much ceremony, set the large carving-knife in the middle of the group with its edge uppermost, and while we expected some conjuring trick, said : " None of you will ever see a knife so laid without thinking of me ; " and then he winked at the prettiest girl.

Thus each of us has some scene which an unlikely, unmeaning incident rekindles. The most remarkable revival of past impressions, however, occurs sometimes at a combination or coincidence of circumstances.

Did you never, for instance, come suddenly across or into a scene which at once is recognised as familiar, though you cannot remember having been present at it before? So strong is the impression at times, that we seem to know what will happen next, as if we had crossed the track of some past life, and, for a moment, were in possession of a little scrap of time, involving future, as well as past and present. No doubt, such an inexplicable appreciation of the view at an unexpected turn in our path has done much to strengthen a belief in the transmigration of souls.

There are sounds and sights which it is impossible to detach from particular ideas, or at least particular states of mind. Whose solemnity will not be disturbed by the squeak, pan-pipe, and drum of Punch? If a waltz could not justify itself at a funeral, it would

disconcert everything else.   The effect of
certain tunes, especially when associated with
national life, is notorious.   In conscript armies
certain airs are obliged to be prohibited, lest
the recruits from the districts where they are
played should turn home-sick.   A particular
succession of notes excites the tarantula dance,
and is not without its impression on the cruel
snake.   The fable of Amphion's influence is
not mere poetic fancy.

It is as difficult to account for the stream
of our waking thoughts, as it is to analyse
dreams ; sometimes the course runs smooth,
and then perhaps the eye rests upon a
particular object, catches a peculiar gesture,
and the whole tide is turned ; some little idea
comes up and takes the reason and the imagination by the nose.   We are not conscious
of anything forced or unnatural in this ; but
we cannot see the association which makes the
change natural.   Occasionally, we ask others
or ourselves : "What made you think of
that?" and we can trace the steps of thought,
but commonly we take them as they come,
without a wish to know the history of their
birth.   There is a moving, endless picture ever
passing before the mind ; we look at, we accept
or dislike it, we can even call for particular

scenes, detain or dismiss them, and think we
provide the show ourselves; meanwhile, sleeping or waking, the moving panorama passes by,
and we cannot tell who is the exhibitor, whose
the secret hand behind the scenes which turns
the crank of life's revolving view.

Association is powerful in office. Let a man
get a place under Government, or be ordained
by the Bishop, and he is changed. He is the
same man; his appetite, memory, power, are
unaltered; he cannot see further, or speak
louder, or reason better the moment he is
admitted to his new office; but he is changed.
In nine cases out of ten, the change appears,
perhaps involuntarily, in more than professional conversation or dress.

Originally, the man made the office; now,
the office makes the man. It is not merely
that his good-will is more valuable when he
has such and such additional influence or
patronage in his power, but the man himself
breathes at once a new atmosphere. He turns
his back upon the world, and sticks up
for his profession. He judges by a professional standard, he accumulates professional
gossip.

I once knew a cat's-meat man who displayed
as keen a professional etiquette, jealousy, and

pride as any member of the most learned
bodies in society.   He had a wooden leg, and
stood upon his dignity with as much grace as
if he had a diploma of knighthood.   When I
made some sensible remark about his business,
he snapped me up, and showed me how little I
knew what I was talking about, with a smile at
my presumption.   Poor fellow! I was glad to
give him that gratification.

The traditional associations of office are
among the strongest, though perhaps least
suspected influences of civilised society.   Conceive the consternation of Mrs. Grundy, if
every soldier, lawyer, parson, doctor, and
merchant said what he thought himself, and
not what he thought would be expected of a
professional man, about war, law, divinity,
physic, and trade.

The official mind is a distinct production
of its age, as unlike others as the uniform
under which it works is unlike our common
dress.

Perhaps there is nothing, however, in which
we are more conscious of the influence of
association than in personal appearance.   We
connect character of the mind with that of the
face, the attitude, the step, the voice, the waistcoat, the umbrella, the boots.   Probably the

waistcoat is the most expressive garment; it is a test of theology and taste; it measures not only our girth, but our social standing, pursuits, and opinions. Does not the black satin vest convey a distinct impression? Is not the waistcoat with sleeves expressive? What do flaps and a multiplication of pockets indicate? In the tightness or otherwise of the waistcoat, we may measure the vanity or good sense of the wearer. It is a great social meter, to those who can read it aright. Boots, again—can we not judge most men fairly by their boots? Indeed, clothes are almost as expressive as faces, which are unexhausted, and will yet produce many a Lavater.

A man of discernment will invariably get near the mark in judging by appearances, and form some accurate opinions about even the details of a stranger's character, from the mere examination of his outside.

Do not let us, however, suppose that there is any law or set of rules by which we could work out an opinion. We don't go deliberately to work—assigning this to the nose, that to the brow, that to the lips, that to the stride; no such thing. But by an undefinable process of association, we come to a conclusion which we are conscious to be just; and yet we are unable to trace, much less explain, the steps which lead to it.

There is really no great triumph in getting a character from a phrenologist off the cast of a Swedish turnip. We laugh at his discomfiture, and then set off at once judging by appearances which we cannot decipher ourselves.

The effect of association is seen remarkably in the case of company or companionship. The man and wife grow alike. The obstinate conservative farmer's head does become at last like the Swedish turnip which he grows. But about man and wife. The approaching similarity of their features, figures, manners, voices, has been too repeatedly noticed to be questioned. There is something in it, a great mystery, which cannot be physically explained.

The rule of contrast often seems to guide the courting. The black bewhiskered Edwin woos the delicate blonde Angelina. But from the day the knot is tied, up to the longest tether of life's rope, they grow less and less unlike, until at last, when the old couple come into the room together, you see that you might often make a magnified Angelina by putting a cap on Edwin's white hair.

There is association in death. Skulls are alike—let the phrenologist say what he will, let the eye and the lip have been ever so diverse. Perhaps that is all we learn from seeing the gradual resemblance between a husband and a wife. It is because they are approaching the great assimilating crucible, and being together, we notice most in them the common converging lines which point to the last focus of life. Indeed, I fancy it must be so. Most old people of the same habits are alike. Look into the workhouse yard, at the shrunken, toddling paupers in the sunny corner. They are associated in decay. Once, one was strong, and another was weak; now, they are all weak together. Their voices, gait, are as similar as the workhouse coat—a trifle looser and more threadbare here or there than the other, but alike throughout.

What period of the man's life fixes his character? What, so to speak, decides his place in the great household? Hardly death, in which not only all the delicate shades of distinction between one and another are often confused, but the most striking contrasts are done away—when the pulse flutters in the athlete and the infant, and the orator and the idiot moan alike.

Look into the penal prison, and see the bullet-headed, close-cropped felons. Here is association in crime. A life of skulking stratagem has set that cunning gleam in the eye; a life of lawless indulgence has stamped that air of sensual abstraction and vile absence of mind upon the lip and brow, which marks the criminal face. These men catch each other's features like small-pox, and all are scarred. How can the comparatively uninfected escape, when the law compels inoculation? You might as well hope to cure an incipient convict in gaol, as to dry damp clothes in a pond.

The licence of crime is notoriously contagious; there is a wicked charm in it almost irresistible. When a man cannot resist it, although free to choose an honest course, how can he do so when brought into daily contact with criminals, and depressed by the loss of personal liberty? Why should prisons be more than tanks to hold our " social sewage," till it be carted off, and spread somewhere upon the soil? It asks to be put into the crucible of Nature, and associated with its freshest material.

One great problem of the day is, where to " deodorise and utilise " our felons. They are "men in the wrong place." It would be something if we could set a thief where he could rob nothing beyond a bird's-nest, and a burglar where he could break into nothing but the ground, where, in short, rogues would have to associate themselves in honest labour or perish outright. Success to the search for such a Reformatory!

But let us leave the felons. The power of association is seen in the influence of the sound man as well as in that of the sick. One fool makes many, so does one hero or saint. Isolated independence is impossible in good as well as in evil, "no man liveth to himself." The solitary devotion of the prophet quickens a thousand pulses. The one brave outspeaker frees the caged-up thoughts of his sympathetic but shrinking kindred—he brings together the hundred drops which hang upon the social window-pane. Thus an opinion gathers weight, and truth makes its way.

This illustration, however, reminds me of a danger. The little raindrops on the window-pane are lost in the big one. As this pursues its zigzag course it grows fat on the bodies of its companions. Not so with the human centres of association. No man, however small a contribution to the great body, can afford to

be lost in it. He is himself throughout, he
cannot be merely the part of another. There
must be a sense of completeness and totality
within his little waistcoat, or he ceases to be
a man. By retaining his individuality, he does
not withhold his support to others ; nay, the
very charm of his support depends upon this.
Let him be lost in another, and he has thence-
forth nothing to give.

But this danger is avoided if we are associated in some principle, and not merely in
support of some man. There must be something common to the whole associated body,
head and members alike, which quickens it.
Take, as example, the words " knit together in
love." There we have one superior motive
life, which holds each up from being lost
in his neighbour's, and yet provides an
irresistible, pervading bond for all.

Some associations, however, are of course
temporary ; men combine to carry out some
definite legislative enactment, to remove some
distinct abuse. It would be well if some of
these societies could be wound up with less
suspicion of disgrace. There ought to be no
more shame in dissolving than in forming an
association. The side at cricket or football is
dispersed when the game is played. But I

fancy there are associations which linger on long after they have done their work, from sheer dread of censure for dying. Some, of course, are kept alive by paid officers, merely for the salaries they produce, but some hang together from the misdirected obstinacy of directors and committees. Wind the thing up, gentlemen ; proclaim your task done ; set yourselves free to take up another ; but do not carry on a work when all about it has grown stale and sour.

True wit depends on association. It lies in the unexpected aptness of ideas, just as false wit lies in odd contrasts or incongruities. False wit is very funny. No one can, for example, remember the Irishman's recipe for a cannon, " Take a long hole, and pour some brass round it," without a little spasm of the chuckling apparatus inside us ; and yet we see it lacks a lesson, which is part of true wit. We will illustrate this by the next familiar example which comes to hand in the mind. Lord P. is asked why he does not get the order of the thistle for Lord Q., and replies : " I'm afraid he would eat it." This old joke is good, but it is more than a joke ; it is full of sense as well as of humour.

Perhaps association is most obviously active

when we travel. Then the ignorant, unobservant man sees without seeing. To him the Forum at Rome is a shabby plot, with shabbier ruins and bullock-carts about it. It touches no store of learning, kindles no dead history within him. In travel, we find the value of accumulated facts, which otherwise would probably lie barren in our memories. Even the dry memories of school-lessons give out a charm to a classical route, which makes us forgive the dreary hours we spent over them. It is all very well, too, to laugh at book-students of nature, but they carry that about with them which gives an interest to every flower, cloud, and stone they see. They see the object, and then, by the magic of association, the true beauty, fitness, history, which surround and accompany it, reveal themselves. A leaf or a bird is but a letter in the great book, which is read only by those who can put letters together; that is, who have the faculty of Association.

 VERY country gentleman came up lately to visit a London friend of mine; my friend trotted him about the streets, got him safely over crossings, and, among other places, took him to the top of St. Paul's. While they were looking down upon the town, the visitor, envying one who had a sight so cheap and grand within easy reach, said to my friend :—" I suppose you often come up here."

This, I take it, is what many of our impulsive country cousins feel when they visit town. What the purple moors and shade-mottled lanes are to us, sick of gas, stucco, and policemen, the shilling-sights are to them. They leave the fresh green of the beech, the lawn, and the nightingale, for Christy's Minstrels and the Exhibitions. Nature's Royal Academy and the May meetings of the summer birds have no chance against the moving spectacles of Regent Street and the voices of Exeter Hall.

Our friends arrive from the station brimful
of excitement, with lists of things to be done
and seen, compiled for the last six weeks out
of the newspapers. They know the different
titles of the Exhibitions, and where they may
be found. For my part, I never can be sure
of the difference between the Old and New
Water-colour. They both seem very bright
to me. Now a days, however, one's power of
distinguishing among the pictures of the season
is sorely tried by their dispersion. Beside the
bonâ fide collections and galleries—and he must
be a sorry artist who cannot get any one of the
rival juries to hang him—single works are
exhibited here and there half over London.
There is, however, much to be said for this
arrangement. What can be more perplexing
to the sight-seer than three or four rooms full
of pictures ? Their number palls the appetite,
and chokes the digestion. As for myself,
though I like paintings as much as most men,
my first impulse, on entering the Academy, is
to shade my eyes ; or, when I have looked well
into two or three works, to shut them, and
carry the impression out of doors carefully, lest
some " Portrait of a Gentleman " should dissi-
pate it altogether. Depend upon it, this exhibition of single works is a sensible plan. One

is glad, nevertheless, on reading the *Times*, to learn that some are occasionally safe out of sight in the provinces. It is pleasant to reflect on the sensation produced in those parts, when we stumble on the curt announcement, "'Eastward Ho!' is at Penzance."

If you can get over the sense of interruption, you will find the crowds at such a place as the Royal Academy not without their interest. Notice the way in which people mar the supposed object of their visit by exchanging salutations, looking out for friends, or watching for a vacant spot on the sparse seats, where they may rest their aching backs, and sink down in a sea of crinoline. It is curious to listen to the comments of sight-seers at an exhibition. Many, if not most, are struck by some peculiarity in the picture which the artist, if a true one, would perhaps have never expressed, if he could have helped it, and would retract on reflection.

Some of the remarks made upon Holman Hunt's "Light of the World," when it was first exhibited, were painful, and yet suggestive. I waited once for a considerable time by it, and watched its effect. Several looked till you could see their eyes fill, and then passed on in befitting silence. Others, mostly in black satin vests, criticised aloud. "Hollo! this is a priest, isn't it?" The picture had not missed him altogether. "What is he doing?" asked another. Some said :—"How pretty!" One detected Puseyism, and walked by with a sniff. Far different was the critique of a genuine dustman I once heard in the National Gallery, before the Martyrdom of St. Sebastian. "Look here, Bill!" he whispered to his mate with genuine respect—"His eye is steadfast, but his soul is stirring"—and then the two gazed long and steadfastly without another word. They had souls above Madame Tussaud.

The cook in *Punch*, who came into her young mistress's studio, and praised the performance on her easel with "Lawk-a-daisy, Miss Mary, if that beant like wax-work a'most," gave a true touch of vulgar taste.

But why should we despise a taste because it is vulgar? Would you not gratify an ass with thistles, even if he sniffed his dislike of nightingale sauce? Who among the crowds that pour along the British Museum on Whitmonday take in the meaning and the value of the sights they see? Would you remove even the mummies, though they do not solemnise the gaping excursionist? He does not think of them as dead. He does not associate the long-enduring calm faces of the Egyptian statues around him with the thought and power of a people who held dissolution in suspense. He does not reflect that the Saurian monster, whose part skeleton he sees, might have gamboled in the mud of the London basin with unprophetic disregard of Pall-mall; to him, it speaks no other message than the case of butterflies caught on Hampstead Heath. It is a bone to him, and nothing more. Bless you! he came there to see the Museum, and will probably recollect nothing more clearly than the umbrella-stand, the great size of the door-mats, and the "silver" cup at the "free drinking-fountain" outside the entrance.

I am sure, though, that those secular philanthropists, who advocate the opening of the British Museum on the day of rest, cannot have tested the proposal in their own persons. There is something in the atmosphere of the place which, in a very short time, develops unexpected possibilities of lumbago, depression, general debility, and all the evils which Du Barry offers to cure with his delicious " Revalenta Arabica." For hard, exhaustive, subduing work, commend me to the British Museum. I wonder that some of our ingenious legislators

have not suggested its use in the matter of
criminal reform.   Send a few gangs of our
surplus stock of felons for a month or two to
the British Museum, request them to move on
slowly about twelve hours a day, and I am
sure that those who survive will never expose
themselves to such a punishment again. Those
who seek instruction there go with an object,
and heed the things in the galleries, through
which they passed to reach it, no more than
they do the houses in Great Russell Street on
their way to the Museum.   But your sight-
seer turns his bewildered eyes on everything,
and thinks it quite a reproach when a companion calls him back to a room with " You
have not seen this."   He sees it in five
minutes.

What a world of thought, however, gathers
round any one object, if you let memory and
fancy play about it for a while ! That Roman
bust, for instance—only recall its history. The
stone, wrenched from the marble cliff, may be,
at Carrara, then set in some old Italian studio
or yard ; the little vanities of the original whose
likeness we have — his spoken and silent
critiques on the disposition of the robe and
hair ; the opinions of his friends or the public
when it was sent home, or set up in the

square; the cost of it—the bill and receipt for the cash. Perhaps it was executed on commission, and paid for with collected money. Where is the subscription list, with its rival generosity? Who gave a penny, who gave a pound? What did Titius set his name down for, what Seius? How long did it stand where it was set? Was it in a hall? Did it see the blue-eyed Goths, or long-armed, low-browed Huns burst in? Did it hear the sack of the city—the shrieks of the household? Was it cast down, and splashed with blood? How came it to be chipped and battered? How long did it lie on the rubbish heap where the lizard sat and sunned itself unmoved? Or was it buried in the cool moist ground, dug up at last by lazy Roman excavators, to look on a changed forum, and find a price once more? The catalogue will tell you who sent it here; at what auction it was knocked down again—going! going! gone. Ay, that is the burden of the story it has witnessed ever since it fell a shapeless, senseless block from the quarry, and was hoisted into the mason's cart by navvies who swore in Latin.

But, after all, that Roman bust! your sightseer would look with twice the interest on a prize-pig's face. Sights! The eye, we are

well told, sees what it brings with it the power
of seeing.

A sight must immediately interest, attract,
or perplex ; at least have the credit of interesting, attracting, or perplexing others.   There
is a marked appreciation of feeble manufacture
by small minds.   Stand outside a doll shop in
Oxford Street, and see how many men will
stop and gape at pink wax babies with heads
much too small for their bodies, sitting uncomfortably upright in real perambulators.   Mrs.
Smith's hulking young footman looks at the
windowful with parted lips and perfect com-
prehension ;   the artizan, cruelly denied a vote,
stops, with tools on shoulder, and stares too.
My dear sir, do you suppose that all those
bearded and hooped people above twenty years
of age you meet with on your way to business
are men and women ? they are mostly children;
and would not be half so happy as they are if
they kept their ears always cocked up for
sensible remarks.   Do you like sensible
remarks yourself—that is, other people's—
which tell you something you didn't know, or
upset something which you thought you did ?
I was walking out of a public meeting the
other day, rather tired, and heard an enthusiastic lady praising the shallowest speaker of

the day. " Wasn't it beautiful ? " said she;
" just what I always think." Exactly, my dear
lady, that is the secret of popular oratory. On
the same principle, sights and the spirit of
sights depend for progress and success upon
those superficial striking qualities which hit a
fool sooner than a philosopher. People don't
like to have the trouble of discovering its
merit themselves ; it must be obviously
interesting and exceptional; a house on fire, a
balloon, even a cab-horse down in the street, is
noticed as he never was before, and yet there
is something to repay study, even in a cab-
horse, unfallen. A dog with a kettle tied to
his tail realises " his day" at last ; so, too,
more honourably, if he can stand on his head
or smoke a pipe ; he is then " a sight ; "
whereas his cousin, who assists the drover, and
fulfils his mission with sagacity and trust, is
overlooked. He is valuable to his master, no
doubt, but would be doubly so if he had eight
legs, for then, though useless, he could be
shown. How many sights owe their fame to
some such equivocal distinction !

One man finds a sight in whatever he sets
his eyes on; he lives in a marvellous, ever-
changing, never-ending exhibition, though he
hardly ever "goes to see" anything at all.

Another, who "goes to see" everything, and is a professed sight-hunter, is ill-instructed, empty, and weak. The one lives on wholesome food, the other spoils his digestion by a perpetual diet of sauce. Indeed, the charm of a sight, as a sight, is its stimulating effect on the curiosity nerves; until at last a man loses the power of application and research, and can perceive only that which is piquant or unnatural.

A "sight," moreover, must be definite and limited. No mere visitor can see London : it takes a sojourn and much patient study to comprehend that; so much has to be accumulated in the mind. So many regiments have to be marched into the field of view, that the mere preparation for the sight occupies years, is in itself an education. There is nothing very striking in London; it disappoints the visitor at first, then stupifies him. He is puzzled, choked, when the real wonders of the place begin to present themselves in crowded confusion to his mind. Regent-street and the exhibitions are no more London than a Life-guardsman is the British army.

There are accounts of London by daylight, gaslight, moonlight, much to see at either time; but another phase is possibly still more strange

—London by early morning light, say at three o'clock in summer. It is quite light, and empty. A gorilla might help himself at the free drinking-fountain in the Oxford-street Circus unnoticed. Cats and rare policemen represent traffic. Rooks caw over Regent-street, as they fly towards Kensington Gardens. More than two million pair of boots are standing somewhere soiled with yesterday's mud, varied in shape, size, and age, but all void. Some twenty million toes are more or less pointing towards the zenith. But London is now a city of dreams. London asleep is a sight well worth seeing. It is curious, though, to traverse much of it, as may be done, even when it is awake, in comparative solitude. Some time ago, I walked from London Bridge to Hungerford Bridge at about seven o'clock in the evening without meeting above a score persons, except when crossing the arteries leading to the bridges. There is a series of streets on the other side of the water close to the river's edge, between huge warehouses; these streets are crowded with waggons, and noisy with rough labour during work-hours, but silent as midnight after six o'clock. As I passed along between the locked storehouses, I could hardly believe it was still day, and that the stream of life was then flowing strong along the Strand.   About opposite St. Clement Danes (I am speaking of my side, the Surrey side of the river, between the great brick blocks of buildings), a little boy had set a trap for sparrows in the middle of the roadway, and was watching it round a corner.   A man might have hung himself unhindered from one of the many gibbet-like cranes which, with their great iron arms, pick up bales all day long, and swing them into doorways high in air.

Then there are the docks—another world; and Wapping with its fierce debauchery, far more glaring than that of the casinos in the West.   Sailors, burned nut brown by tropical suns, just landed, and squandering with eager haste, and cosmopolitan disregard of public opinion in Wapping, the accumulated health and passions of a tedious voyage.   But, my dear country cousins, it is of no use, I tell you, talking about London; you can't see it. Be content and wearied with panoramas and museums.   I don't refer to the regular season visitors, who have a house or address in town. They affect society; they don't trouble themselves about sights; they don't enjoy them; they don't ride on the camel at the Zoological Gardens, or feed the monkeys.   I mean the people who walk much, and take lodgings for a month; who eat ices at Farrance's; who dine once with a friend at a club; whose wives and daughters buy the annual bonnet.

It is a difficult thing to decide how far the benefits of instruction can or should be combined with the pleasures of sight-seeing. The Adelaide Gallery and the first Polytechnic were experiments in this direction; both, I suppose, may be said to have failed. Perhaps there is more benefit to be derived from unmixed *bonâ fide* pleasure than some of our anxious pastors and masters would allow. Lessons are all very well, but I pity the poor boys who are condemned to hear explanations of the things they are taken to enjoy upon a holiday. I see them now in the old dreary chemical Polytechnic, wearily hanging back, and trying to gather some unintelligible amusement for themselves towards the tail of the procession; weary little lads, utterly unenvious of the good boy who, with gloves on, trots beside his master, and exhibits an unnaturally scientific interest in the theory of thunder and lightning connected with the electrical machine. I confess that Tutor, George, and Harry, in the *Parents' Assistant*, never interested me much when a child. They must have been a tedious trio, and I am glad I never took any walks with them. It is hard to find a lesson lurking in a butterfly you have caught after a hearty scramble, and to suffer a description of the various artificial grasses, when your only wish in life is to tumble on a haycock. Let me laugh till I cry without being reminded that tears are the sign of grief as well. I know that, Mr. Tutor; indeed I am inclined to think that the tears of childhood are bitterer than those of any age, as the juice of the gooseberry is sharpest when it is green. Give me a fairy tale without a moral. That is the charm of Grimm's stories; they are stories, and nothing more. Who would like to hear a lecture on digestion after a good dinner?

Talking of instructive sights, I wonder what the majority of visitors to the Crystal Palace get out of those conscientiously representative courts. What a hodge-podge of history they must have cooked in many a brain. It is perplexing even to an educated man to pass through Spain, Nineveh, and Pompeii while you are munching the same bun. What wonder that the observant member of the Mechanics' Institute mixes them altogether, and pictures to himself Sennacherib, in the

Alhambra Palace, sitting on a door-mat inscribed "*cave canem.*"

One of the sights of London is the sunset. I am serious. It shows there as it could show in no town with a smaller canopy of smoke and blacks. The natural western tints combine with them wonderfully at times. I have seen the wildest brown and red effects in the sky looking up Oxford Street towards the Marble Arch, when the wind is in the east, and sweeps the carbon of a thousand fires towards the setting sun.

But then people can see the sun almost anywhere; not so the fireworks of Cremorne, which are much prettier, you must allow, and cost only a shilling. There are histories and legends attaching to both. Phaeton fell, and made some noise in the world; not so a late fire-king of Cremorne. He failed too, and some time ago was a dying pauper in St. James's Workhouse, Poland Street. It is quite true; I gave Mrs. Phaeton half-a-crown myself, and a recommendation to the House of Charity, Rose Street, Soho.

But we sat down to talk of sights, and I have told you of nothing new to be seen, nor indeed of the best way to find and see what is established and old, though you may not have set eyes on it yourself. Have you no guides, however? Is there not Timbs's " Curiosities of London," a notable book, fat, and stuffed with the wonders of the town? Can you not find in these where to go to, and what to see? Are there no printed spectacles to look at, and look with? Have you visited the Museum of the College of Surgeons? any doctor can give you an order. Have you witnessed an operation in one of our hospitals? Have you heard Gladstone speak in the House? Have you witnessed an execution? Have you watched the sun rise in June? No! Then you are lazy, blind, indifferent, and don't deserve the pains I have taken with you. Not but what I dare say you would find something to criticise in either of the several sights I have suggested. Even Mr. Gladstone has a trick of slapping his hand on the table at the end of a telling sentence, so loudly as often to blot out the last word.

The worst of all " Sights" are public executions. I never, I am glad to say, saw a man hanged, though I once came in unexpectedly for a military execution in a foreign town. It was before breakfast. I met a number of people hurrying along, and, pushing myself into the middle of the stream, was

carried at last to the top of a wall, where,
Humpty-Dumpty like, I sat and saw " all the
king's horses and all the king's men" gathered
together in three sides of a square below
me. What was it all about? Presently a
little soldier, with a white cloth over his eyes,
and a whispering priest at his elbow, walked
out and formed the fourth side of the square.
They both knelt down ; then the priest rose,
and covering his face with his hands, moved
aside a few yards. A file of soldiers marched
quickly up to the man, still kneeling in his
gray great-coat and white cloth. They were
so close that the barrels of their muskets converged towards him like the ribs of a fan. It
was all over in a second. He was put into a
military waggon, and they strewed sand over
the place where he fell ; but the dogs still
sniffed about it after the crowd had dispersed.

Hospitals are sights. One of the pleasantest
I ever visited was the Orthopædic. In others,
many patients are sick unto death ; you see
not only pain, but anxiety and despair. But
the sufferers in the Orthopædic are generally
well enough in health, and as the operation
they need is performed directly after they enter
the institution, the worst is past with the

majority. They are almost all getting better; moreover, they are furnished with a test of recovery impossible in ordinary sickness. When we have been ill we often forget how bad we were; and measuring the passing faintness of to-day with the progress of yesterday, fancy we linger longer than we should. On the whole, the tide of disease may be ebbing; but now and then a wave runs up beyond the last, as if it were turning again. We have followed, watching, close at the edge of the retreating malady, and forget the distance we have traversed since the sickness was at its full height; but the patients of the Orthopædic can make no such mistake.

" How are you getting on?" I asked of a girl who was hobbling across the room with bandaged, crooked feet. She said she had been in for months, and was much benefited, and, indeed, was improving every day. "Well, you are hopeful," I thought; and added aloud: " But you are very lame yet."

" Ah, sir!" she replied, " but see what I was!"

This being a common form of speech, I was not prepared to have it realised by her pulling a plaster of Paris model of her legs from under her bed, to which her own were graceful. " See what I was," she said.

Then there was a general exhibition of legs (plaster), and I found each one had an infallible test of progress within reach.

Poor things! they looked on the casts made when they entered the hospital as George Stephenson might at the model of an old stage-coach.

I don't think a hospital, though, generally a pleasant sight, high as its character deservedly is. You are overwhelmed with a consciousness of cleanliness and ventilation. It must be depressing, too, for sick to see sick; moreover, in my humble opinion, hospital walls are too white and staring; I should like to see more colour, and less rigid uniformity of arrangement. But still, even as opportunities for the gaining of experience by young surgeons, which they are, quite as much as anything else, the hospitals of London are sights well worth your going to see; and at least, you may learn from them to thank God for your own bedroom, where you sleep in private peace.

NURSING.

AFTER Miss Nightingale's bright and wise little book about Nursing, it is with some hesitation, on my own account, that I put such a title to my paper. Still, as I have seen a great deal of sickness, and, what is perhaps as much to the purpose, have been nursed myself, we will have, if you please, a little quiet talk about the Principles of Nursing.

I do not profess to set rules for the management of the sick room. I offer no receipt for beef-tea. I give no hint about sanitary laws. I suggest no improved code of hospital regulations. But I venture to say a word about the spirit in which the work of a nurse is to be always done, whether at home or in a public institution; whether by an amateur or an expert.

The first and last requisite in a nurse, is Hope. We are saved by hope. This encourages and ensures life. We enjoy most

that which we have not fully got. We begin
to sicken directly we repose upon success.
Faith and *Hope*, as well as Love, characterise
eternity. These three abide. Such as are
saved are always fed with Hope. There can
be no cure without it. The commonplace
nurse says, "While there is life there is
hope." This is the vulgar maxim. It is
more true to say, "While there is hope there
is life."

Sympathy is so powerful, that next to having
hope in ourselves, it is of the first importance
to have it near us. We catch it.

While nothing can be more bald and dispirit-
ing than the professional smile of a fat old
woman, without stays, who is paid to keep
awake at night (which she does not), there is
nothing more contagious than genuine hope.
I do not mean belief, expressed or not, that
a particular patient will recover, but hopefulness, which is like sunshine, which warms and
cherishes the failing sap of life.

It is the business of the nurse to look, not
to the disease, but to the natural power which
is making a protest against it. She—I use the
feminine gender, though bearded, grizzled men
have nursed with the tenderness of woman—
she must search for the strength there is in

the sick man, and protect that; she must seek
for the little spark of the old fire which lies
under the choked or burned-up heap, and
educate *that*, helping it to circulate again
through the body within which it has shrunk.
Without an eye on that, she may try to soothe
pain in her wisest way, but she will not
succeed; she will be always making some
radical mistake.

I remember once, when recovering from a
fever, becoming very low and wearied. The
unnatural strength which fever gives had left
me. I was helpless as a heap of clothes.
Fever had worn me, like a coat, for weeks, but
now had thrown me off, and gone. As I lay
there, I felt that all I needed was to be let
alone, that the skin might grow over my
nerves again, that the small molecules of life
might accumulate undisturbed, and build themselves quietly up, like coral. Any attempt to
divert or assist me went against the grain.
One day, a kind visitor hearing me say that
I felt tired, began to stroke my arm. It had
the same effect on me that a slow rubbing
has on the edge of a finger-glass. It set up
a thrill of discord which grated all over me.
Then I appreciated the genius of my nurse.
She let the delicate process of silent recovery

go on without comment or curious inspection, and I gathered health with accumulating speed, as by compound interest.

Nurses should remember that almost all patients may be referred to one or other of two classes—those who like, and those who dislike to be noticed. A little observation and tact will soon show to which of these two genera a sick person belongs. The whole management of the case is seriously affected by a mistake in this matter.. One man is pain-fully checked every time you ask him how he is. The little feeler of life which he is pushing on towards recovery, starts back at the question, like the horn of a snail when you touch it. Let the snail alone, if you want it to make progress. Another man frets in-wardly if you don't give him the opportunity of talking about himself. That seems to be Nature's way of freeing him from his malady. Persistent silence puts him in a passion. It clogs the mental pores which should carry the humour off. He suffers from checked moral perspiration. Let him speak about himself. He cannot get rid of his impatient sensations without some receptacle into which to pour them. Then if you, who ought to open the lid of your mind—or at least of your attention—

wide, shut it down, and won't let him pour in his gladness or grief, you are no more fit to nurse a sick man than a pavior is to play the piano. It is a divine rule in all cases, but one of which the spirit ought to be kept most especially with such as are sick and pine for sympathy, to "rejoice with those that rejoice, and weep with those that weep."

Never argue with a sick man. I don't know whether you are wise in doing so with any one, under any circumstances; but it is positively cruel to do so with a man who is weak and ill. I have, however, known people prove that a patient is better, to his teeth, when he affirms otherwise. Now, what can be the good of this? If he is better, he is better; if not, you certainly make him worse. Any argument with him, however reasonable, however clear, is only selfish indulgence on your part. Indeed, the more convincing your logic the more mischievous it is. If the contest of reason is trying to the sick man, the annoyance of conscious defeat is much more so. The struggle may be lightened by the prospect of a triumph, but the humiliation of failure is sheer distress and harm. You walk buoyantly out, buttoning your gloves, and swinging your cane; meanwhile, he remains flushed and weary

beneath the suffocating bed-clothes, or captive
in the stale old room, with all the enfeebling
apparatus of infirmity about him, and, may be,
the sting of your unfeeling argument undoing
the progress which you had tried to persuade
him that he had made. Never argue with a
sick man. The only atonement you can make
is to set the logical top spinning again for a
few minutes, and allow yourself to be cleverly
beaten. If you can manage that speedily,
dexterously, you may as well try it; but perhaps the best plan is to say no more on the
matter.

Oh, what torture have I seen inflicted by
the most conscientious, affectionate friends!
There was no question about their fondness;
but many a time their active anxiety to establish a sanitary conclusion has retarded the
recovery of their beloved one, nay, even sometimes rendered it impossible. There are many
persons fiddled to death, killed with kindness,
if that may be called such which frets the thin
thread of life away, by daily fuss, till it snaps.
Have you never heard in a sick-room :—" I
have been telling him that he must not," &c.
Don't you know the appealing look the patient
lifts to the visitor ? What hours of affectionate
recrimination does not that recall ! How often

the doctor would astonish his clients, if he could speak out! "How do you think he is getting on?" says the friend, just loud enough to be unintelligible to the subject of his inquiry. If the doctor could speak out, he would say:— "Well, my dear Mr. or my dear Mrs. or my dear Miss What-do-ye-call-it, I think he is getting on miserably, thanks to you."

If such people would be openly unkind, they would very likely do less mischief. If the sufferer could feel himself justified in ordering them out of the room, or throwing a physic-bottle at their heads, or otherwise letting off the natural anger they had generated within him, he would take little harm. "You must restrain yourself, my dear," says Mrs. Gosoftly, as she fiddle-faddles about the bed with provoking neatness and quiet. "Ay, there is the rub," the patient thinks :—"restrain myself—it needs health and strength to do that. Please let me fret in comfort; let me have it out; it is there; and if you insist on my corking myself up tight, perhaps I might burst."

Next to hopefulness in a nurse, I would say that *decision* is necessary. Consult your patient's wants, but consult him as little as possible. Your decision need not be very obvious and positive; you will be most deci-

sive, if no one suspects that you are so at all.
It is the triumph of supremacy to become
unconsciously supreme. Nowhere is this decision more blessed than in a sick-room.
Where it exists in its genuineness, the sufferer
is never contradicted, never coerced; all little
victories are assumed. The decisive nurse is
never peremptory, never loud. She is distinct,
it is true—there is nothing more aggravating
to a sick person than a whisper, but she is not
loud. Though quiet, however, she never
walks tip-toe; she never makes gestures; all
is open and above-board. She knows no
diplomacy or *finesse*, and of course her shoes
never creak. Her touch is steady and
encouraging. She does not potter. She
never blows her nose in a subdued, provok-
ingly imperfect, and considerate sort of way,
but honestly, and in a natural tone. She
never looks at you sideways. You never
catch her watching. She never slams the
door, of course, but she never shuts it slowly,
as if she were cracking a nut in the hinge.
She never talks behind it. She never peeps.
She pokes the fire skilfully, with firm judicious
penetration. She caresses one kind of patient
with genuine sympathy; she talks to another
as if he were well. She is never in a hurry.

She is worth her weight in gold, and has a healthy prejudice against physic, which, however, she knows at the right time how to conceal.

The decision of the nurse, moreover, is frequently needed to insist upon real curative quiet in a sick-room. There are people who will sit and talk to a patient, by no means noisily or roughly, but with an air of considerate distinctness which is seriously exhausting to the sufferer. To keep a sick man quiet, you must often do much more than forbid slamming of doors, knocking of furniture, and stumping on passages and floors. Quiet is not altogether a matter of tan and list shoes. There is a still monotonous disturbance of the process of recovery which is as effective as noise and bustle. The looks of the patient do not perhaps pity him. He is evidently getting better. He is out of danger. He will soon be well. But if you sit and talk, pleasantly enough, for an hour or two in the sick-room, you ought to see the symptoms of fatigue accumulating long before the convalescent ventures on a hint for repose. Then the nurse should exert her authority. It is her duty to understand and protect her charge, and, if she knows her business and is honest, she will do so, saving him

even from the friends who pay her wage.
I said, when I began, that the object of the
nurse should be to look to and educate the
shrunken fire of life, and not try too eagerly to
battle against the disease. Nature is doing
that. She wants to be helped, not superseded.
She cannot bear being put second in command ;
to have a great peremptory dose, for instance,
rushing into her bureau or office, and insisting
on this or that result or performance, which she
would have brought about before long in her
own way. No doubt there are occasions in
which, like all other powers, she is glad to
make an alliance with a stranger; but all
measures of this kind must be taken with a
view to her help, not to her deposition or
disturbance. Let the nurse learn this first;
let this be the principle of her action, the
radical motive of her care; and then she will
at least possess that essential without which
all other active qualifications and faculties will
only too frequently make her do mischief.
The disease she is set to watch may not be
bribed, like an old heathen god, by sacrifices of
any kind, for they only established the bad
character of the god, leaving him, in the esti-
mation of the worshipper, more powerful and
dangerous than ever. No ; it is the nurse's

business to realise the sound element in the person under her charge, to encourage the small and weak good, content if it grow of itself, however slowly. She should know how, by silence or cheerful speech, to let the sick man creep out of himself and begin to take interest in something beyond the world of small comforts and medical circumstance. She will not make any remark on the effort she sees, but will quietly clear the way for its progress, or step aside lest she should hinder it.

What I have said refers to the nursing of the sick; it is also applicable to that of infants. There the little one has to be protected, not forced. It would be as foolish to catch a toddling infant up, and run with it across the room—when the object really is to help the child to walk, not merely to gain the opposite corner—as it is to hurry a sick person into counterfeit health by violent medicine and other measures. If the house is on fire, and the brat cannot walk, why, then, pick it up anyhow, by its hair, if it has any, and that comes handiest, and run for its life. But if the house is not on fire—if the journey across the room be desirable only as of the child's performance—then let it go as much by itself

as possible, reducing external help to a mini-
mum, say to the tip of a little finger. So with
a sick man : if there be no pressing and immediate danger, if there be fair prospect of his
being likely to get well, let his infant strength,
like the baby, feel its own way with as small
assistance as can be.

I believe that as many children are injured
through life by careful as by careless nursing.
There is, however, much stupid want of consideration in their dress. They are often not
clad warmly enough, especially about the legs ;
and, though ventilation is a fine thing, a cold
room is not, for a child. Many a little life has
been sacrificed or stunted from a mistaken
attempt to bring up children hardily. But still,
some are helped too much, coddled too much,
kept from tumbling about too much, kept from
crying and romping too much. There is not,
for instance, a more elaborate instrument of
torture than a child's high-backed chair, on
which it sits at meals, if not at other
times, bolt upright, with its legs off the
ground.

What should you think of a woodman who
so shielded the young trees under his care
that they could never feel the wind ? I really
don't know what you would think ; but, as a

matter of fact, he would prove himself a
fool, and ought to have warning. Wind is
exercise to the young trees, ay, and the old
ones too. They can't get up and run about
over the field; they can't play leap-frog or
hop-scotch; their only exercise is swinging
and clapping their hands,—this promotes their
circulation, and opens their chests. They wave
their branches and rustle their leaves. They
play up in the air. Now, children want all
manner of tumbling and rolling about, for
their proper growth; and when I see them set
primly up upon one of those abominable high-
backed chairs, I think of a stunted scanty
seedling standing upright where no breath of
air can come to move its weary stalk. It is
bad enough for any one to be cramped up—
did you ever travel forty-eight hours in a
diligence, wedged in with hot fat foreigners?—
but it is worse for those that are young; they
are intended to wriggle into life. Burn your
high-backed, narrow-seated chairs. How would
you like to get your dinner sitting on the
mantel-shelf?

There is another instrument of torture—a
patent one, I believe—I mean a perambulator.
When I see two babies seated asleep in one,
with their naked legs meeting the wind (which

is always trying in sleep), and their heads
hanging down, backwards, I think of calves
going to market in a butcher's cart. Why
can't babies have a back to lean their heads
against? As it is, they generally hang over
behind, or sideways, like those egg-shaped
balls of rope—I think they call them "fenders"
—which are held over the edge of a steamer
when it is going to bump against the pier.
Poor little baby-heads! I hope some humane
speculator will invent a new carriage or
barrow for you, in which you can go to sleep
without one-half of you overlapping the
other.

But I must have done with the babies. I
want to say a little about the nursing of old
people—the most touching, and perhaps the
most trying branch of the art. Here you have
to eke out the oil in the lamp, knowing that
the vessel is low. The wick must be trimmed
tenderly. You must make it last all its time.
Death is natural, but disease is unnatural.
Nobody has any business to die of anything
but age. God sets us here between birth and
death—equally natural and right. Meanwhile,
what with vice, drains, care, work, over-eating,
drink, dirt, quacks, starvation, and what not, we
create and nourish disease, and have contrived

at last to establish it in human succession and
root it in our nature.

But with the old, you have in some cases
the helplessness and irritability of the baby,
and no gradual unfolding of power to come,
no glimpses of the future manhood, but only
of the past. The leaf is tender, not because
it is a bud, but because it has nearly struggled
from the stem, been nearly fluttered off by the
wind and hail of life. It is for you to keep it
there as long as you can, till some sudden frost
shall come, and it falls down upon the common
ground, where both rose and thistle really mix
at last.

The great difficulty in nursing some very
old people arises, of course, out of their habit
of power and authority. They have been
strong in body and mind, When you are old,
you will perhaps not like to admit to yourself
that you are not what you were, in either.
You will try to set yourself straight with
others by many allusions to decay, but this
is the only concession you will make. You
will probably own to infirmities, and then, as
if the admission exonerated you, act as if you
did not acknowledge them. Thus we see very
old persons sometimes presume upon their
age, and insist on this or that with a pertinacity

they never exhibited before. Of course, this makes the work of nursing them doubly trying and painful, but the old principle holds. Look to what there is of true life and strength, adapt your treatment to it; above all, use it. Learn of the aged; help them by being helped; strengthen by seeking strength. You may depend upon it, though your head may be cool, and your machinery of judgment in first-rate working order, there is an instinctive wisdom granted to old age, when the fruit of experience is mellow and wholesome, when the foot stands upon the very edge of the unseen, and the world-worn spirit feels that this world is not its home after all.

But if the fruit hang beyond its time, as I have seen grapes still upon a vine, shrunk and white with mouldiness before they have been gathered, or dropped of themselves—if you have to nurse the querulous and bitter aged, oh! tend them as if they were sweet.

There is one kindred work, which may, perhaps, be counted as a phase of nursing, about which, as a parson, I want to say a few words before I have done : I mean the religious treatment of the sick. I have pleaded for hope, decision, and quietness in the sick room. But, to many, the presence of the religious element there is one full of anxiety and disturbance. Few men are seriously ill without some apprehension or care about the possible issue of their sickness. Many are then conscious of their immortality, with perhaps a vague but strong conviction that all is not well between themselves and their conscience. To these the minister of good news should be able to give comfort. To all, the ministrations of religion should be welcome. But the greatest care and kindness is needed, lest what should have been for their health become a source of depression or distress. I am afraid that sick people are sometimes sorely vexed and hindered in their recovery by an injudicious application of religious treatment. They are neither restored to health in this world nor helped to enjoy everlasting life in that which is to come. I will venture then, with the consciousness of many years experience in this matter, to say a few words about the nice and important business of spiritual nursing. And what I say applies not only to the official duty of the parson, but to the affectionate endeavours of the religious friends of the sick man.

The spirit in which the sick man should be addressed upon his mental state is set forth in the first words which the minister is directed to use in the office for the Visitation of the Sick. The rule is this. The minister of the parish coming into the sick person's house shall say, " Peace be to this house and to all that dwell in it."

Whether or no the minister shall deem it expedient to use these words, they teach the object and spirit of his business there.

To many he is gladly welcome. And by the exercise of his duty he supplements the work of the physician and the nurse. There are not a few sick persons who long to relieve themselves by confidential intercourse with some one whom they can trust; who can listen to the tale of their mental distress without being shocked, and who has an official claim to hear, if need be, what they would have much hesitation and delicacy in uttering to those with whom they have been intimate all their lives, and whose estimate of their motives might be mistaken.

And this opportunity for spiritual relief greatly assists the physical means being used for their recovery. There are sick people whose soul resents the nursing and doctoring with which they are plied, because they have a mind diseased.

S

One, who knew what was in man, thus addressed a sufferer brought to him for a cure. "Son, be of good cheer, thy sins be forgiven thee." It is hard to heal the body when the soul is obstinately sore. Many a doctor has been puzzled and put out by the apparent stubbornness of a disease, when really the difficulty arose, not from inaccessibility of the affected organ or the nerve, but from a torturing ulcer in the conscience.

Here then there is need of spiritual nursing. And the person who attempts it must use the same principles as I have advocated throughout this paper. He must treat the sufferer with sympathy and hope. He must treat sin as a disease just as truly as fever is, or any other bodily sickness. He must be no more shocked or indignant than the nurse who dresses the sore and cleanses the foul source of the discharge. There is in the worst man, who has gone most clearly against conscience and counsel, a capacity for recovery and spiritual health.

I am not here going to speak of the religious recipe he will apply. I only plead for sympathy and hope in its application. As no good nurse will scold her patient, so no parson who is fit for his post will rebuke the sinful suffering

soul. He will appeal to that spirit divine
which is wholly extinguished in none, and
honestly associate himself with the guiltiest
both in his prayers and exhortations.

I need hardly add that he will avoid, like
poison, any religious dispute by a sick-bed.
How would you, reader, like a theological
argument when you were on your back to
begin with?

If the sick man is hard and quarrelsome, he
will not be softened by a fire of sharp texts.
Of all moral cruelty none seems to me more
devilish than to twit the prostrate sufferer
with his faults, in the name of the Lord; and
to load with condemnation him who is already
burdened with suffering and sin. Love alone,
not mere theological love, but love in the eye
and the voice, can reach, convict, and bring
comfort to the hardened.

But beside the direct application of what
may be called religious treatment, the spiritual
nurse may do very much for the mental
comfort of the sufferer.

We may strip the saying " I was sick and
ye visited me" of all ecclesiastical and con-
ventionally religious dress and yet find it
deeply divine. Spiritual nursing need not
involve the talking to a sick man about his

soul.   It may be done effectually by the con-
tagion of that God-given influence which
flows from a good-hearted man, whose hopeful
presence cheers the sad heart.   The spirit of
the august sentence I have quoted may be
fulfilled by little acts of kindness done from a
heart which stays upon God, acts of kindness
done, not to the poor alone, but to sufferers
among our own kith and kin, in our own
circle, within our own society.

Thus both the parson and the friend may
be in the highest sense a spiritual nurse to the
sick man; where it seems advisable, holding
intimate converse with him about the disease
which affects his soul, but in any case showing
tenderness and comfort fresh from a godly
heart.   For if hopeful, decisive, considerate
treatment is always wholesome in a sick-room,
it is most blessed and contagious when it
springs from deep, conscious communion with
the Great Giver of Peace and Life.

We cannot conclude these thoughts about
nursing without seeing how widely the word
has been used.   We nurse projects, prejudices,
quarrels—and a very vigorous maturity do
these last two sometimes rapidly gain; an
infant grievance, a childish offence, is capable,
with care, of growing up into a war, of setting

the world in flames. How great a matter a little fire kindleth. But I don't want to dwell over these. All I can say is, that if a young suckling of a quarrel be born to you, expose it, strangle it, apply the most effectual form of infanticide you ever heard of, or some day it will grow beyond your management and wish.

But remember, in regard to the nursing of thoughts and projects, that the very same principle as I have advocated still applies. Force nothing, or it will either grow crooked or die soon. Give an infant thought plenty of play ; let it run about in the fields ; and, if it is to grow, the unconscious mother of all growth will help it on. You will find fresh matter accumulate around the original idea ; and some day, the once baby may be sent out into the world full-grown, to make its way with such a constitution and brain-power as it may have inherited from you its parent.

TEMPER.

THERE are many kinds of temper, and I am in no humour to classify them categorically. The moment, however, that I summon the crowd of varieties to my mind, the phlegmatic generally presents itself first (probably because it is too slow to have gone far), as the most permanently irritating. There is no excuse whatever for a man who cannot be provoked. His native excellence is in itself vexatious. Not only does he get a character for good nature under false pretences—being considered amiable by shallow observers—but he is directly and personally objectionable to those who really know him. He sets up a fallacious test of goodness. The mischief he does is double : he perverts the judgment of the multitude, and exhausts the patience of the man. Reflect for a moment. He cannot be provoked. There is some unnatural defect in his constitution. It is small

praise to a broken-legged soldier to say that
he didn't run away; it is equally meaningless
to extol a phlegmatic man for never being
angry. I dare say he would be angry if he
could; but he can't, and I wish I might say
there was an end of the matter. No such
thing : he is as obstructive and provoking as a
street that is blocked up; he checks the rush
of feeling with no soft word, but with dogged
motionless hindrance; he fails in that undefinable but respondent sympathy which is .
mortar to the bricks of society; he is persistently unfeeling; he will be neither with
you nor against you ; and perhaps his only use
is to perfect the temper of saints, who must
not only be tried by the froward and malicious,
but survive the searching ordeal of dull indifference.

I take next a character in many respects
unlike this last, but one with also much nega-
tive power of provocation—I mean the compliant man. He is unpleasantly pleasant ; he
responds, if that may be called response, with
so little capacity for opposition. You deliver
an opinion ; he assents with a smile, and will do
the same to your opponent. The sportsman
does not value a fish which yields immediately
to the pull of the line. An easy capture is an

ill-compliment to the angler; you prize a remonstrant little fish far more than a great scaly
sluggard who suffers himself to be towed at
once into the landing-net, and gapes out immediate submission the moment he feels the point
of your argument.   Just so the compliant man
disappoints you : you suspect your own reasons
when they are at once assented to.   Your wit
is thrown away unless it has a little tussle for
supremacy.   You have said a rich thing ; he
laughs, but in a tone of vacant readiness which
shows that he would have done the same at a
poor one.   You ask him to carry all the umbrellas at a picnic, to ring the bell, to sit at a
side-table, to fill a gap—he complies, gratefully.
Anything to make himself agreeable—forget-
ting, kind soul, that of man's aims and capabilities, this perhaps is not the highest.   However, he piques himself upon his amiability,
and must take the consequence.   I think the
compliant man is most disagreeable when you
try to take him into confidence.   He shuts his
book to listen ; he lays down his knife and fork;
he lets his soup grow cold ; he runs the risk of
losing the train.   Well, you make the first move :
you look oppressed, mysterious, sympathetic,
and you begin.   Before you can disclose your
intentions, he approves of them.   Before you

can deliver your mind, he hugs it in his embrace.
He swallows your words as they come out of
your own mouth, and still yearns with receptive
amiability. Nothing can choke him. He is
affected, interested, he will hear all you want
to say; but you go through him like water
through a sieve. He takes in all you give,
and gets rid of it at once. But perhaps the
worst effect of his compliance is, that you
cannot really gratify him, or do him a kindness.
He has not will enough of his own to appreciate unselfishness or generosity. He is not
obstinate enough for you to do him a civility.
If you ask him, quite sincerely, whether he
will have a leg or a wing, he will resign
the responsibility of the answer. Either—
which you please. Confound him! How can
you please a man who has no choice of
pleasures?

Next, of all people who provoke us, few are
more tiresome than those who will never do
anything thoroughly. Let us call theirs the
hesitating temper. Their actions are incomplete. A natural deficiency of brain-structure
mars their deeds. They leave the door open;
they always remember something to be done
just as they are leaving the house, and spoil
the effect and good augury of the departure

by running back for a pocket-handkerchief, a memorandum-book, or a final order to the waiter. But the worst of it is, they won't let others do what they want right off. A matter has been settled. It is an immense fact and saving of time to accept decisions; it clears the way. A small thing done is sometimes better than a big one prepared or in preparation. These hesitating tempers, however, won't let the small thing do itself. The matter, as I said, has been settled, dismissed. Then they say: Oh! but ——. The luckless decision is caught by the last joint of its tail, just as it was going steadily and safely out of the room—caught by the last joint of its tail, pulled back all flustered and rampant to have a smut rubbed off its nose. Plague on it, let it go with the smut! As it is, the charm of the launch is spoiled.

These people, too, won't eat or drink in a complete way. They put back, ask you to take back a piece. They will have "Only half a glass, please." They will be helped "presently." They affect a combination of meals, tea and dinner, say, and a cloth over half the table. They save the fly-leaves of notes for memoranda, and mourn over a wholesale clearance of old papers. They dread nothing more than a final decision of little things, and whatever they do, leave some part designedly unfinished.

The above defects, however, are infinitely less trying than those of the sulky, uncertain temper. You may depend, in some sense, upon a phlegmatic, compliant, or a minutely cautious man; you know what he will do on any given occasion; you may shape your course accordingly. But the sulky, treacherous temper defies calculation. All at once, a cloud comes over the face. You have unwittingly touched some sore, and he sulks. There is no honest anger, no blaze, but the coals are alight in the mine, and generally you must wait till they are burned out. You can't get at the hidden heat. It smoulders on; all work is stopped, though the outside looks much the same as usual.

Give me a man who, if angry, will flare up. It is very disagreeable and provoking this sometimes; but if the temper is there, let it come to the top as soon as may be, bubble away, boil over, and be gone. It is best, no doubt, to check your anger, and bite it down. It is well to stop it with a jerk, a painful effort, if need be, pulling the curb of the temper sharp. But if it defies your power, or eludes your presence of mind, the sooner it exhausts itself the better. I have heard that there is no remedy for a runaway horse so effective as a flogging. He must needs gallop; well, my friend, then gallop. I have a good pair of spurs on—in they go. I have a whip, hard, pliant, heavy—lay on thick. Here is a nice steep hill—up we go. Here is a deep-ploughed field—Oh yes, keep up your pace, and how do you like it? I remember a horse-dealer, who always cured a fault by indulging it. He had once a brute sent to him which occasionally stood still. Farmer Waistcoat had flogged him, and he would not move for an hour. Well, this man took the beast, put him in his break, and drove off. In ten minutes he came to a dead stand. Breaker said nothing, did nothing. Horse didn't quite know what to reply, tried to look back with his ears, waited half an hour, and then began to move on. No, my friend, said the breaker; you stay here all day. The farmers passed him going to market with uncomplimentary greetings. What, can't *you* make him move? Breaker doesn't look put out, though. Tck! Farmers drive on, show their samples, dine at the ordinary, and jog home a trifle merrier, late in the afternoon. Breaker still there, master of the position. The horse never stopped again.

So may we sometimes treat human temper. Put upon the compliant man till he is ashamed of himself; give the sulky something to sulk about. A soft answer does not turn away all wrath—not, for instance, a bully's wrath ; on the contrary, a hearty blowing up is likely enough to bring him to his senses, if so be it is administered with zest—plainly, unsparingly, without passion or malice, but without any affectation of pity or reserve. Let him get more than he brings. He is a bouncing fool, who will be a tyrant if permitted. Don't permit him, but give him the hardest meta-phorical punch on the head you can. It has a wonderful and speedy effect. He will stop, and gape, and probably end by saying he didn't mean it, which last word may as well be flatly contradicted, to finish him up with.

The respect which is gained, or rather the obedience which is exacted by a cross man, is frequently noticed. It is, however, impos-sible to force it. No good-tempered man can thus act severity and get his own way; you must be naturally cross to succeed. And then, being naturally cross, it becomes a question whether you really enjoy the full flavour of concessions. No; I think you had better rather be put upon sometimes than be always arbitrary and dominant. There is genuine pleasure in yielding to another, in resigning your rights. Of course I don't mean always, because then you would at last have no rights to resign. They must have at least sufficient protection to give a value to their resignation. If you cut off your hand, you can't shake a friend's. But let us pass on.

Talking of temper, have we not all felt how truly fits of anger are called passion. We suffer; it seems as if an alien spirit snatched us up and whisked us out of ourselves before we could stop him. We don't get angry on purpose; we don't light the fire in the boiler, and blow the coals, and listen for the first simmerings of the heat. No. We are in a passion. The mighty mysterious influence, which will, suddenly perhaps, drop us all flustered and ashamed of ourselves, comes on like a squall. Oh yes, we know very well it is wrong; no one suffers from his passion more than the passionate man. It usually thwarts his object, putting him at a disadvantage; it exhausts his energy, and even if he manages to escape a quarrel, leaves him to be angry with himself. He feels his mistakes sooner than others, and, no doubt, for this reason, we sometimes deal more gently with him than with the stubborn, sulky, and compliant. A passionate man is often loved. The impulsiveness which exposes him to the spirit of anger has its influence in promoting generous, unselfish kindness. He is warm-hearted, though he boils over occasionally. The common culinary advice in such a case—namely, to take the pot off the fire—may perhaps convey to him the best lesson in the management of his susceptible temper : he must avoid provocation. When he feels the temperature rising, the best thing he can do is to whisk himself off at once, before it be too late. We must use common vulgar expedients to achieve great results. With a slate and pencil, we may calculate our latitude and longitude ; the pickaxe leads to gold ; the poet-laureate must fill his inkstand ; Stephenson must oil his locomotive, or all his genius is barren. So we may not despise small causes when we try to check or guide anything so important to us as temper. A little paltry care, a word swallowed, a rising sentence stifled or struck down in us by some simple rule, may at least save us from humiliation, if not secure a victory.

NOTHING can be more irritating than the feeble, incomplete way in which some people poke their fires. I cannot bear to look at them. But I don't know which is worse, the indecisive " potter," or the ignorant, inartistic " smash" which batters down the pregnant covering of caked coal into black confusion, letting the precious materials of a blaze escape unignited up the chimney.

To stir a fire *perfectly*, requires the touch of a sculptor, the eye of an architect, and the wrist of a dentist. I never saw it done thoroughly well above a dozen times in my life; and though there are approximations, more or less distant, within the reach of ordinary men, do not suppose that the process is a simple one, capable of being performed in a single operation.

There is the tap, when the fire has eaten into the heart of a big upper boulder-coal, and

its opening chinks require but a slight shock
to part, and let the imprisoned flame spring
forth. There is the lift, when the poker acts
as a lever to the crust, and lets the rich
loosened fragments drop into the red-hot
cavern. There is the stir universal, when the
mass has been left too long, and requires a
thorough mixing. There is the ventilating
poke, when the roof of the fabric has fallen
heavily in, and the struggling flame has hardly
power enough to overcome the incumbent
mass. In this case the poker must be moved
slowly, and left for a minute between the bars
after the movement has been made. In contrast to all this is the procedure of a woman;
who is thus defined by an Irish archbishop:
" woman, a creature who does not reason, and
who *pokes the fire from the top.*"

Then there are side pokes, and indeed many
varieties of treatment adapted to the state of
the patient: for a fire is a living friend, though
a capricious one, and must be managed with
respect and affection. A friend, ay! Does
he not glance a bright welcome when you enter
your room of a morning? Is he not glad and
merry when you come home? Does he not
wink at you out of the window, when you
mount the door-step? Is he not quiet and

considerate in your study or sick chamber?
If you are dreamy, and sit with feet on fender,
does he not sympathise with you, building
fairy grottos, and peopling them with fantastic
shapes, to suit and soothe your mood? A
friend! I should think so. He is kind even
when you turn your back upon him. But I
grieve to see the unfeeling way he is often
treated after months of closest intimacy. You
have sat by his side; you have talked with
him by the hour together; you have held your
hands over him, as if you blessed him; you
have looked into his heart through all the dull
dead winter, and found it ever warm; and
then, when fickle, gaudy summer comes, and
the sun peers into the room, catching the
fire's eye with an insulting stare, is it to be
wondered at if he sometimes slips out in the
sulks? You should have humoured him a little
—drawn down the blind, and not left him
alone to eat his heart up in neglect.

Putting on coals, too, is a delicate process.
A good healthy fire does not much mind a
heavy meal, but a dyspeptic requires to be fed
with caution. The surest way, though a slow
one, is to take up a lump at a time, in the
tongs, and build a loose cairn above the feeble
blaze. How quickly the flames search the

black interstices, and change the dead mass into a pyramid of life! It is marvellous how soon a coy spark may be thus coaxed into a steady unequivocal fire. Coals ought not to be very big, but about the size of potatoes— the smaller ones choke and stunt the natural progress of the flame.

I do not wonder at the freedom of the grate being made a test of friendship. You cannot trust an acquaintance to touch your fire. It is not only impertinent, but often unfeeling in him to attempt it. A hearth is a sacred place. Nothing accounts more easily for the absence of domesticity among many foreigners, than their want of open grates. That can hardly be a home which is warmed by an invisible fire in the bowels of a great dead-looking stove. It is not worth protecting. Who would die fighting for an Arnott? No, no— the successive and contradictory advertisements of patent stoves assure me that the Briton has not yet accommodated himself to so unconstitutional a machine. He cannot find any to suit him, and I humbly trust he never will. Wood fires are better than stoves; they can be poked—indeed, properly managed, they emit an excellent warmth, and crackle well.

But about the right way of burning logs.

Piling them up is simple enough, and a right genial hearty act it is; but many miss the power of a wood fire by having the ashes frequently cleared away. Leave them there —let them accumulate for a week; then, if you will, keep them within bounds; but let there always be a mound or bed on which the log may lie. They warm a room well; indeed, they never go quite out, though they look white and cold by early daylight. Some time ago, when staying at Rome, the frost was very sharp, and we had large wood fires. Dominico, our man, never cleared the ashes away.

The first thing in the morning he used to stick a number of canes into the ash-heap, and, lo; in a few minutes there was a bright blaze. All the associations, too, of a wood fire are pleasant: there is the riving of logs with wedges—work for the brain of a mathematician, as well as exercise for his body; there is the picking up of odd bits of sticks in the plantation, saying, " there, that will do for the fire," and then coming in and feeding it yourself. There is a prosperous look about a woodstack, and well-stored basket of sawn billets in the corner of the room. These materials, indeed, are more pleasing than the best double-screened Wallsend. There is nothing hearty in the appearance of a coal-hole.

I cannot bear polished fire-irons. Polished grates may sometimes add to the effect of a well-built, well-kept fire, but the ends of the tools should be black. Never stuff up the grate with ornaments; hang something in front, if you will, but have the fire always laid. Then, on a wet, chilly, July evening, you can indulge the sudden hunger for a blaze, by the aid of a lucifer, at once. But the poker itself—what an apt, multifarious piece of furniture! Not only has it a normal sphere and use of its own, for which, by the way, it should not be made too blunt at the point, but it is a test of physical power and manual dexterity. Such and such a man, we hear, can break a poker on his arm, or bend it round his neck. In this there is not only the appeal to common experience, for who—what Englishman at least—is ignorant of a poker? but a pleasant vision of the feat. We behold the fire round which the athletes sit, over their wine; we hear the conversation stray to deeds of prowess; we see the ready means of illustration present on the spot—the extemporised performance. Then, too, what a ready weapon of offence or defence is supplied in the poker! What more handy? It is a national instrument—the British poker. When the Yorkshire jury acquitted the man who knocked down his wife with it, giving in their verdict, " Sarved her right," depend upon it, he would· have been hanged if he had done it with the tongs. I wonder whether he was the man who quarrelled with his spouse about the right way of stirring the fire. They had been separated on this account by mutual consent; their friends, however, having brought them together again, they began talking, as they sat by their hearth, on the first evening after their reconciliation, about the folly of falling out on so small a matter, when the lady said : " Foolish, indeed, my dear, especially as *I* was right all the time !"

OMEBODY has remarked that there is the greatest difference in the world between dining and getting your dinner. The world is a large place; suppose we test the saying at some representative spot. What, for instance, is the central point of measurement to us English people? How do we best express our position anywhere on the globe? Are not all distances measured from Greenwich? Does not that town, or some magic spot in that parish, provide the true unit of reckoning, and stand for the starting-post of wanderings and voyages? Is it not the conventional boss or navel of the world? Thence the navigator counts his degrees. Thence the chronometer derives the "time." There, also, we may consult the statute yard—inch and foot. There, also, for a month or two, the gourmand finds the ideal dinner. It is the centre of the culinary system.

Whatever it may be in the "world," there is, at Greenwich, the greatest difference between dining and getting your dinner. I am not going to describe that meal at the Ship or Trafalgar. Mr. Quartermaine would not thank me for a stale version of the result of his elaborate and piquant experience. It must be judged by other powers than the eye or the ear.

How can I explain, even to myself, the succession of dishes which lead the gratified but buoyant appetite up to the culminating, characteristic focus of a whitebait dinner? Can I—though I had the skill of the subtlest analyst—define the combined operation of wines, sauces, and brown bread and butter on the jaded or virgin palate? Epicures would smile at my attempt, hunger would despise my niceness. I will, therefore, let the delicate subject alone, and ask you merely to digest with me some of the reflections which occur to philosophers like ourselves in connection with a dinner at Greenwich.

In the first place, I remark that the prevailing object of the town is to put the satisfaction of even the humblest appetite in as pleasant a light as possible. Do you wish to luxuriate on copper? Walk from the waterside to the park, and listen to the invitations which greet you at every door :—

"Tea, sir; nice tea and a summer-house. Walk in, sir; private apartment—beautiful view!"

The mistresses of these establishments stand at their thresholds, the tea-things are exhibited in the windows. Over-head, hanging like the signs of old London at right angles to your path, on the house-fronts—like more modern advertisements—cunning placards offer silently to the eye what the hostesses pour into the ear. The fare is cheap : you may bring your own tea screwed up in a page of the *London Journal,* and combine it with "hot water and a cool garden, at twopence per head."

Between this and a dinner at the Ship what room for the imaginative palate to wander !— what variety of meals ! Some incapable of classification under any title in use between breakfast and supper, others scientifically distinctive. Some men dine flying—"snatch a mouthful"—we suppose, as the travelling post-office does a bag at a small station, full speed ; others, having no occupation, dawdle on slowly, spreading the sensation over as much time and palate as they can.

Dinners! Think of the omnibus man's, who drives fourteen hours a day—Sundays included—and, when all goes right, gets twenty minutes for that meal; but when all goes wrong, barely ten. Ten minutes for dinner in a period of fourteen hours!—the hinge is too weak—the pivot is too small for such machinery to revolve on. He gets down, though, no inconsiderable bulk of meat and potatoes. Give a cabman ten minutes, elbow room, and a leg of mutton, and you will have a fresh illustration of the value of time.

Critics in eating have remarked, disparagingly, on the sameness of English dinners, as compared, for instance, with French. Their strictures, however, apply only to the feeding of certain classes,—the entertainments which are given in certain society, where the grand set the pattern and the mean hobble after it. Beyond the stereotyped conventional "dinner," the soups, fish, flesh, fowl, &c., there is perhaps a greater variety of meals consumed under that title in England than in France. There the poor man's meal is made to resemble the rich man's in some degree by a change, if not variety of dishes, say by a little meagre soup. They are also related through the accompanying "wine." There is a common ideal to them both.

Take any promiscuous hundred Frenchmen, and their notions of dinner would show much more uniformity than those of a hundred Englishmen.

I was led into this train of thought one day last summer at Greenwich. A friend carried me down there to dine. Where we dined—below, not many yards off—visible from the open window of our room, was a man "getting his dinner" in a coal-barge. His fingers showed black upon the victuals he tore. When he wiped his mouth with his sleeve he partially cleansed the lower part of his face. He was very hot. He drank out of a battered tin can which had been standing in the sun. After that he sighed deeply, and shouldered a sack of coals. Not that he sighed from sorrow, it was from satisfaction; a rude unspoken grace was offered to the lord of work, who had now satisfied his appetite for a time. He shouldered a sack. My friend suggested cigars on the balcony, and the waiter set out some chairs for us.

Now, methought, what a variety of dinners there are between ours and the bargee's. Dinner filled my mind—Greenwich put it into my mouth—so pray forgive a ruminative chat. Dinners : let us see—these are hot and cold;

they are always hot on board steamers. I suppose there is necessarily something more grateful to the palate in a hot joint. The food is tasted without an effort. On this account a bad hot dinner is abominable, and thus packet-dinners are most offensive. The reeking heap of greens and the large, boiled, underdone leg of mutton, which are always prominent on these occasions, have an intensity of flavour such as no two other dishes ever combined.

The cold dinner has a character which it does not deserve; being socially despised, it is often served without care. Such, however, is the way of the world. The man who has little but plain sense to recommend him is made the worst of, like cold boiled mutton, without pickles or grace; he is used, not welcomed, while the sappy joint gathers around it all the care of cookery and support of sauces. Help to the strong; and as for the weak, you may kick him securely—he has got no friends.

Second-rate cookshops have a wonderful power of developing greasiness; every item shines. The very hungry, however, who go there generally need greasy food, I mean physically; fat makes fat and warmth. I confess, though, that on hearing a wise man the other day remark how Greenlanders ate blubber to produce " carbon," I could not help saying (to myself, of course, for he was a great medical authority) that they probably ate it because they could not get anything else.

I am a great believer, nevertheless, in nature as guide and caterer in eating. She not only provides oil and fat for the inhabitant of the Polar regions, but takes away from him the extreme disgust we should feel at such food. Indeed, I believe that the palate is the truest regulator of our diet. What we like best agrees with us best—in moderation—there is the rub. The glutton suffers in the end often as much as the drunkard, and is often more selfish in his sensuality. But he has himself to blame, not his food. Dainty dishes are sometimes abused, because they tempt us to eat too much. Their daintiness is not their defect. The same bulk of nasty food would disagree with us much more than the same bulk of nice food. Some people, indeed, profess that they don't care what they eat. They are generally mistaken; but if not, all I can say is, they ought to be ashamed of themselves.

To affect superiority to one of the senses

God has given us is questionable, but so to change oneself as to be really insensible is unnatural. Don't care what they eat! Take an extreme case. There must be something wrong about a man who would munch with uniform indifference a pine-apple or a carrot. Those, however, who profess not to care for delicacies, when it comes to the proof, are often found to mean that they don't care for what *other people* esteem delicacies, having themselves a particular appetite for and enjoyment in tasting some vulgar dish—such as sheep's-head and trotters. In fact, their boast generally ends in establishing only the coarseness of their own taste.

It would be curious—yes, instructive—to inquire how far epicures help to educate and civilise a people. Man has been defined as a cooking animal. Delicate eating accompanies other refinements. But how far is its cookery the measure of a nation's worth? I leave my readers to pursue these thoughts, noticing myself one apparently good result from dainty and expensive feeding. Every fruit and vegetable sold at a large price is a reward of skilful scientific gardening. Did no one really care for very early peas, or what not, probably few or none would be grown. Horticulture, as a science, would want one of its strongest supports if there were no epicures. Think how much stimulus is given to gardening as well as to cookery by an elaborate and expensive meal. A dinner at so many guineas a-head represents genuine talent and work in several professions, though it may imply much sensuality in the guests.

In forming a fair judgment on the matter we must consider those who produce, quite as much as those who consume. If, as Sydney Smith says, "the object of all government is roast mutton," what the newspapers call "recherché entertainments" may be closely allied with political philosophy, and the Nation's dinner measure the strength of the Cabinet.

There is, no doubt, a waste of supporting power in the cookery of many poor people. I do not refer merely to the material—the meat which is burnt or the gravy which is spilt—but to the small solace and comfort got in proportion to the bulk of food which is prepared at last. It is not so nice, and therefore not so nutritious, as it might be.

Soyer was one of the greatest of philanthropists; but even his shilling book is too elaborate for very uneducated people. The

thousands which have been sold must have
cheered many a home; we want, however,
something simpler—best of all, more practical
elementary teaching about cookery in connection with national schools. If inspectors
required less grammar and had an examination
in (say) boiling potatoes, it would be a step in
the right direction.

I would have the girls bring up their exercises in clean wooden bowls. The children
should be allowed only such cooking means
as they had at home. In the upper classes
there might be prizes for puddings and other
portions, cheap though not nasty.

Indeed, without some practical knowledge of
the art, books on cookery are almost useless,
just as the juiciest description of a dinner is
thrown away on those unnatural people who do
not care what they eat.

As an illustration of the influence of cookery,
I will mention an anecdote which you may
have stumbled on yourself.

A great eater, famed more for capacity than
discernment, bet that he would consume in ten
minutes any two shillings' worth of wholesome
human food, however combined. His adver-
sary took four pots of threepenny ale, and
emptied them into a very large pie-dish,

then he soaked in it twelve penny rolls, and, presenting the result to the eater, with a spoon, bade him begin. He did so, but could not finish the mess within the wagered limit.

Of course there is much more to be said about dinner. Under what forms does dinner appear! The greedy debauch—the prolonged civic feast—the sudden but complete meal, quite French, that which is provided, say, at Macon, for travellers between Paris and Geneva, or Marseilles, where you find the cork of your bottle of wine ready drawn, and see the last plate or two of soup poured out as the train "arrests itself," and the guard says "Macon," "vingt minutes."

Then there is the lunch-dinner,—a delusive compound. The monotonous chop, over which the unimaginative bachelor grins, day after day. The heavy tea—also a mistake. The felon's dinner—rations, sullen hunger, and a scraped pannikin.

Some persons object to the smell of cooking. That depends. Who does not recollect Dickens's description of the stew-pot at the Jolly Sandboys, in "The Old Curiosity Shop"? How, when the cunning landlord took off the lid, and the savour of the mess filled the room,

not a traveller but made up his mind to stop,—
altogether dismissing what feeble thought he
had about pushing on another mile or two that
night. As for the smell of dinner, I say that
depends. One man rings the bell violently,
and is fierce about the kitchen-door; another
sniffs, and is silent.

Which is best? A good appetite, with a
bad dinner; or a bad appetite, with a good
dinner?

Don't answer without thinking. There are
good sauces besides hunger. A bad dinner is
not only unpleasant, but unwholesome. Conceive great appetites and bad dinners universal.
The blacks in Australia will eat eight or ten
pounds of strong kangaroo at one go. There
is much to be said in favour of less hunger and
better· food. Well! I suppose there is a
medium in the matter,—as the hearsay philosopher affirms.

At any rate, please don't pretend a contempt
for cookery. There is nothing in the world,
my good friend, which you could so ill afford
to lose. *You don't care what you eat!*
You deserve to have every spit, range,
and pot pass out of creation, and to die of
scurvy!

Charity dinners are, though not exclusively,

yet eminently English. There is the fact of dinner on which to build, around which the floating philanthropy gathers, under which it develops itself. The feeder of the hungry must first be fed himself. There is thus the realization of the charity in company with the word " dinner," then the actual influence of the food upon the donor.

But I must have done, though I might say much more. The subject is endless : every one is more or less a competent critic. I have been too bold to write on such a theme.

Courteous reader, in rising from the table, let me express a hope that you see a very great difference between "dining" and "getting your dinner." May you never sit down to one without an appetite,—may you never hunger without being able to dine !

WAITERS.

HO knows anything about the natural history of waiters? Present in all lodging-places, with a home in none—moving in the midst of travellers, though never stepping beyond the door of the house in which they live—they form one of the most singular classes in the modern world. Though, probably, on examination, they would be found human enough, yet at first the idea of a waiter shedding tears, making a will or an offer of marriage, or having a tooth drawn, or, in fact, doing anything but wait, could not get itself admitted without a little hitch or hesitation.

Where do they come from? Where do they learn their craft? We see volunteers, nay, sometimes militiamen, at drill. Ploughmen lead the horses before they drive the plough, artisans pass an apprenticeship, surgeons walk the hospital, and even the grand gentlemen who sit in Government offices have an examination in spelling before they draw their salaries; but who ever heard of a school for waiters? Perhaps they are born full-dressed, with napkins under their arms. Once here, they never seem to hesitate or fail; and yet their work is arduous, intricate, and incessant, requiring not only ready wit, but both dexterity and strength of arm. I have, however, often noticed that in advertisements they describe themselves as single-handed, as if a watchman were to beg particular attention to the fact of his having only one eye.

Excluded by professional engagements from the use of conventional meal-times, do waiters sit down to their dinner, or shoot it flying? Where do they sleep, oil their hair, and put on their shirt-fronts? Have they any guilds, lodges, or other brotherly associations and meetings? What are their amusements? A countryman once thought he had found them at their winter play : he noticed a set of men in tail-coats and white ties scudding round a patch of ice on the Serpentine, about the size of a coffee room, but it turned out to be the Skating Club.

Some little time ago I had a good opportunity of observing the movements of a waiter kept in a seaport town. We were in no hurry, and so we stopped there till the rain was over.

There was, as tourists say, nothing to see.
The inn, which was also a station and a
custom-house, had a railway terminus at the
front, and a packet-wharf at the back door.
The land view consisted of saltings; the sea
view, of a muddy tidal harbour—both backed
by bare bleak downs. We arrived late at
night, intending to sail the next morning; but
it blew and rained, and then did both together
so viciously, that we gave it up, and spent a
wet day at the station. Before, however, we
settled to stop, we went on board the steamer,
moved our luggage, took berths, and made up
our minds to bear the usual inconveniences of
a rough passage across the channel in a long
narrow boat, which heaved as if it were
breathing, even in the sheltered harbour. But
the wind still rose, and so we all returned to
the hotel.

It was during the mental parenthesis which
followed, on being suddenly prostrated and set
to begin a new bill at the inn from which we
had just cleared out, that I gave my mind to
the waiter. One could not keep up an interest
all day in the zigzag jerky course of fat raindrops down the window. Some of our fellow-
passengers smoked, some ate incessantly; a
group of wet Frenchmen sat apart, limp and

moody, like barn-door fowls in a shower; some
of the party went to sleep. Not so the waiter
—for there was but one. A double day's work
had come upon him. The last wave of
travellers had been thrown back, and met the
tide from town, until it filled the house.
Having nothing to do, they all wanted something "to take," immediately. Idleness is the
hardest work in the world; the idle man never
knows what it is to rest, and so must be fed.
Accordingly, when. a number of them get
together and help one another, they necessarily
consume a vast amount of victual. But, as I
have said, our waiter multiplied himself, and
met all demands. Waiting is a gift, and
exhibits some most remarkable combinations
of mental power. It is not enough to say that
a waiter has to recollect the different orders
he receives, and execute them at once; this
does not do him justice. On the Continent, his
task is much facilitated by the table-d'hôte, for
in England our insular dissociable habits make
a waiter's post a hundredfold more hard. You
are not conducted to the same spot at the
dinner-table day after day; you do not dine
at a fixed hour, but sit down when and where
you like. The waiter must bear in mind the
number of your room, and connect that with

the various items of your capricious and particular meals. There were a good many people
in our inn; the number of our room was 29,
and that was on the first floor. The second
was also full. Here were a set of new faces to
be learned only for one night. Each tenant
had, say, three meals—dinner, tea, breakfast.
Now, considering that the minute details of all
these had to be remembered, chops to be
associated with A, soup with B, sherry-
and-water with this man, soda-and-brandy
with that, bottled stout or draught ale with a
third—all being of various prices; considering,
too, that the stream of permutations and combinations of customers went on for hours, and
that all had to be presented with so many bills,
without entanglement or substitution, at the
same moment, the next morning, under the
trying pressure of a steamer's departure, and
the arrival of a fresh trainful of passengers,
merely passing through the house, but calling
for goes of this, that, or the other, at the bar
as they hurried by—biscuits, cigars, with " I've
no small change," " I've nothing but French
money," &c., while the amount was being
made out — considering all this, I say it
required an eye and memory of no common
power to perform the duties of a waiter.

Besides being able to fix and arrange a crowd of facts in his mind, the waiter must be able to dismiss them at once; to sponge the slate of his memory, and begin to cover it again immediately with details, whose very similarity is the most dangerous and perplexing part of the business—and this, day after day, week after week. With all these duties, the waiter must not stop to think. With a head full of orders on the point of being discharged, he must submit to be called back for a spoon, or to say where the coat with an umbrella strapped to it, not the shawl with the parasol, was put, when No. 17 came back from the boat, and changed his room to No. 37.

Only a waiter! Why, no prime minister in his place, in presence of a jealous minority, can need greater promptness, accuracy, and elasticity of mind. The waiter, indeed, answers at a disadvantage; he has no notice of questions, but is expected to be always at his post, ready with a reply, in a house where Government business, as well as that of private members, is being conducted through continuous sittings, morning, noon, and night, for the whole period of his holding office. Indeed, a waiter must not only have his wits about him, but wits of a remarkable order. Unlike many earning less than he, he cannot see his work grow under his hand; he cannot hope to perform it mechanically, like a man laying bricks or rowing a boat; he is always beginning intercourse with strangers.

See how grateful he evidently is for kind, considerate treatment! Who would not relieve the anxious monotony of his work with a pleasant word? Who would grudge him the small gratuity, so that he may at last settle down in some business, in which he is not only the jaded medium between the producer and consumer, but a sharer in the main profits along with the trim chamber-maid? Let us hope they may save enough, ere long, to club their fortunes, and to possess, though it be a humble one, a bar of their own.

THE Annual Treat has now become quite an educational institution. The day is prized in the future and in retrospect. The children, with a delicious rejection of all responsibility, magnify the arduousness and specialities of the excursion as the day approaches, and when it has passed recount their extravagance and feats with slowly-fading interest throughout the remainder of the summer. The anxious manager, too, thinks quite as much of the business as the most heedless little trot; he dreads the coming possibilities of accident, and no one walks off with more relief than he when the day is over, and the twenty van-loads of scatterbrained children have been safely emptied into the street by the school, without fracture or loss. It may seem an easy thing, with all the appliances of London, to take from 500 to 1,000 children for a day into the country; but you must not forget that there can be no rehearsal of the proceedings, no preparatory march out, no previous drill. The strong influence which accompanies the present educational system is nowhere more shown than in the power of ordinary every-day discipline to control the child regiment on its one unpractised field-day. True, there are accidents, not unfrequently, but the marvel is there are not more. The exuberance of the children's pleasure comes from the consciousness not only of a holiday, but a holiday as a school, all together, in the country. It is the very nick and crisis of the summer's joy. All provokes amusement. The master smiles, the teachers play. The monitors romp. What wonder that Tommy sprains his ankle among the hundreds thus suddenly plunged into the very opposite of their daily life?

The way in which children delight in running risks is occasionally even absurd, however provoking. Some years ago, I gave about 400 children an excursion to Ealing. We were to play and feast in a big hay-field safely hedged, and studded with large shadow-casting trees. We went in vans, and drove into the meadow at once—so as not to run the risk of losing children by unloading on the common. There were several animals being taken out of the field as we drove in.

Well, the first thing that the first boy did who got off the foremost van, was to pull the tail of the nearest horse. Of course he was kicked down, but, having happened to single out a rheumatic old mare, and having run right upon her hocks, he was simply laid on his back, without being hurt. He could hardly, however, have made speedier arrangements for a serious accident. Sometimes children who have been used to back streets and alleys all their lives, are quite bewildered with their first excursion, and cannot get fairly to play for some time. I remember once taking a number of such poor inexperienced little boys to Hampton Court. It was too much for many of them. A few were stupefied, others ran wild. I never had such a day. The children were mostly strange to me, but I directed the entertainment as the giver of it. Had I not marked each boy with a red calico rosette, I should have lost ever so many among the other schools which were there. We got off very well on the whole, but I was horrified once at finding one fry of urchins bathing in an ornamental basin among the gold fish. Another unintentionally killed a duck with a horse-chestnut, which hit him on the back of the head, etc., etc. However, they were very merry, poor little fellows, and the affair of the duck happily came to nothing. I suppose the guardians considered it accidental death, which it really was. I should remark, in passing, that the performances of that day were quite exceptional, for, having assisted at or superintended many school treats, I must bear witness to the remarkably good behaviour and obedience of the children in our National Schools at their annual excursions.

But let me say a word about the kind of treat which is most liked. It should not be too stiff nor instructive. There should be plenty of running about: a processional excursion loses half its relish. The best place is a large field, with plenty of grass, shade, and liberty within certain boundaries. The commander-in-chief, knowing that children will spend money, should be careful to make an arrangement with the pedlars and donkey boys, who always scent out a school excursion, and present themselves on the ground directly the children come—in most cases fleecing them at once. There should be a regular tariff of prices, or children will pay anything in the first demand for a ride or a swing. It is well, too, to provide a choice of goods and amusements. This divides and protects the children.

For several years I have arranged beforehand for the presence of donkeys, swings, knock'em-downs, print-sellers, archery, &c., at a certain price. A photographic tent, too, with like-nesses at fourpence a-head, frames included, is very popular. Any one taking a large school out of London would find this much appre-ciated. It is better than fruit. There is some-thing to show, and no stomach-ache involved in it. There are itinerant artists who are glad of the chance.

At any rate, let there be something cheap and wholesome which the children can buy, and, whatever is omitted, be sure you get some donkeys. A penny a ride is generally the price, but the men will often neutralize the arrangement, unless you settle how long the "ride" is to be. I always take a policeman with me, and bargain with the owner of the donkeys before him and the children. "From this tree to the corner of the field, and back, for a penny." "Very well, sir," says the master of the obstinate stud. The children all catch the price, screaming in chorus, "The corner of the field and back for a penny." The next moment they secure every donkey, and set off with more enthusiasm than the steeds they bestride. I have known quite expensive excursions comparatively fail for lack of donkeys. Swings, too, are invaluable ; if you really wish the children to enjoy themselves, you should have several of them. A solitary swing is a centre of strife. There should be a small one for the little children alone.

There is a considerable choice of places to go to in the neighbourhood of London. The great thing is to have it as countryfied as possible, and yet with available shelter. This last can often be provided by a rick-cloth, which is much cheaper than a tent, and will cover a host of children. If you can get a good field, with a rick-cloth, donkeys, swings, and other attractions of the sort, ordered for the occasion, you can generally combine all the charms of the so-called " tea-garden " without its attendant drawbacks. The Crystal Palace is too stiff for downright play. Many pleasure-grounds are too ill-conducted. A field with extemporized shelter, and selected camp-followers, is the thing. But suppose you have fixed upon the place, and have not decided how to go there, take my advice and get vans. They consume a long time on the journey, which is half the fun ; they carry the children from the door of the school where

they assemble, right into the field where they
play. They are ready to go or return at your
own hour. Any railway, on the contrary,
involves four marches—one to the station in
the morning, then one to the field; another
back to the station, when the day's play
is over, and, worst of all, another from the
station home, perhaps through crowded streets
at night. There are too many musterings,
and the journey itself is much too short. It
is over directly, whereas a drive in vans of
some only six miles is quite a long business.
Choose a flat road if you employ vans, or the
price of them will be much increased. You
ought to get twenty vans for a guinea a piece
for a day, supposing you go only six or seven
miles out of town. Any gratuity to the
drivers should be made to depend upon their
behaviour, for they are a thirsty race. It is
not a bad plan to give them all tea after the
children; it keeps them together, and weakens
their excuse for drinking at the nearest public-
house. They always take it as a kindness,
and it costs very little.

A word about the packing of vans. The
children should be made into companies of
from thirty to forty, according to their size. It
is advisable to put those who know each

x

other best together; which is done by making
the companies out of the contiguous school-
classes. Each company should have a number
known to the children and the driver of their
van. Thus, when the day's amusement is
over, and the horses are standing harnessed
ready to return, there ought to be no confusion.
The master, having assembled the children,
says, " Now then, No. 1." Up drives No. 1,
and those who belong to No. 1 company get
in : thus the whole are soon seated; all rush
and scrambling is avoided. There ought to
be two teachers or seniors with each van, and
a policeman on the last.

Now about provisions. If your funds are
limited, don't attempt a dinner. Let the
children bring some with them. Give them a
hearty tea between three and four o'clock, and
a bun a piece, with milk-and-water at last. I
have known schools where everything was
provided free, except dinner, and that the
children paid some trifle for. The consequence
was, that the excursion ceased to be a " treat,"
and the parents, if not the children, grumbled
at any failure or omission, as unjust.

There are three ways to cater on these
occasions :—1st. You can carry everything with
you, and make your own tea. 2nd. You can

find some respectable innkeeper near your field to prepare for you. 3rd. You can get the whole thing done by a contractor from town. There are persons who would provide for an excursion of thousands at a few days' notice, and at almost any scale of prices you choose. This saves a vast deal of trouble. The country landlord is seldom experienced in the sort of thing you want; your own commissariat is liable to break down. You forget the knives, the butter, the sugar, or some item which affects the success of the whole affair. A contractor is the best. You can calculate the cost to a penny, and be quite easy about having what you want.

There is a subsidiary treat which many schools within a decent walk of Kensington Gardens might get up, which is very successful and cheap. The most retired part of the gardens are sure to be new to the children. You hardly ever see anybody there. I have witnessed several famous extemporized treats, by taking the whole school to a pleasant open spot among the trees to the north of the round pond. If you speak to a park-keeper he will see that no undesirable people come to interfere with your play. This excursion, too, teaches people to make use of the fresh air and quiet within their reach.   The present retirement of some part of the gardens, off the great lines of thoroughfare, is most remarkable.   I sat on a bench there one day, for half an hour, without seeing a soul except at a distance, and then I left without being interrupted.   Birds were singing in the trees, two or three gardeners belonging to the palace were potting some plants, about fifty yards off, and the only sign of London, beyond the faint hum of distant traffic, was a stray policeman; but he was smoking a pipe.

I always pity the children of the infant school on the day of the annual excursion. You must draw the line somewhere.   You can't take them.   We always have a little appendix or postscript of a "treat" for these, about a week after the great affair.   It really can consist of nothing but tea, and play in the schoolroom; but a few shillings' worth of penny German toys are of priceless value. Imagination does a good deal to give the whole thing a festive character; the chief gratification, however, consists of unlimited noise, and romping in rooms where they are at other times taught to behave quietly.

The character of a school is more affected than many people think by its treats.   Those

who see the train of vans, full of children,
setting out some bright midsummer day, or
hear the chorus of little voices as they come
cheering back at night, sometimes little suspect
the anxiety and enjoyment involved in that one
day's excursion. It is the main theme of some
back dingy streets where hundreds watch the
weather with kind interest, and quite a crowd
awaits the return of the cavalcade. "Here they
are!" is the cry, as the first van comes round
the corner, and the children are soon claimed
by parents, and fast asleep, dreaming of the
real buttercups and daisies of the clean country
meadow where they have spent at least a day,
clear of the smoky, dirty town.

 UNDERSTAND by the above heading the small sport of those who are fond of shooting, but own no preserves, and take out no licence. They are by no means poachers, but follow up a blackbird with an interest unmarred by envy of the great guns ; not but that they sometimes —in the sudden heat of discovery—kill a partridge, pheasant, or a hare, but, as a rule, they do not affect such game, but aim at small results, which they pursue with spirits and success worthy of a tiger-hunt. All birds are fair game to them, with the exception of robins, which are sacred, and rooks, which enjoy a special privilege of destruction, and may not be killed, except young. I am not sure whether a true hedge-popper would kill a wren ; I hardly think he would. Possibly her supposed relationship to cock-robin is a protection to this little bird. Nor would he harm an owl or a swallow. But, with these exceptions,

the hedge-popper lets fly at anything within his
reach.   And why should he be refused a
chronicler? Battues are reported in the *Times;*
the accounts of the moors are published with a
business-like money-article sort of air, some
weeks before the 12th of August; the judges
who go our circuits, and the magistrates who
remain at home, are continually engaged in
adjudicating between poachers and sportsmen;
half the conversation at the squire's table is
about game; the Houses of Parliament are agi-
tated by proposals for the conviction of men who
may be suspected of having pheasants in their
pockets; the governors and the governed are
equally bitter and complaining about preserves.
Why, then, should the humble hedge-popper,
who is happier in his "sport" than the largest
game-owner in the country, be unnoticed?
He is content to enjoy himself without protection; he needs no keepers to set up at night
and have their skulls cracked; he asks for no
army of beaters and markers; he needs no
expensive outfit; he does not buy dogs at fifty
guineas the brace; he is not plagued with a
kennel, abused by tenants, nor covered with
obloquy by the Radical journals.   And yet he
can perfect himself in all that distinguishes a
true sportsman.   He can shoot well—at least he

ought to do so, for he is sharply tested by the specialties and variety of his sport; he must learn to be patient; he sees and should remember the habits of birds; he finds abundant exercise in the pursuit of his amusement, and wastes no money on its artificial support.

Who does not remember the first bird he shot? I do: it was a tomtit on an apple-tree. One afternoon, when I was a naughty little chit in a pinafore, I got possession of a horse-pistol which had been hanging up over the kitchen mantelshelf till it was as rusty as an old rat-trap. After some experimental flashes in the pan, I loaded it, feeling rather guilty and doubtful, with a handful of pease; and seeing cook safely occupied with her own concerns, sallied forth. Then a naughty thought suddenly came into my head. Should I shoot the cat? the temptation was almost irresistible; she sat on a low wall, with her eyes shut, licking the sunshine off her paws. Would it hurt her? Probably. She was a yard off. Would it make much noise? I should think so, cat and all. Would she recover, and tell cook? What should I do with the body, if immediately successful? It was too rash a venture, all things considered; but to this day

she has no idea what a narrow shave it was.
I passed on : there was a small apple-tree
close by, and a tomtit fidgeting about among
its upper twigs. Now, then. With the pistol
held in my two hands, both arms extended,
head thrown back, and teeth shut, I made a
demonstration which at least ought to have
arrested his attention. Not a bit—he fussed
on. Thrice did I cover him with my piece;
as often did it miss fire; but the fourth
time —— Whether it was from the noise or
the pease, or both, is uncertain, but he died.
Pussy reached the kitchen-door with a spang;
cook rushed out; and I, flinging down the
pistol, which smoked like a squib, and clutch-
ing my prey, scampered off to a particular lair
of my own in the shrubbery, where I might
let the first gush of success relieve itself
without interruption. That exploit is one of
the clearest in my memory, and is, I believe,
as deeply cut in the virgin surface of that
material, as many a capital-lettered crisis of my
being.

How confused a record we have of those
years when life's waggon got on the dusty level
road, when one day was like another, as we
toiled on with tedious speed! A man's memory
becomes at last like a long travelled letter,

thick with blotted impress, struck hastily on, as he passed from post to post, covered with confused significance. Whereas of the palmy days of youth —— But, heigho! Let us to hedge-popping.

I believe that most famous "shots" have been hedge-poppers in their time, and, moreover, that some of their pleasantest reminiscences are of early days, when society did not notice their pretensions. Let me try and touch, if it may be, the memories of some bygone days in the respectable bosoms of elderly gentlemen who read these words. I am grey now, and have grave work enough to do, but when I see a boy creeping along under a hedge, with his gun and ears full-cock, I think of the time when my waist was less than it is, and I tore holes in my jacket, stalking the smallest game. Let me look kindly back, and where I see a scene or phase of hedge-popping, put it down here in harmless words.

The young hedge-popper begins almost invariably in the snow or among the gooseberry-bushes. A small boy frequents these bushes when the fruit is ripe, creeping about and looking beneath the low branches, with, of course, far more ease than a man; and there he sees prodigious opportunities of sport. There are great blackbirds hopping about and pecking away, bill-deep, in the central stores of fruit; missel thrushes, showing to the boy-eye as big as partridges; and young robins, which have all the impudence of their race, but are not protected by the badge of red upon their breasts—mean-looking, thievish, voiceless birds, which the hedge-popper does not consider to be robins as yet. On these the young sportsman generally begins, being encouraged by the gardener. His first weapon is a bow and arrow, probably a crossbow made with the aid of the village carpenter. The missile is a heavy bolt, which will fly some thirty yards, and does duty over and over again till it is lost. Armed with this, the boy squats or peeps among the fruit-bushes till he gets a shot at very short range, say three yards. Mostly, the bolt flies wide, causing by its own flight and recovery far more destruction of fruit than any one small bird; occasionally, however, the game is struck and slain, and great is the triumph. Happily, there is less pain and fright suffered by the victim in this than in any other sport. The bird generally hops off, and continues its meal at the next bush, but when struck, receives a fatal blow: once hit with a missile bigger and heavier than itself, it comes to grief suddenly.

But the hedge-popper soon gets beyond the bow and arrow. I remember, when a little lad, thinking another supremely blessed in the possession of a pistol-barrel mounted on a little gunstock, and which once killed a yellow-hammer at the almost incredible distance of twenty-two paces. I had a pistol myself—to this day, I wonder why it was not taken from me—and used to make some very fair practice at eight or ten yards.

But at last we got a gun, and rose towards the higher walks of hedge-popping. Not that the gun was any great matter to shoot, but still it was a gun. You could put it to your shoulder, and take aim. It kicked, which was a great point, and made a prodigious noise. We bought paper screws of shot at the little grocer's in the village, or we cut up sheet-lead into mince-meat with our pocket-knives, and loaded the weapon with that. Of course, we used the bowl of a tobacco-pipe to measure the charge, and employed paper for wadding.

With this implement, we aimed high and low, shot blackbirds thirty yards off, cut up the shrubs, and broke cucumber-lights and hidden garden-glasses. There were, however, two places which almost invariably afforded some sport—one was a tree at the corner of a barn, where the sparrows always retired when disturbed in the farmyard, from whence they made their raids. Every one living in the country knows some such tree, generally a thorn, thick with tangled twigs, and altogether impervious to the eye when covered with leaves. Well, during the winter, there were always some sparrows or finches to be found there, despite of our constant popping. You might stand beneath it the whole afternoon, and find a succession of shots. But the chief tree was a high elm frequented by jackdaws. These birds were pronounced mischievous; and though charged to hold rooks sacred, we were permitted to shoot jackdaws, if we could : not such an easy matter for little boys, who had to get within thirty yards of these birds, and then catch them sitting. They combine, like many busy, chattering people, much cunning with their impudence, and scent a gun as quickly as a thief does a policeman. There was a long wall, however, to our garden, near the end of which stood the jackdaws' tree. When we saw two or three of them fairly perched, we used--hiding the gun—to slip under cover of the wall at some distance off, in an unembarrassed sort of way, as if we were going to gather fruit; then, stooping down, we would creep quickly up behind it till we reached a large lilac opposite the elm-tree. Peeping out of the thick of this over the wall, we too often found that we were detected, and that the birds had flown. If not, if the familiar "jackle, jackle, jackle" was still heard, then resting the piece in the ivy on the wall-top, and taking a long poking aim, one of the rogues was pretty sure to bite the dust. I often think of that masked battery now, when I smell lilac. Of course, those were days in which we could not shoot flying, and a jackdaw was a golden eagle.

We had a man-servant then, named Sam. I remember once his making us boys very jealous by killing two daws at one shot out of this same bush. They had grown very shy, but he got them early one summer morning, and brought them to our room before we were up. We thought it a prodigious feat. Sam was a Weller in his way; and though he occasionally anticipated us in some opportune shot, used to prefer helping us in hedge-popping to doing his work. But he always had an excuse for any failure. I remember his proposing to

catch a rabbit with a fat house-dog we had;
and on returning unsuccessful, "The rabbit,"
he said, "ran so fast, that Mungo had hard
work to keep behind him." Poor Sam! I
forget what became of him; he got into great
scrapes with the authorities for incurable lazi-
ness and impertinence; but he was an enthusiastic assistant in hedge-popping. He never
did anything without some expression of comic
interest in the work. I remember once looking into the kitchen, and seeing Sam crouched
up by the fire, his hands on his knees, mouth
open, eyes half shut, and face as long as a
fiddle-case. The gardener coming in at that
instant, cried out,—

"Hollo, Sam, what are you after?"

"Hush!" replied Sam, cautiously, "I'm
catching a cold;" as if it were an animal
behind the grate, which he expected to bolt,
like a rabbit.

The shrubs at the end of the wall where the
battery was masked for the jackdaws, formed
an excellent practice-ground for snap-shooting
in later boy years. There were always some
blackbirds or thrushes in the shrubbery; but
when disturbed, they never broke cover till
they got to the wall, and then they popped
over with a flip, and I can tell you it is no

such easy matter to catch a bird thus. Some
of your pheasant-butchers would be hard put
to it to knock over a blackbird in such a
glimpse, but we got to be rather dabs at this
quick shooting; and on the first occasion of
my ever shooting at a woodcock, at my first
battue, I knocked one down which was twisting
about among the trees, in the presence of some
eight or nine old sportsmen, with very great
applause.

Woodpigeons are among the hedge-popper's
head game. The best way to get them is to
wait by the plantations to which they resort,
and stand still till they come. But by no
means shoot at one as it approaches you—the
feathers of these birds are so thick upon the
breast that they will often turn off the shot;
wait till they have passed, and then they are
vulnerable enough.

The same rule applies to wild duck, gulls,
&c. Though wild-duck shooting is a high
and separate art, yet the popper is in his glory
on the beach, and about the saltings on the
flat coast. Nowhere does he learn better to
calculate distances, nowhere has he greater
variety of practice, from the curlew going at
full speed down a creek, to an oxbird running
and then rising up just within range, and

needing to be knocked down in an instant,
if touched at all. There is something, though,
about shooting gulls against the grain. They
are the marked companions of our sacred
friends the rooks. With them they follow
the plough, and dot the dark mould with
spots of white, showing bigger than they
really are by their contrast with their black
companions.

But the worst feat of all is to shoot an owl:
there is something ominous of evil in it. Did
you ever see a wounded owl? Its look of
melancholy reproach is most affecting. One
does not wonder at the boy in the story,
whose companion had winged an owl in a
churchyard, and who ran to pick it up. "Oh,
Billy," he cried out when he reached it, "what
have you done? You've been and shot a
cherubim;" a great compliment to the sculptor
of the tombstones he had studied.

There is one rule, too, the hedge-popper
will keep sacredly—he will never shoot in the
breeding-times. Autumn and winter are his
seasons, especially the latter, when the blackbirds are dispersed in the hedges, and the
larks are not packed by too cold weather.
Then even an old sportsman may find abundant occasions for exercise and skill, without

breeding any of the bad blood which too often accompanies the preservation of game, and without slaughtering the numerous little birds which preserve our fields and gardens from the grub.

In revising this little paper, written some time ago, I cannot help feeling how gentle we London parsons should be with the wilder spirits among our street boys, who, too often, have apparently no vent but mischief for letting off their steam. Half the harm they do comes from sheer energy, which wants only to be guided into useful channels.

All honour to the Founders of the Shoe Brigade! Did you ever employ one (not a founder)? The sensation is curious. He pounces on your foot, brushing your trowsers and scratching off the bigger splashes with his nails. It is like putting your toe in the way of a quarrelsome house-terrier, which makes ineffectual attempts to worry the intruder. But Blacky does his work well, though always in a desperate hurry.

" **ELL,** I am going down the Strand, so I will just run in and get it done at once."

So said I innocently of a small square of parchment which came some weeks ago by the Yorkshire post, with a request from my friend C—— that I would get it stamped for him at Somerset House, and leave it with Messrs. Stickfast & Grabfee, the clerical lawyers in Bishop Street. It was the nomination to the incumbency of a poor district in the North, miscalled a "living" by some, but well known to others, with apt reference to the permanent labour and poverty of the place, as a "perpetual curacy." I folded it up in an envelope, and took it at three o'clock that afternoon to Somerset House. Having inquired of an omniscient policeman where stamps were to be obtained, I was guided to a doorway with "Inland Revenue" over it. Passing through this, and turning sharp to the left, I found myself in a street of offices, prepared, as was set forth in large letters outside, to deal with every phase of the deed-stamping process. I had expected a hole in a wall like the ticket-counter at a railway station, a fee of course, a dab with a sort of ink-seal, or a hard pinch under a die with a lever handle, and the speedy completion of my business. But there was no stamping, except up and down the passages. So I made fresh inquiry, and was at last directed to the introductory office. I found counters like a bank, and screened desks with nobody at them. The clerks, or whatever they were, were chatting over an inner fire.

" No use to-day," was the response I got; " no money taken after three o'clock."

" Ah," I replied, " indeed! I have been asked by a clergyman in the country to get this nomination stamped. Will you tell me how to proceed when it may be done?"

" Let us look at it," said the clerk, testily. So I showed it.

" Oh, this must be endorsed by the Ecclesiastical Commissioners; then you must bring it here; then you must take it to the paying-office; then you must claim it at the ——; then you will——"

Seeing in my face that the head of the directions had slipped out of my mind while the tail was going in, he handed me a printed scrap of paper with rules how to get the thing done. I folded it up with the nomination, and went my way, it being too late—three o'clock —to get any step in the process taken then. Next day I sought Messrs. Stickfast & Grabfee, who, on looking over the nomination, told me it was unnecessary to go to the Ecclesiastical Commissioners, as a thirty-shilling stamp alone was required for all perpetual curacies. On repairing to Somerset House, and presenting my parchment in the room where I received the printed directions, the clerk discovered that it was irregular. My friend had resided and done the duty of his parish for two months and *three days*, and the date of the nomination was three days too old.

" Ha!" said the clerk, " he must make an affidavit."

This involved Heaven knows what delay in Yorkshire, so I put in a letter from C——, intended for Messrs. Stickfast & Grabfee, stating that he had been resident, and explaining why he had not been able to send the nomination before.

" Ah, well," replied the clerk, "it's all right," and signed it.

So I went to another office, some way off, to pay the thirty shillings. Handing the parchment across the counter with £1. 10s. upon it, the clerk looked at me with a compassionate smile, and said : "Fill in No. 1," and pointed to a number of printed forms hung against the wall.

Pulling one of these down, I dipped a pen, and found I had first to state the name of " applicant." Thought I, *I* don't want the stamp; I suppose the applicant is my friend. So I asked whether it were not so. Leaning back for a moment, to get a steady look at me, the clerk replied with the air of a counsel who had a witness in a corner : " *You* apply, don't you ? You are applying now."

" Yes," said I, " for information."

" Tt, Tt," he responded, peevishly ; " you have come here——"

" I am here, certainly," said I, " and was here yesterday."

" And apply for a stamp ?"

" Yes," said I ; but added that I applied for a friend, for it was no business of mine.

" *You* are the *applicant*, however, at -this

moment," decided the fop, " and will please fill in the form No. 1."

Then I made a small entry on a foolscap sheet, wrote down my address and name— *surname* only, the paper said—and tried my young swell again with the thirty shillings. I held it towards his right hand.

" The other side, if you please, sir," he replied.

" Confound the puppy !" thought I ; " I shall have to climb over the counter, and cram it down his throat before I go ; " but I did as I was bid, when he graciously accepted the thirty shillings, and told me to deliver my document in the room below. Having dis-covered this, I found a man behind a counter patiently watching a machine like a large mouse-trap, with a glass end to it. This was the mouth of a spout which came down from the upper room, and was emptied as soon as it had caught some half-a-dozen papers. There were about twenty people waiting, like myself, till their papers should be taken out of the trap. Presently, my application descended.

" Blank !" cried the watcher, " No. 500 Queen Street."

" Here you are," said I, and he took my document. Judge of my surprise when he

folded it up with the application, pitched it
away down a hole in the wall, and began
paring his nails. " Hollo!" said I ; " I want
it stamped."

" It'll be done in an hour and a half," he
replied, as if it were a joint, and folded his
knife up, first wiping the blade between his
finger and thumb. Now, an hour and a half
is nothing to a Government clerk ; but, as I
could not wait so long, I called again in three
hours, and found my way down into the
delivery room. A broad, endless band of
canvas, or something of the sort, led into this
from some other place in the department, and
borne upon it came an irregular fleet of
documents, some like barges across the stream,
but all, big and small, moving at equal rate, as
if with the tide. The canvas river tipped
them slowly into a tank, whence a man picked
them out, and read aloud the names on the
outside. Directly I got up to the barrier
which fenced the crowd off him, I asked if
" Blank, 500 Queen Street, thirty shillings,"
had come in.

" No," says he, as a matter of course ; so I
listened in vain for half an hour—no " Blank."

" I've a cab waiting," I remonstrated, " and
was told to be here in an hour and a half,

more than three hours ago. I wish you would look for *Blank, 500 Queen Street, thirty shillings, a parchment.*" Pretending to feel in one or two pigeon-holes, he replied, "Not come," and went on wearily calling out the names of the fresh ships come down with the tide. By this time I had got my elbows over the barrier, and had been trying to catch the fellow's eye for some five or ten minutes. At last he looked up.

" *What* name did you say ? "

" Blank, 500 Queen Street, thirty shillings, small parchment," I repeated.

" Ah, yes," said he, and actually looked for it. " Here it is; it's irregular, though. You must take it back to the first office. The date is wrong."

Now, as I had already got over this hitch, it was hard to begin the whole thing again. However, I ran back with it in haste, for the stream of exhausted clerks was already pouring out fast into the Strand, and I found two or three exquisites just going away.

" Well," said one, testily, "and pray *what* do you want ? "

I forget exactly what I said, but I know that I was very slow, cool, lucid, and, I trust, politely sarcastic.

"Waal," replied he, "certainly it's a baw."

"Yaas," said I, "it's a baw;" for, don't you see, I thought if I spoke the language of the natives I might get redress.

"Ah, you showed it to one of the gentlemen here?"

"Yaas," said I, pointing out his signature, "and he signed it, and said it was all right."

"Ah!" he replied, "I suppose he was very much engaged?"

"Yaas," said I, "he was doing *nothing;* and," I added, "there were two other gentlemen helping him." Mind you, we were quite unmoved throughout the dialogue.

"Waal," said he, "you must take it back." Having said this, and scrawled over it with a pencil an assertion that it was all right, he finished buttoning his gloves, and walked off. Then I found out my weary friend at the mouth of the canvas river again, and depositing the unlucky nomination in his hand, received directions to *call the next day.* "It's too late now," was the answer, "come here to-morrow."

"That I can't," I replied; "I'm going out of town, and shall not be able to come for a week. Will it be ready in a week?"

" Yes," said he, sticking it into a pigeon-hole, where I firmly believe it is now untouched, while I am sitting in a friend's library a hundred and fifty miles away from town ; but when I go back, I intend to take lodgings somewhere near the Strand, and, if possible, see the end of the matter.

Prodigious ! as Dominie Sampson said ; the deed has been stamped at last. Probably, it took less than a quarter of a minute to do it; but it was done, and my attitude of expectancy and complaint is no longer justifiable. Messrs. Stickfast & Grabfee laughed, through their clerk, when I told them the history of the process, and said that even *they* never got a deed stamped without having to send twice. But why, we ask, are not stamps sold ? Why could not I have bought a thirty-shilling one, and, sticking it on the thing with a lick and a pat, have relieved the expectation of my friend C—— at once, though it would have lost me three days' sport in the preserves of Somerset House ?

ID you ever know a path across a level field to be straight, when formed by the feet of wayfarers alone? There is the opposite stile which you seek, there is nothing to turn you to the right hand or to the left but your own swerving fancy; and that makes the field-path crooked, invariably. It seems as if no one could walk straight alone, nor indeed correct himself, once for all, when wrong. The moment he becomes conscious of a deviation from the true track, he leaves it again in the other direction. When the object to be reached is obvious, corrections are more frequently repeated. So it comes to pass that the fresh-stamped path over the mould is never straight, but a calendar of successive mistakes. Thus difficult is it to take the shortest cut. None but a ploughman can do so; and he can do little or nothing, except it be after long years of patient experience. Walking the other day for some miles through fields, in which the track from gate to gate had been marked out by the passengers themselves, and lay always crooked on the ground, I fell into such an entanglement of thought about short cuts that, like as with a tune which you can get rid of only by humming it again and again, I found myself putting some of them on paper when I came home. And if the great excuse for an essay or soliloquy is its power of arousing reflections which the reader accepts as his own, perhaps my familiar reverie may not be uttered without some such effect.

Short cuts : let me first beg the privilege of using them now, and whenever I see a fresh thought, make straight for it, though I may risk a blunder, and leave the correct progress of meditation.

Somebody said once that " there was no royal road to geometry," and that neat reproof to a vulgar king has been caught up by so many, that no doubt there is a great principle involved in the saying. The principle is, that money will not buy genius ; that the splendour of rank does not necessarily make the brain shine. But the philosopher's rebuke is telling only on the assumption that regal power is external alone.

I hold it as certain that there *is* a royal road to most ends, if the traveller be a born king. Every successful short cut is made by a regal mind. Some object has been hitherto approached only by tedious pains. The wise and the weak, alike, labour and wait. All at once the labyrinth in whose turns they are creeping is burst through, and one man's force of brain and will destroys the inviolable hedge. Others follow over the gap; his short cut becomes in a common way but a royal road, for it was a king who first found it out.

Indeed, every true leader and ruler of mankind guides them thus. No nation will ever advance far at the word of command. The national wit stagnates, the schools hang on hand. The tutors teach the old formulas. The pupils thumb the old books. Everything is done, and must be done, with true conservative pains : no princely patronage can quicken the pace or the thought of the workers.

But all at once some mighty mind makes a short cut; invents a steam-engine, say, and the whole nation, prince and all, masters and scholars, tutors and taught, follow in the wake of the new guide.

The four Georges in succession might have patronized, bribed, threatened the united coach-makers of the kingdom, without finding any route from St. James's to Windsor which a well-mounted butcher-boy could not take as well as they.

But at last a great king came, and before long the successors of the Georges and their subjects sat behind Stephenson. There was a short cut : a royal road. Had there been no pains taken before this to carry travellers to their destination at the highest possible speed? Was not the posting system elaborated? Were not the coaches swift? What could you do more? There was a limit to motion. Horses have but four legs, and the suggestive whipcord fails beyond a certain point. But the commanding brain summons an iron steed, swifter and stronger than the fabled Pegasus himself. Possibly, however, some servant may be hereafter found better for our purposes than steam itself.

There is generally a long pause after a discovery. It is as if the energies of invention spend themselves, and need a lapse of years for another effort. The wheel and axle were an incalculable addition to our means of loco-motion. Steam used and developed their powers : may be, however, our successors will see the railroad superseded, and future historians entertain their readers with accounts of the clumsy complication of locomotives, iron ruts, and express trains.

Generally, the royal road becomes at last not only vulgar but tedious, and then the independent genius makes a new short cut. But they must be made naturally. The stream which has to gain the ocean through a long tract of country, may not be taken without danger by a sudden leap into the sea. It may have its waterfalls and rapids, but it has duties to perform by the way; the meadow has to be irrigated, the mill to be turned. The cattle must be watered—nay, the linen must be washed. Don't say that the sole object of the stream is to reach the sea. There is a gain in occasional slowness. So with man's mind, with the progress of the sciences and arts. There may be sudden leaps or waterfalls, but it is well to pause when stage after stage of advance is gained. People must have time to take the good things in as they are found out. When the river has watered the fields of wholesome fruit and food, it takes another plunge; then the short cut is natural and right.

Delay has done its healthy work; the last discovery has been understood and digested— we may make a fresh start. But if you force the journey, you may fail before the end. The river which circles slowly through the flat, receives as much as it gives. Rain and rivulets have time to make an impression, whereas if it goes whisking by in a cataract, it issues from the chasm of smaller bulk than it descended. The fertile stream of progress must give itself time to be fed.

There is another thing which should be remembered about short cuts. You may take them selfishly, uselessly, except as far as you yourself are concerned. The heavy diligence surmounts the Alps by a series of patient zigzags. It grinds on, climbing slowly up above itself with many halts, with much sweat and cracking of whips. Now, of course, if you choose, you can get down and cut off the corners of the road; but you do not thus help the party of travellers; nay, as often as not, you are hotter and more blown than they when at the summit you all take your seats for the descent. Besides, you have broken your shins and torn a large triangular rent in the back of your coat. Short cuts like these are generally mistakes. Indeed, as a rule, any invention which you cannot share with others is no gain in the long run. The construction of the zigzag was a short cut if you will; before that, the pass could be traversed only by men on foot or lines of mules, picking out an ill-marked, circuitous, and jolting route; now that you have made your broad zigzag, however tedious it may seem, you can carry the contents of an hospital or a warehouse over the Splugen. If you are to help others, you must be content to make your short cut with deliberation and breadth. It is the same coming down-hill, if you want to do more than come down, for there are short descending cuts which land you speedily at the bottom, and— break your neck.

There are many other false short cuts. The most deceptive of all is an inherited good fortune or position in society. Don't suppose I am going to jest at these things; they carry genuine influence, and are supposed by many to introduce the possessor at once to legislative and political power. They facilitate intercourse with the wit and wisdom of the country. Much of what others, little people, learn by books, these, fortunately born, acquire in the daily society of their lives. They mix with philosophers, statesmen, and lions. But do the noblest beasts themselves thus grow to be famous? Can you learn to roar merely from living in the Zoological Gardens? Do you suppose a man gets to the head of affairs from being familiar with the celebrities of his day? Have our greatest statesmen risen thus? Did the men who have the greatest influence in Parliament and literature learn it all of philosophers in their boyhood? Pooh! They have generally learnt much more from the toes than the heads of society. Skill in interpreting the complaints of the small, ears to hear, and sense to understand them, give political power more than the wise sentences and maxims of the great. There is no short cut to be made to statesmanship by living in the society of the rulers alone.

Of all short cuts, though, protect us most from any epitome, abbreviation, or analysis of a book. It is sad to think how numerous they are. Crams are the curses of education. If a book is so diffuse that it can be cut down to one-fourth of its size without loss of influence, the residue is probably not worth the trouble bestowed upon it. Reading the analysis of a good book, instead of the book itself, is like swallowing a meal without mastication or decent delay. The facts are there, inside you, no doubt; but the genius of the interior can make nothing of them. They are too solid. They have come in too suddenly. They are dry, tasteless, and unmanageable.

Suppose we had doors to us—like patent stoves—and could put in our dinners, all at once, as we do coals on a fire, with a scoop; do you think we should save either time or digestion? But this is what the cram does. He pops a shovelful of dates, conclusions, formulas, and likely facts into the pupil's head just where he thinks the examiner will dip in his net. They no more belong to the pupil than the goods which are brought over-night by train and are carried away next morning by the van to the goods-station do to the porter. The pupil is no better than he. He is not so good—he is not so honest. The porter merely transfers the parcel from one man to another; the pupil is encouraged to put a new direction on the hamper and make the receiver believe that it came from him,—that it was his; that he packed it full of his own honest property; that it is a sample of his own possessions. In fact, the tutor sends a load of learning to the examiner, with instructions for the bearer to cheat the latter, if he can. Of course the examiner can say nothing if the right answer

is given to the question he puts, though he
may feel sure that it no more comes from the
examinee than a telegram does from the
sparrow which sits upon the wire. The reply
passes under the pert little animal's claw while
his head has no conception of the reservoirs
of intelligence and learning at either end of
the course on which he is perched. He flies
off, when it is all over, in conceited ignorance
of the science whose machinery he has grasped
for a minute.

If the student must have an analysis, let him
make it himself. An epitome is tolerable only
for a grown-up man, whose education has
been fragmentary,—who has got together a
good many facts and gained experience of the
world, but wants some pegs in the storehouse
of his memory to hang his goods upon. But
to a boy, it is like supplying a larder with
nothing but pegs. When dinner-time comes,
lo! the safe is empty. At the most, he has
some dry bones instead of solid ribs of beef
and legs of mutton. I pity the man, however,
who thinks he is compelled, by sheer want of
years, to make any short educational cut. It
is like learning to skate after you are grown
up. You fall heavily, and likely enough make
a fool of yourself, perhaps before your wife

and children. Better stay on the bank and
honestly admire what you cannot, or at least
do not choose to try to perform. Who knows
but that you might have made a famous
skater!

Some short cuts are temporary and legitimate, or at least legal. The barrister must
not unfrequently "cram" the language of a
trade or profession in order to examine a
witness; but in this case the quickly acquired
knowledge is dismissed from the brain without
harm or reproach. It is wanted only for an
hour. It serves its purpose, and may go. It
would be impossible for a man to master
thoroughly the details of any passing business
he might be mixed up in. He has not time
enough for such a course. Instead of it he
cultivates the power of cram; of a vigorous
grasp which can catch the passing situation.
Thus a barrister is retained by a "Patent
Ramoneur Society;" give him a day, and he
will cross-examine an expert among sweeps in
the professional language and details of his
business. Twenty-four hours beforehand,
probably he could not have told you how
often his chimneys were swept: certainly not
what became of the soot.

As the last toast is "the Ladies," I can't

help repeating the stale remark, that women are best in making short, common-sense cuts. They don't reason;—pardon me, I am not rude. They do not find it necessary to set that machinery of judgment in operation of which man is so vain. They have a way of their own—an instinct peculiar to their sex—a gift which elevates them. Within certain limits and on certain subjects they pounce with unerring aim upon a truth. They can't give reasons for their conclusions. They are, at least, very silly if they try to do so, and not improbably disturb the successful impression of their impromptu sentence. If they are wise they give no reasons but an answer; and, if sudden, it is probably right. They have a power of discernment in many things not possessed by man. With them it is no guess, but a common instinctive perception. To most men it is a mysterious faculty, and redeems the short cuts of common life from the general charge of foolhardiness or chance.

MOBS.

ET me, correct reader, be pardoned if I bustle into my subject at once without more ado. The secret of the unpremeditated character of a mob's movements, which changes quickly from rage to laughter, and back again, lies in the loss of individual responsibility felt by those who compose it. Each member yields to the licence of concealment, and follows the last whim; sometimes his neighbour's, sometimes his own. A quick definite proposal is caught in a moment. Each one is ready for anything, having nothing ready himself.

A gentleman, once, being mobbed, and in danger, cried out, "A guinea for whoever will take my side." "Here you are, sir," cried a fellow. "Hit him, boys," retorted the briber; "hit him, boys! he's a traitor." "Hurrah!" shouted the mob, and let their intended victim off, to thrash the substitute thus cleverly supplied. A grin, a wink, will turn a mob, if delivered at some happy pause; but woe betide the man who loses his temper, or attempts to argue with such an audience. It is bad enough to be proved wrong when you are alone, and to have time enough to think of a cunning rejoinder, but when you are lost in a crowd, and are only " a voice," conviction is intolerable.

Unanswerable logic must be bonneted at once, if sternly and correctly urged. It is not fair; combatants must be armed alike, and a mob cannot debate with reason. But do not let us on this account be hard upon mobs. They are an essential part of the British constitution, without which the three estates would fail. Suppress mobs, and you drive the inflammation to the vitals. Mobs are the representative assemblies of those who cannot be otherwise heard.

Philanthropists may plead their destitution and labour for their improvement, but the decorous friends of the people are sometimes too polite. It is all very well to have an honourable member pleading your rights in his place in Parliament, or on the platform, but there is a keen vulgar perception of abuses which he will seldom represent. The bloated aristocrat is, we will say, insensible to reason,

and able to repay satire. Well, then, a plain
coarse joke which he cannot return will set
things straighter; or, if he won't wince at that,
try a rotten egg. If you can't answer his
logic, you may dirty his coat. He has his
fling at the mob in the way which he thinks
most damaging, but how shall the mob reply?
The hustings will be taken down to-morrow.
Time presses. The chance will be gone. You
don't seriously intend to hurt him, but you
must make a hit. A dead kitten is very soft
and nasty. Here goes. And the Honourable
Augustus Fitztwaddle is answered.

The unerring plebeian hand will touch its
hat to him next Christmas, when he goes to
" brush " at the patrician battue, without any
accumulated sense of degradation. Conceive
the restoration of equality between the street-
boy and the magistrate, when the former
reflects upon his summons to the potentate
to " speak up, old boy," which met with
such pronounced success. He can laugh at
his pompous airs now. He shut him up once.

I confess I enjoy the details of electioneering
intelligence, especially of the catechising of a
candidate. I think of the triumph with which
the cobbler reads the account of his shrewd
cross-examination of Lord Foozle. The inde-

pendent, incorruptible reporter jots it all faithfully down, with [continued laughter] in explanatory brackets. Bravo! reporter, you have dispersed a serious accumulation of bile. You have put the parlour of the Cat and Bagpipes into the best of humours with itself, and therewith the Constitution, and things in general. Cobbler does not strap his wife for a month. Local paper is thumbed to rags, and stained with convivial beer.

In melancholy contrast to all this, we read of the police regulations in many parts of the Continent, the arrests of the artisans who sing prohibited songs, pot-house oracles caught discoursing at the corner of the street, impulsive students who march in chorus. Why, an Austrian inspector would drive an English town into open revolution, and sour the politicians of Britain, in a month.

Some time ago I found myself in a foreign mob. Even the little boys had no mischief in them. It was at some races. There was no ragged edge of vagabond amusement to the orthodox business of the day. The people promenaded with the patience of sheep. There was nothing analogous to a knock-'em-down on the course. The inevitable dog did his duty, and galloped over the ground in unpleasant consciousness that he was having his day, but he was the only offender. There was an air of decent respectability about the whole thing which was quite depressing, like the intellectual recreation at the old Polytechnic. It was in France. Depend upon it, this ordinary tractability of French crowds accounts in a great measure for their frantic madness at extraordinary times. It must come out sooner or later.

The vulgarity and licence of an English mob is one of the great safeguards of the nation. It feels that it need not be hurtful if it may have its say. Indeed, it cannot well do much harm. There is seldom severe biting when barking is freely allowed.

The English crowd has no glut of grievances for a revolution, or even a respectable émeute. It lets its steam off too fast. It never meets without being rude. It sets to work at once with goading the nearest policeman, and commits high treason against the Government by its remarks, to begin with. And that not with mere badinage, but downright spleen. Most loud talkers in a mob are quite angry and in earnest. They say the most irritating things they can, on purpose to irritate. A 1 vanquishes them with smiles. You may break his bones with words if you can. But you may not in France. Everybody is expected to be polite; the consequence is that many gather such a store of compressed ill-feeling as some day to burst them, and blow the windows of the constitution out. Let us care nothing for the words of a mob.

But didn't you hear what that great fellow with a hair cap and a stick said? Oh yes! and what do you think he *did?* He went home, gratified beyond measure at having said it, and melted his malice in a pot of beer. I confess that the extraordinary tameness of these Frenchmen left an impression on my mind of deep-rooted dangerousness, rather than of apparent simplicity. There were sores enough inside to have made people more demonstrative; but it is an ill sign when a blister will not " rise." There is mischief within which will show itself some day.

The freedom of a mob, moreover, is not only a wholesome relief to itself, but a suggestive lesson to its butt. You may be sure that those who are coarsely but truly criticised, don't forget the hints they get, even if they affect to despise them. The "voice" at elections generally hits a blot. A man will be shy of displaying offensive peculiarities who knows he may have them shouted out under his nose. It is something for him to feel that he must be civil perforce, though it be only for a day or two, to those whom he would always ride roughshod over, if he could. But he can't, and so he behaves himself. He takes off his hat and smiles.

There is some fallacy in the assertion that most people take an ell if you give them an inch. They don't. They accept the inch. It would be more true to say that the surrender of the less secures the greater. The tub thrown to the whale saves the ship. The bow disarms the man who meditated an insult. " A soft answer turneth away wrath."

There is a deal of truth in mob law, and those who are shocked at the mere mention of it are respectable outsiders. But suppose you belong to the mob yourself (and mobs are made of men, women, and children), how then ? Is there no wholesome gratification in the thought that you, addressed in the riot act, dispersed, moved on, &c., &c., have yet after all a quick rough sense of justice ? Yes, you don't want disorder, but only protest against some passing abuse or petty police encroachment.

The licence of our English mobs is most

useful in resisting this last. One charm of English freedom lies in the paucity or obsoleteness of our laws. You may do almost anything so long as you don't break the ten commandments. But there always will be some fussy, sniffing officials or legislators who try to trim up the Constitution. They won't do anything to annoy the middle classes at first; they begin therefore with some act or regulation about pot-houses, street vagabonds, or some living nuisance. Straightway the nuisances protest with bellowings, menaces, perhaps with a breaking of windows, and indiscriminate pelting of suspected respectability. I a nuisance? says one of them. You are another. Don't you order me off your doorstep when you come home to your dinner, and give me into custody for asking an alms? Don't you pull up the window when I have called a cab for you, and touched my hat? Don't you walk safe and daintily over my crossings free of expense? Don't you speak to me as if I were your slave? Don't you—confound you—ain't you a nuisance, rather, yourself?

And so the vagabonds protest against any extra police regulations, or attempt to legislate away their special offences. And they are right. They are right in striving against the multiplication of social and sumptuary laws. They are the useful house-dogs which indeed wake us sometimes by their barking, and will bite the master himself if provoked enough, but which certainly keep intruders off, and check the itching fingers which would meddle with our personal rights and possessions.

The mob may be disagreeable enough—rude, rank, unreasonable; but it will safely prevent any attempts to drill and trim us up by punctilious legislators or officials. Hands off!—let us be. I button my pocket, feel that my watch is safe, and am much obliged to Demos, who is kind enough to do the dirty work of my citizenship for me.

OME time ago I walked, with occasional lifts, along the western coast
of England, from Weymouth to
Bristol, looking in, as I went, upon the
watering-places which fringe the land. It
was August when I made my tour, and
every place I visited was filled with summer
residents.

Surely, thought I to myself, as I reposed
at home after my round, I have discovered
the uniform invariable state, if not sentiment,
which the old formula would fit. Sea-side life
is led in the same way—" always, everywhere,
and by all." Wherever I went, there were
the same people and the same pursuits.

The scenery varied from the chalk upland
to the rose-tinted rock, from the sandy beach
and treeless downs of Dorset, to the wooded
coombes of South Devon, and the Cornish
black-slate cliff, up which the long Atlantic
wave crept like a tide.

I saw the sea under a hundred forms,

racing round the promontory—asleep in the land-locked bay—flashing with painful brightness, as if the sun had burst and been half spilt on the water. I saw it leaden-coloured—green—flat, like a soft field when it has been rolled—clear, showing the trembling pebbles and wavy weeds which floated from the rock, or rolling folds of mud from the river's mouth. I saw it streaked with flecks of white—I saw it misty and boundless, the great waves looking unnaturally large as they tumbled in out of the fog. I saw it hard-edged, metallic, with stiff little tinkling waves, like a copperplate engraving. I saw it fight, and I saw it play. Everywhere it met me with old welcome, buoyant power, and a fresher grace, filling me with deeper reverence and love. But the human shrimps which capered at its brink presented everywhere the same appearance. They were all doing the same things.

Of course you can't sit on rocks where there are none, nor dig with wooden spades on granite ; but there were some features peculiar to sea-side life which connected every wateringplace, such as donkeys, white bathing-machines, telescopes, mimic nautical phraseology, thumbed novels, and an aimless interest in the reflection of the moon on the water.

" I fear the visitors here lead a very idle life," said a worthy man to me one day, as we had a stray chat on a bench. Being an energetic resident, he did not see that that was the very life they came there to lead. Don't judge a man by his phase of relaxation. There is a fire-engine station at the bottom of my street, close to one of the great thoroughfares of London. When I leave my house, and put out into the great human stream, I always see one man at rest there. He wears a cleaned-up, official sort of undress, and sits on a low stool outside the engine-house door, generally smoking a long new clay pipe. There is nothing more calm than the repose of a fireman. But a breathless house-holder, with a mob of little boys at his heels, comes round the corner. In two minutes our friend is driving fourteen miles an hour against the stream of Regent Street, like a flash of brass and red paint.

Therefore, do not hastily judge the idler by the sea-side: he is reposing. But he can work, at the right time. Last week he fought the fiercest counsel on circuit. Last week he hushed a mob. The day before yesterday he sent in tenders for the construction of a steam-engine seven hundred thousand horse power, and will have it all hammered and rivetted within sound of his office. Yesterday he extracted the diaphragm of a bricklayer's labourer before the College of Surgeons, in one minute and twenty-three seconds. The newspaper that gentleman offered him he saw printed this morning (he came by a mid-day train) amid a crowd of machines and dexterous compositors. With sweat of brain he wrote the rousing novel over which that lady bends and weeps.

He has come for a holiday, and falls into the telescopic pebble-gathering world with grateful acquiescence. Does he trouble himself with the wonders of the seashore? Does he kneel down and grope among the rocks, at low tide, struggling with wretched sea anemones, who hold on for the dear life till some lover of Nature uproots them? How they must hate the season and Mr. Gosse! Poor things! I remember being shown a number of them by a scientific friend, who took them out every morning with a long spoon, and laid them, gasping and limp, on a bench, while he changed the water in their cage. Some were dark and tough, showing that they were used to plenty of daylight or low tides; others were quite fair and blanched from living in the dark depths of the sea. But they were nevertheless herded with their swarthy brethren, and blinked at the sun miserably. I can't help thinking that pseudo-science, however attractive, is often very cruel.

The boiling of lobsters is a process which, however speedy, one does not much like to associate with salad, or supper. The first thrill in the pot must be horrible, but it is soon over. Whereas, a slow death in an aquarium, with great eyes looking at you and offering quantities of unsuitable food, together with the puzzling resistance of the glass, like the mysterious detention of a dream, must altogether make the last hours of a "specimen" hideous. It must be as bad as dying of nightmare. "Oh! my lovely star-fish are all dead!" says charming Angelina, as she joins the breakfast-table, after nine hours of the soundest, rosiest sleep. "They are only just dead, I think," says she, with her mouth full of toast and butter. "I saw one of them move a little"—very likely. But what a night for the star-fish!

Now, your busy man, or rather your man who really works hard in his profession, will, if he be wise and brave, leave the wonders of the seashore alone when he comes to rest.

Lying on the rounded shingle, he lets his mind
uncoil and gather unconsciously suppleness and
strength ; he lets it stretch and sun itself without interruption.   And he is no loser, for so
surely as he is content and not ashamed to sit
maybe for a whole bright forenoon, doing
nothing, thinking of nothing, the unfolded
mind will have filled itself like a sleeping net ;
and when afterwards he gropes within for
thought and illustration he will find good store.
The dusty, faded chambers of his brain will
have become wholesome and fresh.   He will
return to the operating-room, the law court,
the editor's den, with an atmosphere of salt
and sunshine about him.   Of course, some
active minds must grub about the rocks and
fish in the clear pools of brine left by the tide,
but I beg once for all to protest against the
sweeping   condemnation   uttered   .by   some
people, who would employ every idle saun-
terer on a fruitful beach.

Let them whip the *bonâ-fide* lounger, the
man who never works.   Ay! there is something in that ; or, better still, let them try to
save him.   Seize the moment when the dull
mind is touched with fresh thought, when the
sleepiness of the daily inland routine is somewhat rubbed off, and arouse a new interest in

a crab if you can. There are people who have been plucked from a life of blindness by the wonders of the shore. The only danger is of a relapse, as if the "littoral zone" were really more wonderful than the brook round the meadow, or the glade in the wood.

Therefore do I like to see—though they be only faint—flashes of thought (like summer lightning) quickened in the drowsy mind by some popular revelation of the beach; nay, I like to see even a persevering reliance on the brightness of wet pebble. True, the gems are opaque in the morning—not to say gritty—and will probably be found by the next comer to the lodgings in the drawer of the dressing-table; but they have rubbed a human mind as well as one another. They have perhaps made some crafty soul childlike for a day. Childlike! Give me either science or simplicity. Either a seeing eye, which, however ignorant of geological details, recognises the progress of the world as it rests on a cliff; or the eye which loves the cliff, without a reason indeed, though none the less for that—perhaps the more.

Preserve me from the distilled prattle of the conscientious quack who grinds up facts out of a printed book, and then repeats them at

haphazard, because he thinks educated society
expects some acquaintance with the phraseology of science. Protect me from him, I
should only put him out; let him enjoy himself
in his own way, I in mine, out of shot. Perhaps, while I am peopling a flat valley with
ancient monsters, smacking the slime with their
great tails, gobbling, sleeping, snorting, fighting
—while I hear the shriek and the rustle of
strange birds in the air, but see the same
blessed sun above our heads, the same harvest
moon, though rising on the unreaped earth—
while I am thus out of date, or may be pictur-
ing to myself the naked battle around the
barrows on the windy downs, my friend with
the book shouts to me that he thinks he has
found a *Coleopterum ridiculosum* in the shingle.
Will I come and see? And the inspected
beast bounds off his open palm with an elastic
" spang,"—very like a shrimp, as I tell him,—
and is gone past verification; is probably at
the moment hastily shoving himself, at great
risk of bruises, deep down among his native
stones. But my friend says, contemptuously, that
it cannot be a shrimp—because shrimps are red.

There is one subject in which all sea-side
visitors are expected to take an interest, and
that is the annual regatta. Nine-tenths of

them don't know a brig from a schooner, but
they talk as if they had built the winning
boat, screwing away at everything with their
telescopes throughout the day. There are,
however, moments in a regatta which the
uninitiated may enjoy, as when a number of
white-sailed yachts open their wings together
like rising gulls; but, to most, the duck-hunt
at the end affords a sensible relief. They have
been bewildered with the banging of signal
guns and sudden jaunty appearance of all the
craft in the harbour, which string up every
scrap of bunting they have on board for the
occasion. The "million" have never any
clear idea of the merits of the boats, get sorely
deceived about time races, and, as I said,
gladly welcome the "duck-hunt" and "greased
bowsprit." Paterfamilias—caught enjoying it
on the sly—says the latter is vulgar, as if he
had not hit upon the very thing in it which,
despite of his protest, is amusing his refined
mind far more than the great race of the day.
My dear sir, why not accept heartily a piece of
vulgar play? Did you ever see two boys
swallow respectively, in rival gulps, a tumbler
of water and a bun—the water to be taken
with a spoon? You set the boys on a table
in two chairs facing each other—One, two,

three, off! That is vulgar, but highly
ludicrous. Squaretoes may look another way,
but I choose to see it out with unaffected
interest. Which do you think won? Try it,
and be popular for an evening.

Another invariable feature of sea-side life
is the arrival of the steamer. People living in
Euston Square never go to see the Express
from Liverpool unload in the terminus hard
by, but while down at Ramsmouth will get
up from their luncheons and hurry out, if the
vessel should arrive before its time. There
is no variety in the crowd of passengers—the
same people seem to come every time,
especially in rough weather, when they are all
wretched alike, and are quite reckless whether
their bonnets be tumbled or hats crushed, so
long as they can join the mocking crowd upon
the steady shore; but they are stared at like
Esquimaux as they land. The people who
enjoy the sea-side most are the real men of
business and children, who come alike to play.
I cannot conceal my dislike of the prigs, both
male and female, who come to dress and be
admired. Their intention is an insult to the
sensible shabby visitors. But the children,
with inexhaustible wealth of sand, as good as
gold, and suddenly discovered licence to wet

their feet!—for there is a favourite myth current
among even nervous mothers and nurses that
" salt water does not give cold "—look at the
children digging, where mischief is impossible,
defying the recollection of sanitary advice with
unfading ecstacy, by walking into the water
simply to get their feet wet whenever they
feel dry. See them all at their early dinner
through the open parlour window of the
lodgings—what a gust of healthy, tanned
appetite comes out as you pass !

I don't know which is best, shingle or sand.
There is something in the freshness of the
flat hard beach, which no rolled gravel or con-
crete can approach, though the sea break at
your feet. There is a grateful sense of escape
from the dull road, where your own footprints
are the first upon the shore. It seems as if
you were a discoverer; you are severed from
the world of men; you have left it behind; no
one has wandered there before. But you
cannot sit down on sand—not comfortably,
at least—much less can you lie down upon it
on your back, and turn the world topsy-turvy
by gazing into skies beneath you. You can't
lie flat down on the sand, and enjoy it. You
look for a big stone, the stump of an old pile,
or unfold a camp stool.

Now shingle, on the contrary, affords the most perfect rest you can enjoy. A bank of dry shingle, resolutely sat upon, makes a lounge which Messrs. Gillow would do well to measure and model. Be you lean or fat, short in the thigh, or long in the back, the shingle bank takes your shape. Then shingle is clean: you do not rise as gritty as if you had been knocked down on a turnpike-road. Moreover, you are lulled by the delicious drawl of the retiring wave, to me inexpressibly soothing. But you can't walk upon shingle—not, at least, without great fatigue. On the whole, though, I think it is better than sand, as you can always get exercise on firm ground further ashore, if you want it, whereas nothing but shingle gives the seat and couch.

In my tramp round the coast I confess to great disappointment at some of the most famous watering-places. You see the sea, it is true, and there are beautiful walks made upon the cliffs and among the rocks, but very often, as in the north of Devon, for instance, the impression is that you can't get down to the water; you can't throw stones into it; you can't get your feet wet; you behold it from afar, like a goat: and that is all, unless you repair to some small patch of beach, monopolised by a bathing-machine.

Not that patches of beach are bad; give me a shore with hidden little bays, where you may wander alone if you like, and then· go back to the beauty and fashion on the promenade. Nothing is worse than one public walk, where you cannot get away from people, and where a conspicuous figure, say some staring snob, with a white hat in half mourning, meets you on every tack; even without him it is dreary work to be confined to the same pier, up and down, like the bubble in a spirit level.

There is one class of the population at most watering-places which I pity with all my heart. I don't mean the donkeys, who affect an expression of patience I am convinced they don't feel; but the goats. Goats in harness, towed by young plebeians in front, and worried by young gentlemen passengers from behind. I can't conceive a more unhappy, inappropriate fortune befalling any animal. I wonder whether they derive any malicious satisfaction from the consciousness of being goats, and that a ride behind them must displace even the fresh smell of the sea. But I don't believe they think of it themselves.

Let me say a word about bathing, and I will have done.

In many respects they manage this better abroad. If you have your dip in public there you are obliged to wear a " costume ; " and the machines are often not shoved into the water ; but the arrangements are convenient and decorous. The bathing at many of our watering-places is anything but this last. Perhaps it is more outrageous at Margate than elsewhere. The first time I saw it I was reminded of some old picture of the landing of the Romans, when the beach was lined with naked natives, half in and half out of the water. There is, moreover, something inexpressibly dismal in the unrobing within a machine, in the flapping of the spray at the outer door, and the shivering station on the gritty ladder, before the leap. This and the treacherous recall of the machine to the beach while you are standing on one leg, tugging at a sticky boot, make the whole process intolerable. If I must bathe, give me a clear header from a rock, and sunshine to dress in.

The young lady's amusement in the water seems to consist in a quick succession of deep perpendicular curtsies, and an attempt to tug the machine in after her by its tail.

Sea-fishing is generally a failure ; one or two are partially successful, the rest are sick. So with aimless sails, at a shilling an hour ; the boatmen are extortionate and oracular, the excursionists wretched.

By the sea-side, however, as everywhere else, those only enjoy themselves as they might who dare seek recreation as the innocent whim may lead them ; who defy the dressiness of the prigs and puppies, in easy clothing and old shoes indoors and out ; who are not ashamed to roll or lounge on the shingle, unattracted by the band and the esplanade ; who, having come to rest, idle wisely, with perpetual acted protest against the fuss of affected science and fashionable propriety.

SAW it at St. Malo, where it is said to flourish. There was nothing very particular in the shape of the machines which were drawn up on the beach. Except that they were made of canvas instead of wood, and had much lower wheels than ours, they had the same bald, gritty look which those vehicles generally wear. They were twenty or thirty yards from the edge of the water, and therefore, as I was not thinking much about bathers, but idling along in a promiscuous sort of way, I supposed that the day's dipping was over. Judge of my surprise when, on passing close by a machine, the door opened, and a short, stout gentleman, in a jacket and drawers of a large staring check flannel, stepped out with a smile and a shudder —like a clown. I almost expected him to put his head on one side, and say " Here we are again," before turning a summersault.

But it was the mayor. The Mayor of St.

Malo, going to bathe. Or, if it was not the mayor, it was as good, for I saw him afterwards, and he had a red ribbon in his buttonhole, to which no end of people took off their hats. Perhaps he was a préfet. At any rate, he had on nothing but breeches and a shortish jacket, of flaring check flannel, and proceeded to paddle down to the water after a few minutes, with Mrs. M., who popped out of a neighbouring machine similarly dressed, on his arm; and I can assure you Mrs. M. did not owe all her charms to crinoline.

Bless my heart, I said to myself, this is worth coming to France to see. So I brisked up, opened my eyes, got a chair for a sou, sat down, and took it all in. Let me reflect—no, not reflect—but consult my notes, which I made on the sly, lest a ferocious gendarme, who paced about, should suspect me of sketching a fort, and sabre me on the spot.

Let me see. There were about fifty or sixty machines in this village, all of canvas, and upon very low wheels, the floor of the hut not being above a foot from the ground. They are seldom, if ever, taken into the water, and, of course, a plunge from one of them is impossible even then, as they cannot draw above six inches.

There are, however, rafts moored at different distances from the brink, so that those bathers who want to take headers may be suited— there being always a raft in about three or four feet water, and another further on.

But whatever you do when you are fairly afloat, you must paddle in like a goose.

The ladies and gentlemen all bathe together, often walking down to the sea, or up from it, arm in arm. When Mr. and Mrs. M. came out thus, and his aldermanic proportions were more developed by the clinging of the wet flannel (I won't mention her), the effect was so odd, the contrast to English habits so grotesque, that I laughed—respectfully. At first, I thought several figures in the water were boys, but they turned out at last to be young ladies—who came up dripping from the ocean, like so many Venuses in flannel dittoes.

Many of them evidently wore their own bathing-dresses, which fitted so jauntily, and were so prettily trimmed and ornamented, that I have no doubt they were made to measure—women tailors, I presume. When I came to think about it, and had seen through the novelty of the " costume," as it is called on the beach, I saw how decent and sensible it was. The suit was really nothing but Bloomer, in many cases a trifle more close fitting and short-skirted ; but the lines of the model were Bloomerian. Many of the men wore dresses as tight as an acrobat's; and, indeed, looked so like them, that you half expected to see the mat and pole produced; or, at least, a "pyramid" made. By the time I had sat there an hour, the number of bathers increased fast. There was quite a crowd of expectants and friends. The former, with their dresses rolled up under their arms, ready to get into the next vacant machine, the latter reading, working, or sitting in chairs, idly waiting till the bath should be over. Fresh bathers paddled down in twos or threes, while others continually emerged, and came up the beach dripping ; the suit was so complete in some cases, that the wet figure looked as if the bath had been taken by accident, not choice.

Everything was well organised. There were three or four sunburnt women with bare feet, and hats with " Service des Bains " on the band, like the name of a ship; and men who gave lessons in swimming, or helped to shove the heads of recusant children under water.

A " Buvette" on the beach provided glasses

of liqueur to those who wanted to take the chill off themselves, and there was a large copper of hot water on wheels, to supply bathers who wished to wash their feet after walking across the dry sand to their machines. One tremendous woman, who was mistress of the ceremonies, directed her crew where to take these little addenda of baths, and dispensed the dresses to those who brought none of their own. Moreover, she arranged the order of procedure, and insisted strictly on the rule, "first come, first served." She was a tremendous woman, with a voice like a speaking-trumpet, and knitted rapidly all the time she was giving her orders, or listening to the petitions of bathers. But she had a tender heart.

All at once—I may as well give the cries and conversation in English, for though you can scramble on with French—after a sort—you may honestly funk the spelling of short conversational speeches with unnecessary *y's* in them,—all at once, then, there was a great shriek, and the idle crowd rushed to the edge of the water, wildly excited in a moment. Two children had got out of their depth, and were being carried out and under by the tide; their little black dots of heads sunk beneath

the surface. Then the big woman's colour
went, she stopped her knitting, and putting
her right hand to her side, I thought she
would have fainted, as she cried in a half-
choked voice :—

"Help! help! the poor little infants! look!
Oh—O——h!"

But the acrobats splashed in, and plucked
them out, for they were as yet only in five feet
water. This episode over, the directress went
on with her knitting, and shouted out directions
to the bathing men in the water, two hundred
yards off.

To-morrow, thought I, I will come and have
a dip here myself, for I was eager to experience
the whole sensation. When I went back
to our hotel, and told my wife how they
bathed in France, she thought it shocking,
but after two or three visits admitted that
the arrangements were both convenient and
decorous.

But about my own bath. Next day I
repaired to the beach, and going to a place
like an Aldershot hut, with a notice outside,
" Billets pour les Bains," found an old man
with a big book at a desk just within the
entrance, taking down names; he had two
large bunches of tin labels before him hung on

wire, like keys. The building was fitted up like a large bottle-rack, on the shelves of which lay bathing suits, rolled up, accessible and dry. When the old gentleman had, with a great display of precision, disposed of the group which was being served when I entered, I went up to his desk, and asked him for a ticket.

" One ? " says he.

" One," said I. " And ' costume,' " I added, and he repeated.

Then he slowly took two of the tin labels, one from each ring—his hands were rheumatic —put down their numbers in his book, looked over his spectacles, and said—

" Eighteen sous."

So I paid him, and he handed me the tickets, with directions to get them cashed on the beach. The big one represented a machine. The little one a suit. Then I sought out the Amazon, and presented my credentials. For the smaller "billet" I got a suit with a towel rolled up inside it. The other was exchanged for a fresh ticket, marked No. 5.

" You will have the fifth chance," said the Amazon, so I attached myself to her at once. As the machines become vacant, she called out the name of the next number loud enough to be heard by the whole crowd, for there were many bathers, and the edge of the water was alive.

" Nu—m—ber two!" she cried, pronouncing the numeral short and sharp. "Not there! You must look sharp, or lose your turn. Num—ber three! likewise out of the way. Num—ber four!"

An elegant lady, with a servant following her, and a long train of muslin, too, responded to the summons, and squeezed herself into the machine, which she must have filled when she got in.

" Num—ber five!"

" Here you are," says I, and entered the next tent to my grand lady's.

When I stepped out, in a short suit of mauve check, I saw Madame also emerge, seriously thinned. I never felt more odd and incongruous in my life. There were knots of well-dressed, fashionable people, through whom I had to pass before I reached the water. It was like escaping from a fire at night—only it was broad day—but the oddest thing was that nobody noticed me.

The scene in the water was most absurd. Whole families were bathing together in a circle, hand in hand. Where I went in, Mr.

and Mrs. Briggs, just their figures, and all the little Briggses, were crowing and splashing in a shallow. Now and then, you could see friends meet, and acquaintances bow; a young lady who thus met some partner at the last ball, making a fashionable sweep in the water. Sometimes a party of young men would come down together, full run, and dash in like mermen who had been confined in the town, tumbling head over heels, and otherwise throwing themselves into the arms of the sea.

The tide advanced so much while I was in the water that the machines were all drawn off the beach on to the paved road beneath the walls of the town before I came out. It was a spring-tide, which rises very high here. The result, however, was most grotesque when the dripping bathers emerged, and in several cases could not find their machines again for some time, wandering about in the crowd, sticky and cross. Mine was high and dry on the pavement. It was something like bathing in the Thames, and coming out to dress inside a cab in the Strand. However, I was more fortunate than several, for my wife had followed the machine, and showed me where it was.

The inconvenience of grit, from walking across the sand, is, as I said, removed by a little tub of water—hot or cold—for which last you pay a sou, or halfpenny, extra. I do not know, however, what Robinson Crusoe would have said to the beach, when he was so much astonished at the print of *one* naked foot. The place was dimpled with toe-holes.

When I had recovered from the novelty of the thing—from seeing ladies of all builds, from Mrs. Gamp to Ophelia, paddling down in scanty Bloomers, without shoes or stockings—when I felt that these gentlemen in check shorts were neither acrobats nor clowns, but sober, steady men of business who bathed on principle (for the liveliest and more sportsmanlike of swimmers went to some distance where they could enjoy themselves without encumbrance), I decided in favour of the French fashion over the English. There is nothing indecorous or inconvenient in it. The system is well arranged. The ladies' dresses must be much more comfortable than the shifts of freize which they wear in our watering-places, and they are more completely *dresses*.

Much care is used to prevent accidents; there is generally a boat some short distance off where the water begins to deepen. Every-body is served in turn, and the greatest pains are taken by the attendants to make the bathers comfortable. By dressing in machines which are drawn up, the disagreeable access to them by plank is avoided, and the toilette is never spoilt by a wave bursting the door open and floating out your shoes. This dressing on shore, too, enables servants to come and assist their mistresses more easily.

The machines are comfortable and roomy; there is a hanging-place for your watch, a pin-cushion, and looking-glass, beside abundance of pegs; moreover, being of canvas, you do not knock the skin off your knuckles when flourishing about with the towel.

You may depend upon it that—much, as I confess, Mr. and Mrs. Mayor astonished me when I first went down to the beach at St. Malo—the French method of sea-bathing, as practised in public, is far preferable to that which is common in England.

ALIKE in origin, for they share the blood of the earliest recorded inhabitants of our land; alike in ancient tongue, for the " Vraie Bretagne Brettonnante," as Froissart calls it, is allied to our Welsh and Cornish; alike in name to the present day, these distant cousins live upon the same sea, but almost in another world. Perhaps no Europeans are more unlike each other than they. They differ more widely than plain French and English, for the Breton exhibits in caricature those habits and customs which mark the contrast most strongly between our neighbours and ourselves. He is far more bigoted, dirty, and ignorant than the average of his countrymen.

During a recent visit to Brittany I noted down on a sheet of paper some of those peculiarities which always strike John Bull most; and now, on looking over my list, I find it so long that I am tempted to serve it up in such a shape as may give information to some, and perhaps recall a few pleasant whiffs of continental recollections to those who are acquainted with France. Of course, in using the materials which are before me, some will be found—indeed, I see already that they are —common to the whole country. Perhaps not many are really peculiar to Brittany, but they struck me as being exaggerated in that province. For instance, I think that the Breton breakfast-cups are heavier and have thicker lips than those anywhere else—a sip from one is a mouthful; their dinner-plates are colder and congeal the gravy quicker than others; their carriages are dustier and more tinkered; their mixture of meats is more surprising to an English stomach than any in Gaul. The other day we had for breakfast, at a good inn, these principal viands—tripe, raw artichokes, and cider. Not that there were no other dishes—the meal was abundant and good; but these were more distinctly and unhesitatingly consumed, along with slices from huge coarse country loaves—no *petit pain*, or crisp white rolls, so sweet and common in Paris. Yet we were in a good hotel, at a town which contains several thousand inhabitants, and is much visited in the summer. It is a striking place, with rain-worn granite walls and towers

which redden in the sunset over rows of green
young trees; dark little gateways which look
quite impassable to the lumbering diligence,
with its three straggling white horses abreast,
and luggage like a load of hay; quaint old
houses which have been peeping round corners
and nodding their heads at one another across
the street any time these last three hundred
years; houses with projecting first-floors standing on stone pillars; streets, narrow, tortuous,
interlacing, paved up to the walls with cruel
stones, and each with a trickling black drain
in the middle, where the ducks rummage;
shops which nobody seems to enter, with small
windows of bad glass—blue cotton, wood, and
tobacco being the commonest merchandise;
old women (and you can have no idea of the
unpleasantness which may be associated with
one till you visit France), little creeping
mummies, who beg with voices of unalterable
misery; dark, shaven priests in shovel-hats,
cassocks, and black bands, who glide about
with thumbed, gilt-edged books under their
arms; gorgeous gendarmes, with quantities of
white rigging about their coats, who saunter
down the middle of the street, in perpetual
contrast with the squalor around them; little
bevies of nuns, with their hands folded, baskets

on their arms, and a low gust of small talk as they patter by; bullet-headed children, with tight nightcaps tied under their chins; men in straw hats and blue blouses lounging at the café doors; and some small-faced soldiers in red trousers, sitting on a low wall under the shade.

Not that we saw many soldiers in Brittany. But there was, what struck me often, a great scarcity of youths; the male population consisted of old or middle-aged men and boys. Some lads of eighteen or nineteen years of age, whom I noticed as exceptions, were lame, badly cross-eyed, or crippled in some way. The youth of the place was with the army. This gap in the ages of the populace became more evident as I observed and reflected. There is hardly an able-bodied man in France who is not, at one time or another, connected with the camp.

I have said that almost every street has its central drain. This made the ordinary stenches numerous and powerful. But one day, when I walked down to the river-bank, and happened to pass the spot where their united contributions flowed into the stream, I met with an odour which, for pungent liveliness and original piquancy of flavour, excelled any I have ever smelt, and yet there was a woman with a beautifully clean white cap on, sitting alive and ruddy on a doorstep in the very thick of the stench.

By the way, these Breton caps are considered curious. The women generally wear *sabots* (or wooden shoes) not over-clean, but their head-dresses are scrupulously spotless. As to shape, they are so varied that they really seem to have no idea in common. Perhaps, though, I can convey a better notion of these finials by comparing them to dinner napkins, starched, and folded on the head according to the wearer's fancy, but always with great flaps or wings ; these last being sometimes turned up or back, sometimes cast loose and left to float on either side, like the banks of oars depicted in ancient galleys.

There are no street lamps in ——. Strange as it may seem, the town is not lit with gas or oil. There is no pretence made of lighting it. If you want to see your way you must take a lantern or wait for the moon—nay, better still, for the sun. Other towns in these parts have, it is true, some lamps hung with cord in the middle of the streets at rare intervals, but —— is left at night as dark as an old coalmine, or London in the time of the Saxons.

There are a good many beggars in the place; they look wretched enough, and have not the professional power of their class in London. Indeed, the beggars here are frequently very destitute, and a few sous may be charitably bestowed upon them.

There is no poor-law proper in France. A lone and needy man, past his work, must beg or die. It is true that he is most generally provided for by the " brethren " or the " sisters " —some religious orders being devoted to the support of the aged and helpless. But when he receives their help he is a recipient of charity. There is no parish to which he can apply as a right. There is no law for him but (thank God for that!) the codeless law of love. He is utterly dependent on the charitable. Thus there is much more excuse to be made for beggars here; and I confess that an old crippled body past its work generally gets one of my coppers. " Bad thing!" I hear Mr. Squaretoes say. " Bad advice!" But, sir, I don't give to children—at least, only to those in their second childhood; and, should you ever come to that, and want a penny, if you would not ask for it from your fellow-Christians, for the love of God, you would show a worse opinion of your brethren in the faith than you give yourself credit for now. Ah, me! there must be some genuine beggars, I suppose, and their state here is not such an enviable one that we should be very angry at it, as if they were getting all the good things to themselves.

Look at these foreign paupers, at their faces, their clothes. Don't you think they would gladly earn money if they could? Don't you suppose it possible that many of them are so stupid, so ignorant, so awkward, that they never could master a handicraft, and have come to what they are after spending the prime of their lives in the lowest brute-like toil?

Professional beggars, on the other hand, are generally bad. You must have noticed that they are seldom very old or thin, but lusty tramps, often with a capital pulse in their veins, and a kettle of rich stew on the hob at home. These rob the poor more than the rich, and I am sure that the habitual copper-giver, who buys selfish blessings from their profane lips, does thereby far more harm than good to his race.

The Bretons have the character of being very impulsive, though they are rather a stolid-looking race, for French. But they swear horribly, using oaths which are as curious as they are incessant. They also drink to excess.

Cider is the beverage of the country, but brandy is abundant and strong. Wine they seldom touch. The cider is drunk out of very large teacups, like common blue slop-basins with handles. Passing the common cafés or public-houses you may often see three or four rough men in *sabots* sitting round a table and clicking these basins together before their draught, in good fellow-ship, as if they were carousing in coffee or tea.

The Breton works hard, and, I should fancy, produces the least possible result with the greatest amount of labour. He tries to get antagonistic crops out of the soil at the same time, planting his wheat-land thick with apple-trees, and therefore injuring both. The fields are very small, and the holdings also. I have seen a couple tilling their land together, like Adam and Eve, or getting up their harvest with one ricketty cart drawn by a donkey, the farmer and his wife " loading and leading."

Then, too, Darby and Joan often thresh their crop themselves on the bare earth outside the door, winnowing the result by pouring it out of the basin in the wind. As they stand opposite one another, flail in hand, and lay on thick, the effect, a little way off, is that of a " matrimonial difference"—you hear the blows distinctly.

What they do with the grit and dirt the corn picks up, I don't know: grind their teeth down, I suppose. Of course, these poor people employ no labour and lay no capital out on the land. They do their own work, and get food enough to carry life on, at a snail's pace, throughout the monotonous years.

The face of Brittany is seamed and wrinkled with a thousand narrow lanes which waste the soil and bewilder the traveller. The country has been compared to a " rabbit warren " with the turf flayed off, and all the burrows laid bare.

The highways are excellent, and skirted by an electric telegraph. They are as unlike the ordinary roads of the country as the Great Northern is to a cow-path; but will, I suppose, in time be superseded by the rail.

You never see what we understand by a gentleman's carriage anywhere in these parts. There are vehicles which cost more than the others, and are driven by their owners in good clothes, or coachmen in laced hats; but there is a varnished second-hand look about the best of them, which spoils the effect they are evidently intended to produce.

Inns are tolerably good, and the fare is sufficient. The two meals of the day are a *table-d'hôte* breakfast at ten, and dinner at six. Great decanters of cider are placed on the board at both, the French generally taking neither coffee nor tea then. Many have a cup at six or seven, and breakfast after a few hours, heavily.

One speciality of the country is its cattle. The horses are mostly grey, and hard as nails. The cows are becoming familiar to us in England, being just now the fashion for gentlemen's parks. They are very small. There was a cow-market at Dinan while I was there, and I found that very many of the animals were no higher than the bottom of my waistcoat. Women came in from the country dragging full-grown cows no bigger than our calves.

There were about 200 horses for sale at the same time,—strong serviceable beasts, with great heads and long tails. A good animal fetched about £30. I looked in vain among the farmers and drovers who attended the market for men of a superior class. They were apparently all dirty, close-fisted, and profane, sacr-r-r-r-ing away at one another, at themselves, and at nothing, all the day. The patois of the Bretons is horrible. In some districts they have, I am told, still a peculiar language, preserving their Celtic tongue, and being, intelligible to genuine Welshmen.

Those who visit this country for scenery ought to be fond of apple-trees, for they fill a great part of the land. Some views, such as that from Avranches over the bay of St. Michel, are very striking; most, however, are praised; not because they are good, but because the others are bad. A squinting hillock is a mountain among flats.

The charm of the province is its number of quaint towns and occasional coast scenery. The former are very picturesque and offensive. But if you have been living in the bustle of the nineteenth century, and fussing yourself with schemes of progress or the like, you cannot get a greater change than by putting the clock of your observation back some hundred years or so among the lesser towns of the Bretons. You will return not only refreshed by the bodily recreation, but ready to appreciate still better the state of civilisation which Britons have reached.

NE drawback to the interest with which you visit many celebrated spots is the difficulty of identifying them when they are small, or of taking them in at a glance when they are extensive. " Tradition," says the guide-book, " assigns the exploits of —— to this locality." There is the hitch. Whereabouts did the gulf open in the forum ? Here is the forum, but where was the cleft ? Did the patriotic Roman who rode into it, look east or west, when he put spurs to his horse for the leap ? Descend into the Mamertine prison; tradition says that St. Paul was confined there. He was a prisoner somewhere in Rome, and—that is all —tradition does the rest. It has a ragged edge, has tradition. It has led to mistakes in everything. It has perverted histories and religions without end ; it has lured and hood-winked the keenest antiquaries. But it is so probable, so attractive, however uncertain, that it saves as much trouble as it gives. Since the majority of mankind prefer a respectable tradition, received without pains, to a fact which needs to be established by labour, learning, and patience, we need not wonder at traditions generally carrying the day. " The cleft was here," says the cicerone, drawing a line on the ground with his stick. Give me a fearless, uncompromising, positive cicerone. But a conscientious guide, who scratches his head and thinks ! what can be more provoking ?

I fell into this train of thought this morning, while I sat upon the rampart of Avranches, and looked down upon the singular rock of St. Michel, standing up as clear as a ship out of a sea of quicksand—standing up there more than 500 feet high, looking round upon the coasts of Normandy and Brittany, as much as to say : " Ah ! you have a history, no doubt, but your accounts are all in a muddle. I am like the dot of an i above an obliterated line. There is no mistake about me; I have preserved my pedigree distinct; I am where I have always been, though I may not be what I was."

The rock of St. Michel, famous in the border history of England and France, is a many-pointed granite pile, about three thousand feet in circumference, and five hundred and eighty feet high, rising abruptly in an immense expanse of sea and flat sand in the bay of Avranches)—like a solitary cruet-stand in the middle of a large round dining-room table. There it *is*. No tradition ever helped to identify its position. How irregularly fortune has scattered her marks over the world! Here is one district which no book of history can pass without allusion; there is another which no historian has ever troubled himself to refer to. This mountain is a calendar of events; that has offered itself to the notice of a thousand generations, un-marked, disregarded.

Perhaps there never was a spot round which, considering its littleness and seclusion, more local history has gathered than round this Mont St. Michel. Like the small point of an electrical machine, about which the stream of magic fluid buzzes, while the rest, though charged, is still, so this granite peak drew the streams of war and peace from a wide circle for two long thousand years—as a sanctuary and centre of the Druids; as a temple of Jupiter, and Roman military station; as a con-vent, towards which long lines of pilgrims converged from afar; as a fortress which never

was taken—never, till the Revolution whirl-
wind spun over Brittany, and turned St.
Michel, for the first time, inside out. What
visions of the past came floating up as I sat
and dreamed on the rampart of Avranches, on
that still summer day! The straight dusty
road towards Granville lay like a white ribbon
across the green country. Peasants cut the
wheat and barley in the little fields beneath;
a parcel of small children in sabots were
playing in the shade, at the catholic game of
dirt pies, in French; one or two sails notched
the horizon far beyond the bay in which
St. Michel's rock had stood for ages past com-
pute. The very shape and character of the
coast had changed. The rock was once surrounded by wood—people have dug up the
trunks of trees—though modern history has
known it only as the rock amid the quicksands.
Its position makes it, or rather made it, im-
pregnable; for a Whitworth gun would now
sit up on the shore of the mainland, and pitch
solid shot and shell into it, like a butt. It is
neither on the land nor in the water; twice a
day the tide surrounds it. Boats, of old, could
approach it only at certain times. They could
not blockade it; but coming near enough to
be injured, would be obliged to retire at once,

or be left more defenceless than geese on a common. Armies on foot would be equally at a loss; there was no regular besieging of St. Michel; whoever took it, must do so by assault, at low-water.

Some people say that there is nothing like the inspiration of necessity; but for the troops to know that the work must be done in six hours at the most, if done at all—that the limit was laid down, not by the bravado of a commander, but by the laws of the imperial tide—that after a certain hour the water would surge swiftly up (the tide advances rapidly over these flats), and then wash the survivors away, unless they had forced an entrance through these unbreached granite walls; in any case, drowning the wounded : all this must have operated as a great contingent difficulty to the besiegers, and succour to the besieged. The flag of St. Michel was never taken. When Henry V. fought the battle of Agincourt, and Brittany lay at his feet, the fortress of St. Michel held so successfully out, that when the English brought big cannon to cripple the place, the French took them, and there they may be seen to this day—cannon which threw balls of granite a foot in diameter. Beside the sudden alternatives of sea and land, fatal to the prolonged operations of an army or a fleet, St. Michel is defended during the short intervals of tide by the quicksands which surround the rock. It is difficult to say at sight which sands are dead and which are quick, but the latter have a profundity of appetite horrible to reflect upon.

Some time ago, a few curious persons, wishing to know how deep the quicksands really were, threw upon them a great stone with a hundred feet of cord attached to it. The stone was soon gone, and the cord began to follow. In twenty-four hours the last inch of this long tail had disappeared. Whether the stone rested then, tradition cannot say, but the descent of one hundred feet is an "established fact."

No wonder the place was never taken, with such a character around it.

Of course I am indebted to Murray—I read Murray on the rampart. I had also another book with a long account of St. Michel—I read that. I don't affect contempt for information at second hand—I read translations. The best book in the world is a translation. So don't suppose I wish to cover the fact of my having got a help out of Murray, though I dish it up in my own foolish way. Still

I may say that when a child I was a constant devourer of Froissart. I love his pictures, quaintly out of perspective, with great cannon-balls going out of the cannons' mouths like footballs, and horses smothered with trappings, intricate crossbows, warriors in wonderful boots, and trumpets with flags to them ; so I flatter myself I have an under-current of undistinguishable original information about Normandy and Brittany.

Well, then, a great slice of the land of Froissart lay beneath me—lies beneath me, I should say, for I am writing out of doors. Let me first go back a while. Once that curious rugged cone of rock was the centre of Druidical influence in these parts. When naked painted sailors crept from point to point in wicker-boats covered with hide, they used to go to that rock, before they set foot in their slippery creaking craft, for magic arrows, which, when discharged by youths who had never known the passion of love, were supposed capable of laying storms. My authority does not say what happened when these were shot against the threatening skies in vain ; probably, the youths were taken to task for having deceived the crew ; but when the recipe was successful, when the clouds cleared off, or the wind fell after the mystic archery, the youths, on their return, presented themselves at St. Michel's rock, and the Druidical priestesses rewarded them by their love—testifying the extent of their affection by the number of golden shells they fastened to their garments. The barometrical changes must have been watched with great, if not scientific, interest, by these amorous damsels, since the changeable mercury supplied them with relays of gallants. Where can I find an authentic account of these Druids ? They were learned, influential, but who taught them ?

Now the scene changes. Straight Roman roads have streaked the face of Gaul. Regiments, with their bright armour, high floating plumes, and spears with broad glancing heads a foot and a half in length, have marched and countermarched throughout the conquered land, glittering among the trees as the road dips into the valley, now showing like a long brazen serpent as the column tops the hill. There is a temple of Jupiter on Mont St. Michel. Bronzed, hooknosed Romans sacrifice and consult. Legionaries discuss among themselves the *pros* and *cons* of a British invasion, lounging in the shade of the mount.

The scene shifts again. Building, busy

monks have colonised the rock. Day after day goes on the chip and blow of mason's chisel and hammer—cranes, long since rotted, hoist the graven stones ; the convent walls creep up, the mount is crowned with a Christian Church ; masses are sung, and bells are rung. The convent grows famous. Sun-burned pilgrims thread the roads of France towards St. Michel, thanking God when they see at last the view beneath my eyes ; sitting down to rest may be on some such place as this, and then, staff in hand, once more setting their sandalled dusty feet upon the road.

The monks are rich and warlike. In their council-chamber there, I see them sit in high debate ; William of Normandy proposes an invasion of England. How many ships shall they fit out to help him ? They equip six. After a while, a courier comes with tidings of the battle of Hastings ; and the brethren gladly talk to one another of it, not without grateful mention of the piety of their Norman soldiery before the fight. Then they have their projects in England too. There is a mount in Cornwall placed somewhat like their own ; they establish a dependency there, a second St. Michel's Mount, as seen to this day.

Ages go by: the strong austerity of old times has passed away—the monks are sensual and fat. Here, in their stronghold, however, they smile at reformation, so long as they can keep superiors in good-humour. Here they linger on, rebuked at times, but undisturbed, until a sharper power than the German monk's awakes the land. The Revolution has begun. The brethren—first incredulous, then terrified, impotent—hear reports which grow louder and nearer. The *bonnet rouge* crosses the sands of Avranches, and confusion fills St. Michel. Three hundred aged priests were confined to the dungeons for the remainder of their lives; the convent was suppressed, and the place became a jail. Politicians who survived the doctrines of the Revolution, without recanting them, were sent here before they were transferred to Cayenne; and now criminals weave and work drearily within the once sumptuous abbey-walls, and eat their stinted rations in the church. The Mont St. Michel is a penal prison; and whoever wants to see the prisoners, and the ins and outs of their long-famous place, must get a written order from the sous-préfecture, gritty with sand, "pour visiter les objets les plus curi eux."

Thus have I let my pen wander on, as the

distant sight of St. Michel suggests the changing scenes which have passed within it.
Meanwhile, the sky, just now so bright, has
become clouded, and a drop or two of rain
has fallen pat upon my paper. We must go
in. Bah! I have forgotten the umbrella. We
will get this same order from the sous-
préfecture, and, if the day be fine to-morrow, enter the place itself. But I don't
much fancy it. Nearness often dispels the
charm of reflection; and the positive pipe-
clayed form of a gendarme, however polite,
will be sure to occupy all the space which, to
my eye, has this last hour been so pleasantly
filled by successive generations of the inhabitants of Mont St. Michel.

I thought so. I have just come back from
the place—it is full of convicts and red trousers,
sullen work and sharp military supervision. I
called on the sous-préfet, who, in a white linen
coat, with his clerks, had his office on a bald
first floor. He most politely filled up a printed
form, and then, puffing out his lips in the true
magisterial way, held the wet order over a
bowl of sand, poured a large wooden spoonful
over it, like gravy, and bowed me out. We
got a chaise with one brown horse, and a
driver in blue; the whole turn-out mended

intricately with cord and string, down to the coachman's pipe. Why are carriages never washed in France? Our driver tried to make up for his horse's want of energy by his own; but though, on closing one's eyes, the pace sounded frantic, actual observation gave something between five and six miles an hour. We descended to the coast by some zigzags, and then a straight highway, and, after skirting it for some time, found ourselves getting gradually into a world of white sand. The road was sand, the fields little else. At some remote time, the sea had burst in upon this whole district, and smothered it. Soon we left nearly all the trees behind us, and continued jolting along close by the side of the bay.

All the while, the Mont St. Michel seemed nearly as far off as it did from Avranches, for we were obliged to make a great round before reaching that part of the sands which can be traversed by wheels. At last, we came to an open space where the road disappeared on the beach; St. Michel rose before us, about a mile off, across what appeared to be water quite as much as land. The tide was out, but here and there were little pools, brushed into small waves by a fresh breeze from the sea. There was no track, except from two or three vehicles which had crossed to the rock that day; following these, we left the bump and rattle of the road, and steered straight across the great wet waste towards the mount.

There is a causeway for foot-passengers, of rough stones, for no one could walk across the sands without getting wetted ankle-deep.

After we had creaked some distance, a bare-legged old man came splashing hastily towards us, as if he were bringing some bad news about the tide; but he was only a guide, though we did not want him in the least; however, he did his best to earn a franc.

We drove up to the town-gate from the sea, like Neptune; and, after a short lunch, ascended the steep narrow street of the town, which lies beneath the old abbey-walls. The people seemed a very cheerful, cleanly set; indeed, they could hardly be otherwise than the latter, as they live in sand and water, and necessarily scrub their feet whenever they take a walk. I could not help thinking that some of them must be as gritty within as without, for we passed one or two farm-yards on the main shore, where the corn was being thrashed on the bare sandy ground, by a number to the town.　Having hunted up our driver, we were launched again into the sand sea, and steered for the shore.　We met many of the inhabitants coming back from fishing—sturdy, bare-legged Tritons they were, splashing along. One old man, with his trousers rolled up to his knees, made a military salute in passing, and cried : " Vive l'Empereur ! "

" He is a fool," said our driver, cracking his whip ; by which I understood him to mean, not the Emperor, but his unseasonable admirer.

The drive to Avranches took three hours— twice as long as it need.　Our poor old brown horse, though, had a lift coming back—at least so he seemed to view it—but it consisted merely in the privilege of putting his nose against the hind boot of another returning carriage.　He began to trot directly he found this chance ; and when the other vehicle parted company, it carried away, on the outside of its rumble, a dusty impression of his head.

All the Druids, Roman soldiers and priests, middle-age monks and men-at arms, had faded away during our visit ; warders and felons had complete possession ; and it was not till I had gone back to my old place on the ramparts, that I could revive the scenes which I had associated with my first long look at Mont St. Michel, and bring back the lengthened train of its historical tenants.

of men and women, who surrounded it in a
circle, as if they were playing " Bull in the
Park."

When we had threaded the little town of St.
Michel, which contains 400 inhabitants, we
reached the old gate of the abbey, and gave
in our order.   A woman who was knitting in
the deep shadow of the gateway, just inside,
then led us to read a notice by which we were
expressly forbidden to offer any gratuity to the
warder, who would presently come to show us
round the prison.   We sat down on a bench
till he arrived, as he soon did, with a bunch of
large keys.

Then we went over the prison.   All these
old prisons, or buildings made into them, seem,
to my eye, alike.   There is a penal atmosphere about them which swallows up lesser
distinctions; there are the same heavy doors,
huge locks, monotonous walls, and felon uni-
forms.   We were taken through a wilderness
of crypts and passages, ending in several
places with *oubliettes*, now boarded over, and
black as night.   At times, through stone port-
holes, we caught glimpses of the sea of sand
in which the rock stood; and the wind whistled
through the place like a ship.   One other
sound alone was heard, like the hoofs of a

troop of horse walking down a paved street.
I inquired, and it proved to be the ceaseless
clicking of the prisoners' looms. Most of
them work at these. The large hall of the
abbey is filled with them, wearily weaving out
their term of imprisonment. Down below, in
the town, you can hear the incessant clatter.
The nave of the church is used as a dining-
room for the convicts, and was full of wooden
benches and pannikins.

On a small terrace, commanding a wide sea
and land view, was a string of prisoners
walking silently round and round, headed by
a yellow old man, with his chin hanging on
his breast.

" These," said the warder, "are the sick,"—
and sick they looked, circling there. Though
the sun was bright and the breeze fresh,
one could almost have thought that the sight
of the green country and the open sea added
to their misery.

" Are most of the prisoners here sentenced
for long periods ? " I asked.

" Many for life," replied the warder, looking
at the crawling circle as if they were a box of
caterpillars.

We went to the top of the church, and then
descended the different strata of the building

WHAT is the good of it? says old Grimsire, whose hat, when off duty, is always on a peg, either in the office or at home. To racket about anywhere is bad enough, but to do it in a crowd of jabbering foreigners is humiliating as well as tiresome. Others, again, assert that the great good of it is felt in the relish with which one enjoys home afterwards. There is something in that; but the pleasure does not spring from mere contrast, or home might be made sweeter by a month at the workhouse, or a tour on the treadmill. Travelling, however, is intrinsically pleasant to some, or they would stay at home. Those who have tried it once almost invariably repeat the experiment, until it becomes a habit. The desire comes to almost all—the fruition to an increasing number. Did not the promoters of the Exhibition of 1862 tell us that the railways could bring into London six times as many per day as they could in 1851?

This is a striking proof of the growing multitude of tourists, as well as of the increase in goods traffic. The objection to travelling, based upon our grandfathers' indifference to it, might be urged with equal force against the use of the penny-postage or the pocket-handkerchief. We could live without either—and many do. But it is a great relief to get clear away from our work, though it be only for a week or less. There is a kind of hunger for recreation, which nothing but a change of scene can satisfy. You cannot sufficiently detach yourself from the instruments and apparatus of business without leaving them. The miller's man could not enjoy a whole holiday in a mill, though others carried the sacks and furled the sails. The sailor would not be refreshed by a cruise. We always see country folks run up to town for relaxation, and townspeople escape to the country for the same purpose. Who fill the exhibitions, great and small? Who wander through the British Museum in June? Who dive into the Thames Tunnel, and whisper in the Gallery of St. Paul's? Who spend weeks in seeing London sights? Cockneys? Not they. Let the barrister loose from court and chambers, give the clerk a month's respite from the office—

where will you find them in a week? On the top of Monte Rosa, or among the Cumberland lakes. I put up last summer at an out-of-the-way châlet six thousand feet up in one of the Alpine chains, and found a dissenting minister from Glasgow, an inspector of schools, and a London police magistrate, in wide-awakes, to say nothing of an archdeacon in highlows and a flannel shirt, discussing the shortest climb to a neighbouring peak. The charm of travelling is its total change from our daily drudgery and stale scenes. The very houses of London are breaking out on all sides, away from the rattle of omnibuses and cabs. From whatever side you approach the metropolis, you meet a number of prim villas coming out to take the air in double lines, like school girls on a walk —like them, too, dressed in the last fashion, and unengaged.

Of all travelling, that on the Continent is the most refreshing. It has its supposed drawbacks, no doubt. The steam-packet is the first. This is like the bitter taste of the medicine from which we promise ourselves relief.

Another supposed drawback to a tour on the Continent, is often the tourist's ignorance of any language beside his own. I believe, however, that, almost anywhere, if you talk English, somebody will come. But suppose he does not, I really think that the sensation of not being understood is rather entertaining than otherwise; it makes the change you are seeking more complete. You have always a good reason for helping yourself to what you want, and can persist in small excursions, intrusions, and general indulgences, on the ground of prohibitions being unintelligible.

Moreover, when you travel, say by carriage, and fail to satisfy a succession of hostlers and discontented *garçons*, you have the greatest advantage in not understanding them. Their satire, both direct and indirect, may be withering, but you don't know it. They can't insult you except by gestures and grimaces, which are often worth money to see, instead of being the reward and consequence of a just economy. You pay your bill with good coin, and add what you know to be a sufficient douceur. What if you are entertained with a pantomime at your departure? Then, again, when you are angry yourself, what a relief to abuse the offender in the strongest language you can command! He is none the worse for it, while you are all the better. He does not understand a word, and you would have been sorry, half an hour afterwards, if he could.   Since it must take two to make a quarrel, and the re- joinder is more irritating than the original insult, all dangerous provocation is neutralised, and yet the excess of steam is blown off by both.   It is a great thing for a reply to be unintelligible.

Most of the ills of travelling are made by tourists themselves.   In the first place, they frequently settle beforehand where they will go, and mark out their route.   Now, I would by no means dissuade them from this.   Let them study books and maps before they start; let them ask experienced friends; for thus they realise the coming pleasure.   Yet the most elaborate plans are better discarded; it is better not to follow the proposed route.   It is delicious to defy the arrangements of a cam- paign, and revel in the consciousness of errant independence.   Many people, I am afraid, not only draw out their route beforehand, but follow it, and so create a fund of reproachful conscien- tiousness and apprehensive responsibility.

These are the wretched people, too, who conceive themselves expected to see the lions of every place they visit.

The visitation of churches, especially, is a great feature in their movements.   Half of

them don't know the difference between Etrus-
can and Chinese architecture, and yet you may
hear them after breakfast asking waiters out of
a phrase-book the nearest way to St. Pierre's,
and at dinner, telling one another of the curious monuments they have seen, and the old
women at prayers they have interrupted.
Nothing, it has often been remarked, makes a
sensitive Englishman more ashamed of himself
indirectly, than the irreverent behaviour of his
fellow-countrymen in foreign countries, and
their ill-concealed, too often openly displayed,
contempt of the devotions they witness. I
heard, two years ago, when I was in Switzerland, of sound Protestant principles being
carried out to a remarkable extent. A tourist
found himself one cold evening at the monas-
tery of St. Bernard. The monks, it is well
known, give food and shelter freely to all
comers with noble catholicity. There is a box
in the chapel, with a little slit in it, where you
may drop a donation ; but your attention is not
drawn to it. No one asks or knows whether
any particular traveller gives anything or not.
Well, our friend warmed himself at the fire, ate
his fill, drank his fill, tucked himself into bed,
slept his fill, got up the next morning, said his
prayers, had his breakfast, picked his teeth,

and then proclaimed that he should give nothing to the monks, lest he should countenance Popery!

Picture galleries are often a snare. How deeply have I pitied the haggard groups who gape listlessly along the galleries of the Pitti Palace and the Louvre! Why will a man who knows nothing about them, not have the courage to refuse to look at pictures? There he is, working wearily through the catalogue, often misapplying its directions, and shading his eyes at a daub, when he thinks he is admiring a Rubens. Collections of prints sometimes cause sudden discomfiture to pseudo-connoisseurs. I knew a man who went to the famous collection of engravings in the Corsini Palace at Rome. He drove to the door, and was shown up into the room where they are kept, when a polite custodian asked him *what* he would like to see. They were all in portfolios; and, for the life of him, he could not hit all at once upon the name of an artist to cover his confusion, and be quite sure he didn't mistake a painter for an engraver. He didn't dare ask that clerical-looking librarian, in a cassock and black velvet skull-cap, for " Cruikshank "—first, because it looked unlikely; and, secondly, because he didn't know how to put it in Italian. What, then, should a man look at, if he has no real interest in churches, palaces, or museums? There is an endless fund of gratification, if he will draw upon it, in merely prowling about, with his eyes open. Let him only feel in his conscience that he is not playing the hypocrite, and he will find everything interesting.

There is another piece of advice I would give to every traveller: smile at the bills. Take one with another, and the expense will barely exceed your estimate at the worst. But never suffer little extortions to annoy you. You are, we will suppose, charged double the intrinsic value of your meal; well, if you will keep on calculating the price of mutton, you had better have stayed at home, and stuck to the shop. At any rate, Boniface must live; and what better opportunity for him to realise this resolution, when he hears a hungry moneyed Englishman ask: " Esker voo zavey kelker shose poor deenay?" Half the year he is without customers, unless you count those who order coffee, call for a toothpick, smoke their own cigars, and spit on the floor. He can't live on *them*. Somebody must help to pay the rent and feed the little ones.

There are those who say that, if you want

to travel with comfort and economy, you should go to the second-rate inns, and live on the best. The tariff is lower, and you squint proudly among the blind. You are welcomed and dismissed with attention. This may happen sometimes, but an inferior hotel is often dear as well as bad.

Seldom travel first-class abroad, or you will find yourself in the company of English invalids. To me, the travelling in the society of foreigners provides continuous matter for odd observations. Their hats, their queer articles of luggage, their patient respect for the arrangements of the road, and the officials, are always surprising. See them flattening their noses against the window of the waiting-room, as the train pulls up; notice the submissive way in which they show their tickets to the porter, and the politeness with which they touch their hats to society when they enter the carriage. We might take a leaf out of their book here.

Then, when the journey is done, how patiently they wait for the luggage, which the porters will not let them touch till the van is emptied, and all is arranged under the initial letters of the passengers' names, or the different points of their departure. That great moustached fellow will watch the process without a murmur, though he has only a tight little hair-trunk, with slips of wood nailed on it, and sees it deposited, close by, among the first. He must wait, perhaps, for twenty minutes, while the porters jabber over illegible directions, and arrange a whole waggon-load of packages with provoking conscientiousness. He must wait; he has no *Times* to write to— he must wait, though his dinner be doing the very same thing in the next street.

One often, however, forgets the obedience due to regulations. I recollect that once last year—I forget at what station—believing myself rather late, I tapped at the window of the ticket-office. Up rushed an elderly official, and checked me with horrified gestures. Had I offered to sneeze while kissing the emperor's hand, he could not have shown a greater sense of the impropriety; so I blushed, and waited half an hour.

In dining at *table-d'hôtes* always take something of what is offered, however disguised. Otherwise, when you have missed several opportunities, you may all at once find yourself pulled up with *compote*, and left with nothing between you and starvation but a tureen of stewed plums. Those *table-d'hôte* dinners have a trick of sudden finality; the meal comes to an abrupt end; and there is not even bread and cheese wherewith to fill the vacuum which you abhor. Chickens and salad are generally the last course; when they come, it is then or never. Do not be coy, however tempted to let the chance slip by, while you are wondering why French fowls have always four legs, to say nothing of duplicate drumsticks, as if they had been lame, and used crutches, which were cooked at the patient's decease.

The secret of all travelling is to be unfettered—to cast off those conventional irritating restraints which are necessary at home, and to move about when, how, and where we like, in our own foolish, easy way. This allows both body and mind to uncoil themselves: thus we get that without which labour and rest are insufficient, however carefully balanced—namely, recreation.

BACK again to dear, old, misty, grumbling England—back again to London fog and mud, and sturdy snobbishness, from the glittering Alpine snow, and the deep-blue Italian lake, and the bowing, close-cropped Monsieur. Hurrah! for home, after a summer away on the paper-sanded, flimsy-journaled, many-hatted, harness-roped, table-d'hôted Continent. The run back was delicious. I had had some business to do abroad, and therefore could not return directly the whim took me. I was bound to remain up to a certain date, whether I grew tired of foreign scenery and cooks or not. But directly the term of my engagement was up, I hastened back, partly because I had pressing business at home, partly because I was getting rather bored by Monsieur. Excellent fellow! we English owe him more than we can repay; we give him a change, no doubt, when he visits us, but small entertainment. We are too glum to be immediately ridiculous, and too expensive to permit economy. Monsieur begins to spend more, and laugh less, directly he crosses the Channel. One thing, however, we do for him : we whet the love of home; in that we mutually interchange good offices.

When I sat down in the great salle-à-manger at Belladogana for the last time, and for the last time the waiter skated up, and said, " X," which I gratified him every day by understanding as an inquiry whether I would have eggs for breakfast—when, as I say, I sat there for the last time, and thought that the wheels of the diligence were probably being already greased, preparatory to its carrying me away at eleven o'clock, a.m., that very day, I was glad. I had seen the season begin and end; I had chatted with the early tourists, and bon-voyaged the late; I had seen them come pale and dapper, and go away sun-burned and travel-stained; I had watched the transition from a modest spirit of inexperience to one of insolent cynicism; and now they had all gone. The small Swiss inns were shut up, the big ones in the towns nearly empty. The bustling crowd had melted down to a few loiterers working their way homewards, or now and then a family passing into Italy for the winter, before the snow got too deep on the passes for Paterfamilias. There were but a few trickling drops in the channel of the great summer-touring stream. My wife and I found ourselves alone on several occasions at the breakfast hour in the largest hotels, and took our meal in a corner of a huge apartment, like two mice in a barn. Most of the waiters, who were hired for the summer, had left; the small remnant read the papers openly in the salon, or smoked without rebuke at the door of the inn.

Our last resting-place was one of the large establishments in the Italian lake district. The low hills round Como and Maggiore were powdered with snow; the chestnuts were all beaten down and housed; the paths which in the height of summer were checkered with the shade of interlacing boughs, now rustled with withered leaves; the winter service of diligences, &c. was begun; guides had no one to follow them : but the scenery of the lake district was far more lovely than in the full-blooded autumn, with its heat and dust.

It was very lovely, but we were glad to be gone ; and the nearer we got to England the faster we went. It seemed as if the speed was accelerated as we approached the busiest metropolis of Europe. At first, we crunched slowly up the old familiar Alpine road, now white with snow, and hedged with icicles, the hoar-frost dusting our shaggy horses as we crossed the summit. The trot down the other side was followed by a passage in a lake steamer, whence, again, the pace was increased on a Swiss railway. A long express took us with more safety than swiftness to Paris, and a shorter one whisked us at very tolerable speed to our port of departure. Once at Dover, however, and seated in the carriage, we were reminded of English expedition by our tickets being immediately collected; and then, phit! the engine screamed, and we ran smack into London without a pause, the Sydenham Palace having apparently been moved to the entrance of the tunnel under Shakespeare's Cliff.

Perhaps the first sensation of surprise on a return to England, after even a few months' absence, is caused by the great proficiency in the English language exhibited by illiterate people. Railway guards, cabmen, and little rude street-boys converse in it without hesitation; it is most remarkable.

But let us to our retrospect—back again. Now that I have kicked the carpet-bag into a corner, and tasted the first returning sense of possession, let me think what contrasts strike me with the freshest force.

Imprimis, London is the cleanest town I know; yes, in fog, mud, or thaw. Think of its smells—what are they? Have they any peculiar edge or striking variety? No doubt, in some hot summers, the Thames has produced a steady mass of odour; but, as a rule, the streets are scentless. As to the slums, as they are called, I visit them every day, but I never come across anything so keen and nasty as I do even in renovated Paris. As for Rome, pheugh! ramble about a ruin, but hold your nose. As for Naples, is not the deep blue of the Mediterranean tinged—no, not tinged, but grossly dyed with sewerage in face of the town? Walk along the beach of that tideless sea, but do not attempt to sit down on it. As there is no smoke without fire, so the dirt of continental towns can be detected by most unmistakable symptoms. Mischievous dirt betrays itself. Nature did not give us noses merely to blow, or adorn a profile; they tell us what is bad to breathe and see; but in the most frequented parts of London they seldom convey a warning of the presence of dirt, because there is none. Simple mud is harmless enough; it is a witness of clouds and

water-carts ; but it is clean : we don't shudder
when it sticks to us.

Another continental fallacy is touching the
politeness of foreigners.   Tompkins converses
after a fashion with the conductor of a diligence or the boatmen on a lake.   He is struck
with the native ease and pleasantry of their
manner ; he compares them to those of cabby
or the steersman of a penny-boat, and remarks
to Mrs. Simpkins that the lower orders abroad
are infinitely more courteous and conversable
than those at home.   Well, I suppose you are
a judge of good manners, Mr. Tompkins, and
I hope you always speak civilly to your
" inferiors," when not checked by an imperfect
acquaintance with the language you employ ;
but I suspect that half your impressions are
influenced by your very partial knowledge
of French or German.   You don't know how
to be coarse and arbitrary in these tongues
yourself; and much of what you take for
natural ease in the *conducteur*, would be vulgar
familiarity, if you only understood what he
said.   Translate the gallant speeches of the
cicerone to signora into flippant cockney, and
you would call him an impertinent rascal to
speak so to your wife.

As to the good manners of the middle

classes, we cannot call them conspicuous at
meals. There is an apparent wantonness of
indelicacy in some which no custom can excuse
—a greedy, noisy process of eating, which
could hardly be found in their grade in
England. See how Monsieur will gnaw the
bones of a fowl—and he always has some to
exhibit on—or watch him cut up his portion
into swallowable pieces, preparatory to an uninterrupted disposal of it, and then reconsider
your sentence about his politeness. He wins
the character mainly by bowing; there he
excels us; a pot-boy takes off his hat to
another pot-boy. We associate the gesture
with ceremonious courtesy; practice makes
him perfect in the obeisance; and we compare
his salutation with the gruff greeting or in-
elegant nod of the corresponding Briton.
You may see a Frenchman uncover his head
when he goes into a neighbour's shop, but
you don't see an Englishman spit on the
floor when he makes a morning call. There—
that will do; let us turn to a different test of
good taste.

Somewhere or another, I read some strictures on the vulgarity which distinguishes our
countrymen in writing their names on monuments and walls. But here he is utterly

distanced by Monsieur. Every available inch about continental sights is scribbled over with foreign names. The other day I was on the top of Milan Cathedral; the highest landing-place is dingy with signatures, the statues even being covered with a coat of black-lead. I noticed this to our attendant, and he said it was no use washing them, they were defaced again at once. Let us be fair; give our neighbours their due; and let our own good taste and feeling express themselves in corresponding manners; but do not let us cry down the defects in English courtesy which we notice at once, because our ignorance of the language, or want of presence of mind, prevents our observing the drawbacks to foreign politeness.

A word as to foreign food. I was struck with its monotonous variety. There is always an embarrassing amount of dishes with a want of hearty material. The dinner at the *table-d'hôte* impresses the simple tourist at first, but in time it loses its effect. For genuine soups and solids, commend me to an English cook; but I grant you that the intermediate class of dishes, neither liquid nor substantial, are to be found in their unsatisfactory abundance far more plentifully in the produce of a foreign kitchen.

It is notorious, however, that we claim excellence in comfort. After all, says the traveller, give me English comfort. Paterfamilias, fresh from the Continent, embraces his bed, and smiles upon his soap-dish with genuine affection. But we must not be too sharp about this notion of comfort. In many respects, the comfort of English travellers is studied more abroad than at home. Compare the scalding gulp at our railway refreshment-room with the well-proportioned meal provided on your journey in France. Compare their carriages with some of ours, and—among many minor luxuries—the facilities for smoking. Moreover, do you not travel with less anxiety about luggage abroad? Does not it add to your comfort to know that you are not responsible for anything when once you have that limp, gritty little record in your purse of the weight, number, and fare of your articles of luggage? Is not the arrival at an inn on the Continent more comfortable than in England? Are not the beds—yes, I say it, however devoted Paterfamilias may be to his four-poster—are not the beds generally delicious?

The fallacy lies in this—we compare *foreign hotel* comforts with those of our own *house.* I believe the contrast would be greater if we had to pay the bills and submit to the vexations of English inns.

But leaving this question of comforts, what other contrasts have left their impressions still fresh upon the mind? I was struck in entering London with the sodden, wretched look of one particular class amongst the poor. I came in by gas-light, and saw them about the public-houses. There was a staleness of face, and air of soiled limp finery about them, which I did not see abroad. No doubt, the beggars of the Continent are often disgusting; but they chatter and squabble with a vivacity which saves them from despair. But these poor English people I mean are not beggars; they slip and slouch about in silent, dogged wretchedness, their force of temper coming occasionally to a head in a sudden exchange of loud-shrieked abuse and a duet of curses. I confess this saddened me. Merry England? No; that is not the adjective. We must be content with our privilege and characteristic of grumbling. An Englishman is never happy without a grievance. He affects to rejoice in being free, and secretly wonders that a tattered Mossoo of the third estate, with his accumulation of social and religious restrictions, can grin and caper about as he does. Wonder? Why wonder? Is not the child happy on the nursery floor? Does not he smile through his tears? So with the subject of these foreign " paternal " governments, which, whatever their faults, certainly do try to make things immediately pleasant to the very poor; witness Bomba's patronage of the lazzaroni. Ignorance *is* often bliss, though wisdom be not folly.

But of all the retrospects—now that I am sitting in my own study, with my papers about me within, and my work to do without—nothing touches me with so deep a feeling of compassion as the case of permanent residents abroad. I don't mean the invalids, whose search for health occupies and interests them, but the listless, chattering people who live at hotels, and have nothing to do. There is something more than dreary, something appalling in their state. They are the centre of no family, no village, no circle, no set even of tradesmen—nothing abides by them. They move from inn to inn with less hold on the human race than the postboys who help to drive them. Even the very courier, who seems as detached a dot of humanity as any man, is earning his bread by flitting from place to place, and wearing out the signs of his distinctive nationality. He earns his bread by severing himself from his home; but he has probably a wife somewhere, and children who send him letters in large printed characters, with their love and a kiss. Your wandering inn-haunter, however, is earning nothing, loving nothing. In most cases, he is pleasing, voluble, and heartless. He makes the acquaintance of everybody, talks about everything, and will some day be found sick and frightened by the waiter, and die alone in a crowded hotel, to the disgust of the landlord, who will smuggle out his corpse by night, and take care that all the household look as if nothing were the matter.

But joy to the man who has a welcome home, and faces the old familiar work with fresh and buoyant heart. Nothing like a pause, and a view of our position from a distance. If you would see the battle, you must mount a hill; and as each man is more or less his own general, it is well for him to step aside out of the smoke and noise for a while, and see how matters look from without. The whole of a scheme reveals itself: we see the tendency of some favourite plan; we decide on cutting off that, on dropping this, on securing such and such a result. We have time to breathe and look about us; we know where objects lie when we return to the battle, our short excursion has shown us a map of the field; we spare our strength, and are stronger still; we work not only with freshened spirits, but with a far clearer understanding of what we are about, when we come " back again."

THE END.

COX AND WYMAN, PRINTERS, GREAT QUEEN STREET, LONDON, W.C.

USEFUL WORKS.

The Grasses of Great Britain

(Completion of). Now ready, in 1 vol., containing life-size, full-coloured Drawings, with magnified Organs, of 144 British Grasses, and Observations on their Natural History and Uses. Described by C. P. JOHNSON. Illustrated by J. E. SOWERBY. Royal 8vo., price £1. 14s. Parts XIV. to XXXI. may still be had.

The Useful Plants of Great Britain.

A Treatise upon the principal Native Vegetables capable of Application as Food or Medicine, or in the Arts and Manufactures. By C. P. JOHNSON. Illustrated by J. E. SOWERBY. 300 coloured Illustrations. Complete, in cloth, price £1. 7s.

The British Ferns

(a Plain and Easy Account of): together with their Classification, Arrangement of Genera, Structure, and Functions, Directions for Out-door and In-door Cultivation, &c. By Mrs. LANKESTER. Fully illustrated, price 4s., coloured by hand; 2s. 6d. plain.

"Not only plain and easy, but elegantly illustrated."—*Athenæum*.

The British Fungi

(a Plain and Easy Account of): with especial reference to the Esculent and other Economic Species. By M. C. COOKE. With coloured plates of 40 Species. Fcap. 8vo., price 6s.

"The book is a very useful one, supplying, for a few shillings, information not hitherto attainable except at a much larger cost."—*Field*.

A Manual of Botanic Terms.

By M. C. COOKE. With more than 300 Illustrations. Fcap. 8vo., cloth, price 2s. 6d.

"This elegant little volume will be a welcome boon to all botanical students. It contains intelligible descriptions of all the terms used in botanical science, with a collection of beautifully-executed illustrations at the end of the volume. To all who do not but are willing to know the full value of such terms as Campylospermous, Sterigmate, and Perichætium, this volume may be safely recommended."—*Critic*.

A Manual of Structural Botany.

By M. C. COOKE, Author of "Seven Sisters of Sleep," &c. Illustrated by more than 200 woodcuts. Price 1s.; bound 1s. 6d.

"Condensed yet clear, comprehensive but brief, it affords to the learner a distinct view."—*Globe*.

Wild Flowers worth Notice:

a Selection from the British Flora of some of our Native Plants which are most attractive for their Beauty, Uses, or Associations. By Mrs. LANKESTER. Illustrated by J. E. SOWERBY. Fcap. 8vo., cloth, coloured by hand, 4s.; plain, 2s. 6d.

"We are so frequently asked by our country friends to recommend books on Flowers and Ferns that shall be interesting without being too scientific, that we are heartily glad to have the opportunity of so doing which the present elegant but cheap little volume affords."—*Practical Farmers' Chronicle*.

The Fern Collector's Album:

a Descriptive Folio for the reception of Natural Specimens; containing, on the right-hand page, a description of each Fern printed in colours, the opposite page being left blank, for the collector to affix the dried specimen, forming, when filled, an elegant and complete collection of this interesting family of plants. Size of the Small Edition, 11¾ by 8½ in.; Large Edition, 17½ by 11 in. Handsomely bound, price One Guinea. A Large Edition, without descriptive letterpress, One Guinea.

Old Bones; or, Notes for Young Naturalists.

By the Rev. W. S. SYMONDS, Rector of Pendock, Author of "Stones of the Valley," &c. Second Edition, much improved and enlarged. Fcap. 8vo., price 2s. 6d. Fully illustrated.

Half-hours with the Microscope.

By EDWIN LANKESTER, M.D. Illustrated by 250 Drawings from Nature, by TUFFEN WEST. New Edition, much enlarged, with full Description of the various parts of the Instrument. Price 2s. 6d. plain; 4s. coloured.

Half-an-hour on Structure.	Half-an-hour at the Pond-side.
Half-an-hour in the Garden.	Half-an-hour at the Sea-side.
Half-an-hour in the Country.	Half-an-hour In-doors.

APPENDIX.—The Preparation and Mounting of Objects.

The Mounting and Preparation of Microscopic Objects.

By THOMAS DAVIES. Fcap. 8vo., price 2s. 6d. This Manual comprises all the most approved methods of mounting, together with the results of the Author's experience, and that of many of his Friends, in every department of Microscopic Manipulation, and as it is intended to assist the beginner as well as the advanced student, the very rudiments of the art have not been omitted.

Chap. I. Apparatus.	Chap. V. Sections, and how to cut
,, II. To prepare and mount objects dry.	them, with some remarks on Dissection.
,, III. Mounting in Canada Balsam.	,, VI. Injection.
,, IV. Preservative Liquids, &c.	,, VII. Miscellaneous.
	Index.

Hints on the Formation of Local Museums.

By the Treasurer of the Wimbledon Museum Committee. 18mo. price 1s. illustrated.

Waste Products and Undeveloped Substances;

or, Hints for Enterprise in Neglected Fields. By P. L. SIMMONDS, Author of "Products of the Vegetable Kingdom," &c. Fcap. 8vo. cloth, price 6s.

Metamorphoses of Man and of Animals.

Describing the changes which Mammals, Batrachians, Insects, Myriapods, Crustacea, Annelids, and Zoophytes undergo whilst in the egg; also the series of Metamorphoses which these beings are subject to in after life. Alternate Generation, Parthenogenesis and General Reproduction treated *in extenso*. With Notes, giving references to the works of Naturalists who have written upon the subject. By A. DE QUATREFAGES, Membre de l'Institut (Académie des Sciences), Professeur au Muséum d'Histoire Naturelle. Translated by HENRY LAWSON, M.D., Professor of Physiology in Queen's College, Birmingham.

Prof. Huxley's Lectures "On the Origin of Species."

1. The Present Condition of Organic Nature.—2. The Past Condition.—3. The Method by which the Causes of the Present and Past Conditions of Organic Nature are to be discovered. The Origination of Living Beings.—4. The Perpetuation of Living Beings, Hereditary Transmission, and Variation.—5. The Condition of Existence as affecting the Perpetuation of Living Beings.—6. A Critical Examination of the Position of Mr. Darwin's Work "On the Origin of Species," in relation to the complete Theory of the Causes of the Phenomena of Organic Nature. Crown 8vo., price 2s. 6d.

PUBLICATIONS OF THE RAY SOCIETY.

BRITISH ENTOMOSTRACOUS CRUSTACEA.—A Monograph, with 36 plates (most of them coloured), of all the species of the. By Dr. Baird, F.L.S. 8vo. pp. 364. £1. 1s.

BRITISH ANGIOCARPOUS LICHENS. A Monograph of the. With 30 coloured plates. By the Rev. W. A. Leighton, M.A. 8vo. pp. 100. 10s. 6d.

CIRRIPEDIA. A Monograph of the family. By C. Darwin, Esq., M.A., F.R.S. 8vo. Vol. I. pp. 400, 10 plates, 16s. Vol. II. pp. 684, 30 plates, £1. 6s.

BRITISH FRESH-WATER POLYZOA. A Monograph of the. By Professor Allman, F.R.S. With 11 plates (10 coloured). Imp. 4to. pp. 119. £1. 11s. 6d.

RECENT FORAMINIFERA OF GREAT BRITAIN. A Monograph of the. By Professor Williamson. With 7 plates. Imp. 4to. pp. 100. £1. 11s. 6d.

OCEANIC HYDROZOA. On the. By Professor Huxley, F.R.S. With 12 plates. Imp. 4to. pp. 141. £1. 11s. 6d.

BURMEISTER ON THE ORGANIZATION OF TRILOBITES. With 6 plates; translated from the German, and edited by Professors Bell and E. Forbes. Imp. 4to. pp. 136. 15s.

A SYNOPSIS OF THE BRITISH NAKED-EYED PULMOGRADE MEDUSÆ. With 13 coloured Plates, drawings of all the species. By Professor E. Forbes, F.R.S. Imp. 4to. £1. 1s.

BRITISH NUDIBRANCHIATE MOLLUSCA. A Monograph of the (with coloured drawings of every species). By Messrs. Alder and Hancock. Imp. 4to. Part I. £1. 10s. Part II. £1. 10s. Part III. £1. 10s. Part IV. £1. 10s. Part V. £1. 10s. Part VI. £1. 1s. Part VII. £1. 1s.

THE BRITISH SPIDERS. A History of the Spiders of Great Britain and Ireland. By John Blackwall, F.L.S. Two Parts, coloured by hand. Folio, £3. 13s. 6d.

INTRODUCTION TO THE STUDY OF THE FORAMINIFERA. By W. B. Carpenter, M.D., F.R.S., F.L.S., &c.; assisted by W. K. Parker, Esq., and T. Rupert Jones, Esq., F.G.S. In 1 vol. Imp. 4to. pp. 319, with 22 plates. £1. 11s. 6d.

ON THE GERMINATION, DEVELOPMENT, AND FRUCTIFICATION OF THE HIGHER CRYPTOGAMIA, AND ON THE FRUCTIFICATION OF THE CONIFERÆ. By Dr. Wilhelm Hofmeister. Translated by Frederick Currey, M.A., F.R.S., Sec. L.S. In 1 vol. 8vo. cloth, pp. 506, with 65 plates. £1. 5s. 6d.

Fully Illustrated, well printed, wonderfully cheap.

CHYMISTRY (An INTRODUCTION to). 144 pages, price 6d. ; or, Three Parts, 2d. each. Uniform with the above—

MECHANICS. Complete, 4d. ; Two parts, 2d. each.	WALKINGHAME'S ARITHMETIC. 4d
HYDROSTATICS. Complete, 2d.	MACKENZIE'S TABLES. 2d.
HYDRAULICS. Complete, 2d.	BOOKKEEPING. Complete, 2d.
MURRAY'S GRAMMAR. Complete, 2d.	MAVOR'S SPELLING. 4d.
	PHRENOLOGY. 2d.
	SHORTHAND. 2d.

Published Annually, Second Year of publication; Price £1. 16s.

The County Families of the United Kingdom.

Or, *Royal Manual of the Titled and Untitled Aristocracy of Great Britain and Ireland*, containing a brief notice of the Descent, Birth, Marriage, Education, and Appointments of each Person, his Heir Apparent or Presumptive, as also a Record of the Offices which he has hitherto held, together with his **Town Address** and **Country Residences**. By EDWARD WALFORD, M.A., late Scholar of Balliol College, Oxford, and Fellow of the Genealogical and Historical Society of Great Britain.

" We find in this most convenient handbook the living representatives of those who have earned rank for themselves and for their descendants. We have records of the military or naval services in the titles of Wellington, Marlborough, Howden, Amherst, Anglesey, Cadogan, Charlemont, Cathcart, Dartmouth, Dorchester, Gardner, Gough, Hardinge, Harris, Hill, Huntly, Keane, Powis, Raglan, Seaton, Stamford, Stanhope, Stratford, Vivian, Nelson, St. Vincent, Camperdown, De Saumarez, Hood, Exmouth, Hawke, Mulgrave, and Sandwich. Official services are represented by Clifford, Albemarle, Dunfermline, Sidmouth, Congleton, Glenelg, Holland, Lauderdale, Monteagle, Onslow, Oxford, Melville, Ripon, Salisbury, Shannon, and Sydney. Success in commerce and trade is represented in Fitzwilliam, Leigh, Petre, Darnley, Carrington, Overstone, Leeds, Craven, Greville, Radnor, Ducie, Pomfret, Tankerville, Dormer, Coventry, Romney, Dudlow, Dacres, and Ashburton. Political services have elevated Lowther and Massareene ; diplomatic services, Berwick, Cowley, Durham, Malmesbury, Granville, Harrington, Heytesbury, Rivers, and Stratford de Redcliffe. The fortunate lawyers have contributed Tenterden, Thurlow, Eldon, Plunket, Redesdale, Rosslyn, Walsingham, Campbell, Stratheden, St. Leonards, Lyndhurst, Truro, Ellenborough, North, Hardwicke, Cottenham, Cowper, Kenyon, Lovelace, Manchester, and Manners. The ' Romance of the Peerage' is written in titles such as these. The mercer, the skinner, and the silk-merchant, the merchant tailor, the draper, the wool-stapler, the cloth-worker, the Calais or Cheapside merchant, the banker, the jeweller, the goldsmith, and the apothecary (Smithson), like the gallant admiral, the general, and the gentlemen of the long robe or of red tape, have, when enterprising and energetic, founded noble families."—*Literary Gazette.*

" It possesses advantages which no other work of the kind that we know of has offered hitherto. Containing all that is to be found in others, it furnishes information respecting families of distinction which are not to be found in the latter. It will prove to be invaluable in the library and drawing-room."—*Spectator.*

" To produce such a work in the perfection which characterizes ' County Families,' must have been an almost Herculean task. It is sufficient for us to say that accuracy even in the minutest details appears to have been the aim of Mr. Walford, and the errors are so few and slight, that they may readily be passed over."—*Weekly Register.*

By the same Author,

The Shilling Peerage ;
The Shilling Baronetage ;
The Shilling Knightage ; and
The Shilling House of Commons.

By E. WALFORD, M.A., Balliol College, Oxford. New Edition, for 1864, just published.

Crown 8vo. price 6s., Seventh Edition,

Our Social Bees.

Pictures of Town and Country, and other Papers.   By
ANDREW WYNTER, M.D.

CONTENTS :—The Post-office.—London Smoke.—Mock Auctions.—
Hyde Park.—The Suction Post.—St. George and the Dragon.—The
India-rubber Artist.—Our Peck of Dirt.—The Artificial Man.—
Britannia's Smelling-bottle.—The Hunterian Museum at the College of
Surgeons.—A Chapter on Shop Windows.—Commercial Grief.—
Orchards in Cheapside.—The Wedding Bonnet.—Aërated Bread.—The
German Fair.—Club Chambers for the Married.—Needle-making.—
Preserved Meats.—London Stout.—Palace Lights, Club Cards, and
Bank Pens.—The Great Military Clothing Establishment at Pimlico.
—Thoughts about London Beggars.—Wenham Lake Ice.—Candle
Making.—Woman's Work.—The Turkish Bath.—The Nervous System
of the Metropolis.—Who is Mr. Reuter?—Our Modern Mercury.—
The Sewing Machine.—The *Times'* Advertising Sheet.—Old Things by
New Names.—A Suburban Fair.—A Fortnight in North Wales.—The
Aristocratic Rooks.—The Englishman Abroad.—A Gossip about the
Lakes.—Sensations of a Summer Night and Morning.—Physical
Antipathies.—The Philosophy of Babydom.—Brain Difficulties.—
Human Hair.

"The papers are treated in such a manner as to form not merely an interesting,
but an instructive contribution to the stock of popular literature, and the volume is
therefore a welcome contribution to our current literature."—*Observer.*

"The 'Curiosities of Civilization' contained so many amusing and important
details, that a second selection will be accepted at once with the utmost gratification
by the many readers who have already been fascinated by Dr. Wynter's agreeable
style, and the characteristic details of men and manners by which he has rendered his
name popular. Sometimes the first dish is more palatable than the second,—the
newest *entremet* serving to take off the pleasant taste of its predecessor. In this
instance it is not so, since Dr. Wynter has kept back the better portion for a second
course."—*Bell's Weekly Messenger.*

"Crowded with facts and sparkling with fancy; written in a cheerful and philo-
sophic spirit. The writer is never unapproachable in his ideal, but shrewd, sensible,
and thoughtful in his mode of narration and in his way of marshalling facts."—
Literary Gazette.

"On the whole, we prefer this volume, as a book of amusement, and even instruction, to the 'Curiosities of Civilization,' which has enjoyed a good name and
sale. Dr. Wynter is an accomplished and well-informed man; he writes well, has
much to tell, and even his lightest sketches convey substantial thoughts or facts in
their delicate outlines. This volume contains more than forty papers gleaned from
first-rate periodicals. It would have been a literary loss had they not been so gathered
and preserved. Sometimes there is a quaintness in some of the essays which recalls
the immortal Charles Lamb."—*Era.*

"These papers are characterized by the same breadth of view, the same felicity
of language, the same acuteness of thought, which distinguished the 'Curiosities of
Civilization.' So long as Dr. Wynter continues to write papers similar to those in the
volume before us, and in 'Curiosities of Civilization,' so long will the republication of
those papers be welcomed by the public."—*Standard.*

Seventh Edition, Crown 8vo. price 6s.

Curiosities of Civilization.

Being Essays from the Quarterly and Edinburgh Reviews. By DR. ANDREW WYNTER.

CONTENTS.

The London Commissariat.
Food and its Adulterations.
Advertisements.
The Zoological Gardens.
Rats.
Woolwich Arsenal.
Shipwrecks.

Lodging, Food, and Dress of Soldiers.
The Electric Telegraph.
Fires and Fire Insurance.
The Police and the Thieves.
Mortality in Trades and Professions.
Lunatic Asylums.

" We shall look in vain, for example, two centuries back, for anything like an equivalent to the volume before us. Some of the articles are mainly derived from observations made in the course of professional studies ; others are at least cognate to the subjects which occupy a physician's hourly thoughts ; all are more or less instructive as to certain phases of our civilization, and the strange elements it holds in suspension. Some of the incidents are of unparalleled magnitude, quite as striking as anything contained in the wonder-books of our ancestors."—*Times.*

" Dr. Wynter's papers show that he has made deep researches, and that he brings to bear upon them the acumen of a well-stored mind—a perfect kaleidoscopic array of subjects."—*Morning Post.*

" Dr. Wynter has both industry and skill. He investigates all branches of his subjects, and tells us the result easily and unaffectedly. In short, a better book of miscellaneous reading has not come under our notice for a long while."—*Daily News.*

" One of the most amusing and best-executed works of its kind that ever came under our notice. Every subject that Dr. Wynter handles, even if it refers to scientific matters, is ground down so very fine, that it is hardly competent to human stupidity to fail to understand it."—*Saturday Review.*

" These articles form a delightful inventory of facts, in which every reader has a direct personal interest, for they are such as may or do affect him and his at every moment of their lives, and collectively they form a very curious insight into the anatomy of some parts of our civilization past and present. Seldom have the fruits of so much labour been converted into more easy and pleasant reading."—*Spectator.*

" It would have been a pity if so much that is useful and entertaining had been entombed in the pages of a review. The subject-matter was worthy of being put into a book, and we are glad that it is done."—*Illustrated News.*

"Among the various Essays by eminent and brilliant writers, none surpass Dr. Wynter in instructiveness, amusing information, and easy cleverness of style. If any one ' wants to know' how our great Babylon is supplied, with unerring certainty and sound calculation, with food and drink, day after day and year after year ; how that food is systematically and universally doctored and adulterated; how our thieves operate, flourish, come to grief, and are affected by the police who are employed to detect or capture them; how men are slowly murdered by unhealthy trades, and how the professions kill or keep alive their members; how fires influence fire insurance, and fire insurance influences fires ; how and what sort of people dwell in lunatic asylums ; how many romantic and least-imagined things can be learnt by studying the shipwrecks which have occurred during the last few years; how—but we will stop, and simply add, that whoever wants a *fireside* book this winter, rich in useful facts, and written in a manner clear, fascinating, and original, had better purchase Dr. Wynter's *Curiosities of Civilization.*"—*Mining Review.*

USEFUL WORKS.

Peter Schlemihl.

From the German of ADELBERT VON CHAMISSO. Translated by Sir JOHN BOWRING, LL.D., &c. Crown 8vo., cloth, with Illustrations by George Cruikshank, price 2s. 6d.; the Illustrations on India paper, price 5s.

Whist.

The Laws and Practice of Whist, as played at the London Clubs. By COELEBS. With coloured Frontispiece. 16mo., cloth, gilt edges, price 2s. 6d.

Horse Warranty:

A Plain and Comprehensive Guide to the Various Points to oe noted, showing which are Essential and which are Unimportant. With Forms of Warranty. By PETER HOWDEN, V.S. Fcap. 8vo., cloth, price 3s. 6d.

Graceful Riding:

A Pocket Manual for Equestrians. By S. C. WAITE. With Illustrations. Fcap. 8vo., cloth, price 2s. 6d.

"In the school, on the road, on the course, or across country, this little book will he invaluable; and we heartily recommend it."—*Morning Post*.

The Plagues of our Domestic Animals, and their Prevention.

Being Lectures delivered by Professor GAMGEE at the Royal Agricultural College, Cirencester. To which is added the Report of the Congress of Veterinary Surgeons held at Hamburg in 1863.

The Science and Practice of Farm Cultivation.

By Professor BUCKMAN, F.L.S., F.G.S. Fully Illustrated, price 7s. 6d., bound in cloth; each part separately, price 1s.

1. How to Grow Good Roots.	5. How to Grow Good Hedges.
2. How to Grow Good Grasses.	6. How to Grow Good Timber.
3. How to Grow Good Clover.	7. How to Grow Good Orchards.
4. How to Grow Good Corn.	

Hardwicke's Shilling Handy-Book of London.

An Easy and Comprehensive Guide to Everything worth Seeing and Hearing. Royal 32mo., cloth, price 1s.

CONTENTS.

Bazaars.	Omnibuses.
Ball-rooms.	Palaces.
Cathedrals.	Parks.
Dining-rooms.	Passport Offices.
Exhibitions.	Picture Galleries.
Mansions of Nobility.	Popular Entertainments.
Markets.	Police-courts.
Money-order Offices.	Prisons.